Mackenzie McKade

THE Charade
ECSTASY

ELLORA'S CAVE
ROMANTICA PUBLISHING

What the critics are saying...

છ

5 Angels "*The Charade* instantly grabs the reader's attention with an alarming, startling suspense and maintains an intriguing interest until the very end. [...] Overall, *The Charade* deserves the highest Fallen Angel Reviews Award of 5 Angels and a Recommended Read because it provided me with the ultimate satisfaction–both physically and emotionally. I can hardly wait until Ms. McKade's next Ecstasy installment. If you desire an outstanding suspenseful read with a BDSM factor, then *The Charade* is the perfect book to loose yourself in. Enjoy!" ~ *Fallen Angel Reviews*

4 Hearts "Readers will experience the same befuddlement that Ciarra does as she awakens to a horror of a situation. The details of her escape were inspired and her subsequent sexual odyssey will certainly keep readers attention firmly glued to the story. [...] This can be read as a stand alone book but is richer for having read its predecessor, *The Game*. Readers should be aware that there are scenes with ménage a trois, f/f, and of course BDSM." ~ *Love Romances and More Reviews*

An Ellora's Cave Romantica Publication

www.ellorascave.com

The Charade

ISBN 9781419958816
ALL RIGHTS RESERVED.
The Charade Copyright © 2006 Mackenzie McKade
Edited by Sue-Ellen Gower.
Cover art by Syneca.

This book printed in the U.S.A. by Jasmine–Jade Enterprises, LLC.

Electronic book Publication July 2006
Trade paperback Publication February 2009

THE CHARADE

જી

*D*edication

ഌ

To my beautiful daughters Tia, Samantha and Ashley. I love you dearly.

*T*rademarks *A*cknowledgement

ഌ

The author acknowledges the trademarked status and trademark owners of the following wordmarks mentioned in this work of fiction:

Cinemax: Time Warner Entertainment Company, L.P.

Jacuzzi: Jacuzzi Inc.

Chapter One

෨

Jolted awake by a screaming alarm, Ciarra Storm was instantly aware of three things —

She was naked.

A dead man was beside her.

And three — she clutched a dagger in her right hand.

With a startled jerk, she snapped into a sitting position. The room spun, seesawing up and down, making her eyes feel like two tiny spaceships trapped in a meteor shower. Her stomach pitched and acid burned up her throat. With a thud she fell flat on her back amongst the tangled sheets and blood.

Dream. Dream. It had to be a dream.

More like a fucking nightmare.

She attempted to ease her rapid pulse, inhaling deeply, releasing slowly. Once again she pushed into a sitting position, the screech of the alarm now a blaring pounding in her head.

Her heart stuttered. Real. This was real. And the man *was* dead. The cold, heavy weight of his leg tossed over her thigh, pinning her to the blood-soaked bed, confirmed it.

"*Ohgod-Ohgod-Ohgod!*" The knife fell from her hand, landing with a dull *clunk* on the marble floor. Desperately she shoved at the man's lifeless limb, kicking her feet, thrusting his leg away and flinging herself from the bed. She tumbled onto her hands and knees, pain exploding on contact. Struggling to gain footing, she slipped, her naked body sliding across the polished stone. The floor was cold as she clambered to her feet. Standing in the middle of the room, she wildly swung around, looking one way then the other.

Where the hell am I? What's going on?

Her heart pummeled her chest, over and over, desperate beats. A chill iced her spine. The taste of something foul and bitter in her mouth caused her to swallow hard. She swiped her tongue between dry lips.

Nothing was familiar. The hotel room was masculine, the mood of seduction burned in a dozen lit candles. Cinnamon lightly perfumed the air mingling with a metallic scent she refused to identify. Two half-filled crystal goblets and a wine decanter atop a dark wood end table. The lip impressions of *Mauve Heaven*, her lipstick color, graced one glass. The mark jumped out at her in warning.

A strong fire blazed in a fireplace. Orange-red flames flickered, crackled and popped — their warmth lost to Ciarra in her frenzy.

She took a step, her ankle slightly twisting, as her foot landed on something hard, a shoe — her red stiletto. Another lay several feet away. To her disbelief, her silk evening dress was crumpled in a corner, bra, panties and stockings skewed about the elegant hotel room…and they were covered in blood.

She trembled as if caught bare-assed in a raging snowstorm. Nothing she did, not briskly rubbing her palms up and down her arms or folding them tightly around her, took away the chill.

And still the alarm screeched.

What if someone hears the alarm? Panic-stricken, she ran to the nightstand and with a shaky hand silenced the alarm. Of course, all she really had to do was to have said, "Alarm off." Everything was voice activated these days. But she wasn't thinking clearly.

Where was she?

Ciarra gaped around what looked like a large room. She took in the marble fireplace, the elaborate furnishings and paintings draping the walls. But too soon, her gaze went right back to the corpse lying on the bed. His large brown eyes stared accusingly, vacant of all life and vitality. There was an angry, two-inch, vertical puncture wound below his right nipple the size of the serrated blade now lying upon the floor. Drying blood covered his chest, soaking into the sheets, turning them almost black.

Recognition dawned. It was Stan Mayhem, an influential client of Kohler's Advertising Agency, her new place of employment. Their accidental meeting in the *skytron* moving from floor to floor had been brief, but memorable. When the elevator made an abrupt stop, he had spilled hot coffee, chocolate mocha from the rich scent, down the front of her suit. Apologizing, he nearly molested her in the process as he took a handkerchief from his suit pocket and swiped haphazardly down the front of her ruined shirt.

But how did she get here? And what had happened? Blindly she searched her memory.

A party...a drink...then nothing. Absolutely nothing.

She pressed a fist to her mouth restraining the scream that built with horrifying speed in her throat. She couldn't possibly have killed this man.

Could she?

But when Ciarra pulled back her hand from her mouth, the dark evidence was on her fingers, her palm. Drying blood crusted her wrist. The metallic taste upon her lips made her stomach roll.

The rapid pounding of her heart took on a wild and erratic rhythm. Again acid flooded her throat. Eyes wide, she darted for the first door that came into her line of sight, thankfully the bathroom.

Feet unsteady beneath her, Ciarra barely made it to the commode before her shoulders convulsed and she spewed the contents in her belly. When she had nothing left to throw up, her knees gave out. She slithered to the floor, her arms desperately hugging the toilet for support.

This can't be happening.

She'd killed a man.

Hot tears raced down her cheeks. Why? How?

For what seemed like forever she just sat there. The penetrating cold from the marble beneath her numbed her ass, her legs and her heart.

How could she have done something so horrible? She never drank excessively. Never lost control. She didn't dare, not with her family's history. Ciarra clenched her teeth, fighting the old memory that surfaced.

Eight years old, she'd hidden behind the couch in the living room, hands over her ears to drown out the screaming. Her father was drunk again. Her mother was angry.

A crash—*thud*—followed by a curse. Then her mother burst into the living room in a panic—eyes wide—a scream upon her lips. There was a loud pop! Her mother's body flew through the air carried by an unseen force. When she fell to the floor, a red spot appeared on her back.

The image of that red spot growing larger and larger, like it had so many years ago, turned Ciarra's vision dark.

She was alone. Her only living relative was the man who killed her mother those eighteen years ago.

Alone took on a whole new depth.

No family. No friends. She couldn't even return to New York. Not after pissing off Morris.

In the hallways, outside her office, he had propositioned her. When she ignored him and walked away, he had grabbed her. Who knew that the man she had slapped was the owner of the company she worked for? Not to mention, an extremely influential person.

From that point on he had made her life miserable at work and home, calling her constantly. Of course, he promised to call it even between them, if she fucked him.

"When hell freezes over," she had told him. She was fired on the spot.

Thank God, the headhunter who called the following day had offered her a plushy job in California. An opportunity to become a copywriter, the money and promise for growth was something she just couldn't turn down—and wouldn't.

Yet it was hard coming home night after night for two weeks to a dark, empty apartment. Last night she had only wanted to fit in—have a little fun. So she accepted a coworker's invitation to a party.

Ciarra hung her head and brushed her hair out of her face. The bitter smell of vomit rising from the toilet twisted her stomach. If she didn't move away she would lose it again. She pushed from the commode and stood on rubbery legs, using the counter and sink for support. The swishing sound, water swirling as the automatic toilet activated made her jump.

Red-rimmed blue eyes stared back from the mirror. Her flaming red hair was a mess torn from the neat bun she had twisted it into earlier that night. Thick tresses hung loosely over her shoulders, tickling her ass as she swayed.

And the blood.

Her body was covered in it as if it had been painted on in long brush strokes. She shuddered, needing to get clean, to wash away the evidence—the shame.

As she staggered into the shower, a glass enclosure large enough to house at least six people, she pressed her finger to the activator.

"Good Morning, Miss Storm," the sexy female voice of the activator spoke. "Your preferred temperature has been dialed into my memory. It is a pleasure to have you visit again. Will you be alone or will Stan be joining you?"

Again? Ciarra had been here before and with Stan?

The shower computer continued, "Should you require adjustments to temperature or water pressure, please let me know. I am here to serve you."

Even before Ciarra stepped beneath the pulsating beat, she grabbed a loofah hanging on one wall, and her hands moved rapidly over her body. She had to get the blood off—now. In quick, frantic movements, she scrubbed so fast, so hard, that her skin burned. Before the coppery water finished swirling down the drain she was out of there, tossing down the sponge and stripping a towel off the heating rack. She ran the cloth aimlessly over her damp hair and then wound it around her head turban-style, before she pulled another towel from the rack.

This wasn't a dream. She briskly rubbed the warm towel over her body. She had murdered someone—like her father had.

Where would she go? What would she do?

Her hands stilled, the towel coming to a stop. Her arms drifted to her sides as her shoulders drooped.

She was fucked.

If Ciarra called the police she'd be incarcerated. No one would believe her, not with her family history. In 2106 people were isolated on the moon, left to die—alone. She'd been there once to visit her father. Huge mountains and flat plains of nothingness as far as the eye could see. The dome erected during the mid-twenty-first century did nothing to erase the cold gray matter or the hopelessness of its inhabitants. Her father appeared as one of the walking dead, barely able to speak, much less answer the many questions she had. Every question left unanswered, including how she felt about the man who killed her mother. The fact was it was hard to hate a lifeless entity, someone who apparently didn't really exist any longer. And it had been a horrible experience.

She didn't want to end up like her father. But if she ran she'd be a fugitive. The wonderful new job at Kohler's Advertising Agency had promised her a new start. In the end it looked to be costing her freedom.

Ciarra's footsteps faltered as she made her way into the bedroom. God, how she wished she'd stayed in New York. No, that wouldn't have been smart either. Morris Dawson was an influential man. No one crossed him.

Like a magnet her vision was drawn to the bed. Just the sight of the pale, lifeless body made a tight knot form in her throat and she gagged, almost throwing up again.

Had she fucked Stan, and then showed her gratitude by driving a knife into his heart?

Hot tears streamed down her cheeks. If only she could disappear forever, not face the truth. But the facts were before her—a dead man not more than ten feet away. She'd been covered in blood—his blood. She'd been holding a knife.

She had killed a man. The thought replayed over and over again in her mind. His void expression couldn't hide the accusation in his lifeless eyes…

Her fingers curled into fists, twisting the towel into a knot. Panic bubbled like hot lava through her veins. She had to get out of there and fast. She couldn't go to the penal colony. She couldn't!

As if someone switched her to autopilot, she scanned the room for evidence, something—anything that would incriminate her. Gathering up her blood-drenched clothes, lingerie and shoes, she tossed them in the fireplace. Sparks flew. A bitter metallic stench mingled with burning silk.

As the flames hungrily consumed her favorite dress, she murmured, "Damn," and started to retrieve the garment. Heat scorched her hands before she could grasp the red silk. She jerked her hand back. The smell of singed hair filled her nostrils. It was too late.

Now what am I going to wear? A naked redhead running from a building would definitely draw attention. Perhaps not as much as one covered in blood, but still…

Forget the dress. First I've got to get rid of the rest of the evidence.

Moving frantically across the room, she grabbed the wineglass with traces of her lipstick and raced for the bathroom. Empting the contents in the sink, she ran the water and flushed the red wine down the drain as she washed the glass. After drying it, she hastened back into the bedroom. Glancing around, she located a wine cart containing other glasses. She placed hers among them.

Pulling the towel from around her head she began to wipe down anything she might have touched, including the commode and the shower. Finally, she wiped away her bloody footprints and other smears on the floor before tossing the towel into the fire. The damn thing was wet. Smoke smoldered. She prayed it would not set off the fire alarm. When hot flames began to consume the towel she breathed a sigh of relief. A breath that caught in her throat when her eyes landed on the bloody knife lying on the floor.

For a moment she stared at the ominous weapon. Then she snatched up the dagger and ran back into the bathroom. As cold water rushed over the knife, she noticed something familiar about the handle. A tight scream pushed between her lips. It was one of the knives from a set she had purchased several years ago. If she left it behind would they be able to trace it to her?

God, what should she do?

Shit. She would have to take it with her. She picked up a washcloth, returned to the bedroom, wrapped the weapon, and placed it on the end table.

Now for clothes.

The naked man lying on the bed was big, too big for her to fit into any of his clothing. Still she might find something. Entering his closet she noticed that on one side was men's attire, the other women's.

Her heart stuttered. Had she killed someone's husband, someone's father? She closed her eyes as shame heated her face. How was she going to live with herself?

No. I couldn't have. I couldn't have! Something is wrong here. I'm not like my father.

But the evidence was all around her.

Pushing the closet's retractor button, the motor hummed, sending dresses, pants, shirts, and array of other clothing by her. Whoever this woman was, she wore risqué clothing, because there wasn't much fabric to any of the ensembles passing by Ciarra's eyes. Finally, she stopped the flow of clothes, selected a skin-tight, black one-piece pantsuit. She only prayed it would fit.

As she wiggled her hips, pulling the damnable outfit over her thighs, past her waist, she pushed her arms through the long sleeves. She wondered briefly whether she had put the thing on backwards, because it barely covered her breasts. One sneeze and her nipples would be playing peekaboo.

Below, where the outfit had hung in the closet, was a pair of ankle boots with spike heels and a gold chain around the front. As she slipped her feet into them they adjusted to her size. From a shelf she grabbed the matching handbag and gave a choked laugh. Just like a woman to remember to accessorize, even when she is fleeing from a murder scene.

Next she extracted from a hanger, a strip of black silk with gold threading. Without looking, she laced it through her dampened hair, weaving it so that her long tresses were piled atop her head. She tied the cloth off and headed for the door when she pulled to an abrupt halt.

The weapon.

She turned her head achingly slow. Glanced over her shoulder hoping the night had been just a horrible dream…

No. It's all too real.

A dead man still sprawled across the bed — the weapon of his demise was wrapped in a small white washcloth lying upon the table.

Real. Not a dream.

The heels of her boots clicked across the marble floor as she retraced her steps. Her outstretched hand trembled as her fingers folded around the bundle. For a moment she closed her eyes. Her chest rose and fell on an audible breath.

Lord, what am I doing? she thought, just before opening her eyes and cramming the dagger into her purse, clutching it to her chest. She took one more look around. Had she forgotten anything? Regret squeezed her heart as her vision focused on the bed and the man lying on it.

"I'm so sorry, Stan," she whispered, before running to the door, opening it and rushing through then quietly shutting it behind herself.

Ciarra looked down the long hallway—one direction and then the other. The word "exit" shone in neon lights at each end of the corridor. To the right was the *skytron*, to the left the stairs.

What floor was she on? Hell, it didn't matter. The stairs would be safer.

In a flurry of movements, she made it down four flights of stairs, only meeting a little old lady who smiled and said hello in passing. It seemed odd that an elderly woman would use the stairs instead of the *skytron*, but her speculation dissolved like smoke on a windy day—Ciarra had bigger problems. She had no idea where she was going. Hell, she didn't even know where she was.

The last step led her straight to the automotive cage, housing for the tenants' transportation vehicles. From there she could find her way out of the building. Moving down the dimly lit corridor, the smell of oil and other scents associated with machines and aeromechanics assaulted her. As she stepped forward off the curb, Ciarra came to an abrupt stop.

Parked right outside the stair entrance was her sleek, black turbo-sedan. "How?" she murmured. In recognition of her presence the engine purred to life and its dual exhaust jets, shiny and silver, lengthened from beneath the car releasing *aeriform*, a colorless liquid that burst into flames followed by a light bitter scent. Perplexed, she stood for a moment watching the light blue blaze shoot from the pipes, and then she took the necessary steps to reach her vehicle. A press of her thumb against the identification pad confirmed her identity and activated the doors, causing them to lift like a bird in flight. She climbed in and with a *thud*, metal met metal, closing her inside.

"Good morning, Ciarra, you hot *thang*," the southern twang of her turbo's male voice welcomed her. Her signing bonus at Kohler's Advertising Agency had paid the down payment on the posh vehicle. "Are we still scheduled to go to the LA Transport Station?"

"LA Transport Station?" She stumbled over the repeated words, then startled as her seat belt slithered across her waist and chest to entrap her as she set the purse containing the knife beside her. The temperature regulator hummed lightly, adjusting to her specifications, and her favorite scent of sunflowers filled the air.

"Yes, ma'am. You scheduled the destination prior to putting me to bed last night." The sexy sedan's tone and insinuations, not to mention the mighty fine looking man in cowboy hat, boots, jeans and no shirt smiling back at her from the simulator monitor, usually made her heart pitter-patter. But not today. Now all she could do was second-guess herself. All indications were that she had planned this horrible deed...and her escape.

"Yes, Brody, the station. I don't know what else to do," she added in a whisper.

The man's image in the monitor drew his cowboy hat low over seductive eyes. He cupped the bulge between his thighs. "I could take you for a long drive, we could park beneath a tree, that vibrator in the glove compartment—"

"I didn't mean that." Ciarra rolled her eyes skyward. When you spoke to computers they took you so literally.

He nudged his hat up a notch. "Then hold on, little filly." With a jolt, Brody's engine shifted into first and they were off.

What was she doing? Where was she going? She leaned back, closing her eyes, and didn't open them again until Brody came to a stop.

"We've arrived, Ciarra." Then the sedan's voice deepened. "I'll miss you. When are you coming home?"

How pitiful was it when you only had a car to come home to?

An invisible vise squeezed her heart. She might never be returning to Earth, much less her barren and lonely apartment. "I don't know, Brody."

"Do you wish for me to remain at the transport station or return home?"

She sucked in her bottom lip, biting hard to quell the rising emotion. "Home. Wait for me at home." She grabbed her purse and scooted over.

"Then enjoy yourself." His engine purred, then hummed low, "Don't do anything I wouldn't."

You know that's never going to happen now, Ciarra.

When she climbed out, his doors automatically closed. An overwhelming melancholy gripped her. She fought back tears beating against her eyelids as she watched her black sedan speed away and disappear around a corner.

Alone, again.

Inside, the LA Transport Station was a madhouse. The huge dome with steel braces overhead echoed every sound. Ciarra had forgotten just how chaotic it was as people prepared to leave Earth and travel to stars and planets in the heavens. She passed a couple who reeked of being newlyweds. The lip-lock they held made her wonder if they would ever come up for air. A family with two toddlers, a boy and girl, passed by and sorrow engulfed Ciarra. She'd never experience the unity with another, the thrill of holding a child to her breast. Last night had taken all of that away from her.

Then it dawned on her...why was she here? She didn't have a flight voucher unless that too, had been prearranged. Had she left it in her sedan? No. Brody would have reminded her. This meant she'd have to stand in line and wait to discover if a reserved voucher existed. But to where?

Anxiety slithered across her skin. She could actually feel the passage of time as if it had actual substance and it slid through her grasp. And it felt like her time was quickly drawing to an end.

When it was her turn to speak with the Voucher Express System, she stepped forward. "Yes, do you have a ticket for Ciarra Storm?"

"Your destination?" the machine asked.

"I don't know," she whispered, so those behind her couldn't hear.

"Could you please speak up?" the computer requested.

"I don't know," she repeated louder this time through jaws so tight she expected her bones to shatter at any time.

"Can you please be more specific?" the voice in the damnable box insisted.

What was she to do? She had no idea where she was heading. If she wired money, her whereabouts could be traced. Without commenting she shoved away from the counter, receiving confused stares from several travelers behind her.

Panic welled inside, but she pushed past it, clutching her purse to her side. There was no time for her to lose it, especially not around a crowd of people. As she began to walk she saw a galactic-officer coming toward her. His metallic uniform glistened beneath the halogen lights. He had a stun wand strapped to his side next to a set of static handcuffs that Ciarra swore had her name on them. And he was looking right at her.

Adrenaline exploded through her body. Her heart pounded as if it would burst. Without thinking she darted toward the nearest door, which happened to be the women's bathroom.

A flashy blonde was leaning against the counter talking on a trans-communicator pressed to her ear.

"Fuck! Can't you imbeciles do anything yourself? This deal is big, huge, and I will have it *my* way." She paused, listening. An expression of pure disdain hardened her classic features. "I've had this vacation planned for six months. The hotel is paid for—no refunds. The transport is paid for—no refunds. My luggage has even been loaded." The blonde glanced at her wristwatch. When she turned her back in a huff, the woman's eyes met Ciarra's. For a brief moment she was silent, a forewarning flashed in her brown depths. Then her voice stuttered like she was having a moment of indecision, then it dipped, lowered into a growl. "The shuttle leaves in ten minutes from Platform Twelve. What am I suppose to do with the fucking voucher?"

Ciarra wanted to yell, "I'll take it!" Instead she activated the water, selecting cold and began to splash cool water on her face.

"Heads will roll." The menace in the woman's voice left no doubt, as she slammed the trans-communicator closed. Then, without so much as an afterthought, she tossed the voucher in the nearest trash receptacle. When the woman sharply pivoted, a pair of gloves fell from her purse. Ciarra's mouth opened and then snapped shut—jaws clinking together.

As the door slid closed behind the angry blonde, Ciarra lunged for the trash receptacle. She latched on to the plastic voucher.

How lucky could she be?

Ciarra stooped and swiped up the gloves. They were the newest in *Impressionist*, the thinnest and most reliable material molding a person's fingerprints into their folds, so they didn't have to be taken off to enter or exit a building. She held the woman's identity in her hands. With no problem, Ciarra would be able to get past the stewards, onto the transport, and far away from Earth.

What a freaking coincidence. She crammed the gloves into her purse, touching the knife and sending a chill up her spine. Her fingers closed around the weapon. She needed to get rid of the weapon. As she started to pull it from her purse a woman walked in. The short brunette went straight for the mirror. Her large purse made a thud as she dropped in on the counter. Without delay the woman began to refresh her makeup. Slowly, Ciarra released the knife and it fell back to the bottom of her bag.

Later.

When she exited the restroom and started down the corridor, the fresh breath of hope filling Ciarra's lungs turned sour as she nearly tripped over her feet to come to a halt. The blonde stood twenty feet away and was speaking to the galactic-officer. Concern was etched in the lines creasing her forehead.

Had the woman already realized that she lost her gloves?

Ciarra's pulse raced. Her frantic gaze searched for an escape route. To the left were the loading platforms. Multiple aisles led in several directions, each dead-ends. To the right lay freedom blocked by the woman and the officer standing before the exit.

Ciarra tried to ease the pounding of her heart. Surely Stan's body hadn't been found yet. If the blonde knew she dropped her gloves in the restroom they would have met in passing. There was nothing to connect her to the woman.

When the officer leaned forward and whispered something in the blonde's ear, the tightness in her features softened. Then together they moved through the open doors, disappearing around a corner.

Ciarra released her repressed breath. *That was a close call.* Without another moment's delay, she pivoted and headed for Platform Twelve.

The transport was early, people were already boarding. Shaking, she pulled on the gloves, one hand then the other. Her pulse quickened as an elderly teleporter approached. He said nothing, just stuck the identifier in front of her. She pressed a palm on the small box's monitor. The name Kitty Carmichael appeared in glowing green letters across the screen.

Kitty? That woman is a Kitty?

"Follow me, Ms. Carmichael," the teleporter said with as much enthusiasm as a wet dog.

As the tall, thin man escorted her through the dining hall and down a corridor, Ciarra wondered if she would get away with impersonating the nasty blonde.

When a door slid open and she was ushered into a plush chamber, Ciarra managed a smile. Nothing but the best for little Miss Blonde *Thang,* and for now it was all Ciarra's.

Chapter Two

ဢ

Shawn Thorenson stood with his legs shoulder-width apart, arms crossed over his broad chest, as he scrutinized the new clients—slaves and Masters—arriving on Zygoman, Ecstasy Island.

A gust of air from the transport revving its ion engine brushed back his shoulder-length blond hair. Radiant energy, heat waves, streamed from beneath the sleek, silver conveyor, releasing a metallic scent that always reminded him of his youth. He had loved to travel. His parents searched far and wide for the perfect place to raise a family and to build a business. This small planet had been the answer to his parents' prayers.

He moved across the granite platform, past a rubber tree that had crawled like a vine along the wall and ceiling, to get a better look at the people he would spend the next two weeks with on an intimate basis.

The onset of the season was always exciting and promising. Anticipation stirred his blood. He was a man who enjoyed pleasure and Ecstasy Island was his very own playground… Well, his and his two older brothers, Tor and Terrance. Together they owned the most exclusive pleasure planet in the universe.

He grinned, watching six women filter through the slave entrance. Two men followed, then seven or eight more women. In the distance, his two brothers were escorting several influential men and one woman through the Masters portal.

Business had risen sharply after the erotic game show, Voyeur II, had featured the explosive reuniting of two prominent ex-lovers on Ecstasy Island. Seth Allen, 2104's Astral-ball Champion, and of course, Chastity Ambrose.

Just the thought of the beautiful brunette model made his smile falter, and a wave of disappointment shimmered over him. He had desperately wanted to brand the woman and make her his. She was everything he had imagined a woman should be — and more.

For a while now Shawn had been missing something in his life. Another two women exited the transport and headed for the slave entrance. Their laughter filled the air as well as their rich womanly perfume. He could never quite put his finger on it, but somehow Chastity had made him feel whole again, had filled the void in him if only for a moment in time.

Just as the thought left his mind, a tall, statuesque woman disembarked from the transport. Her legs were long and lean, her hips softly rounded with a nipped-in waist. A sense of familiarity crawled across Shawn's skin. Drawn by the sensation, he unconsciously took a step toward her.

If he didn't know better he would have thought Chastity had returned. An uneasy chuckle left his taut lips.

When the woman spun around, he flinched. She wasn't Chastity, but could definitely pass as her sister, except that her hair was red, like the last dying embers of a warm summer day peeking beneath the wrap that hid her tresses. The one-piece outfit she wore set his hormones raging. Skintight, the garment clung to her as if seducing each curve. And she clutched a purse in front of her as if it were a shield.

The palms of his hands itched. Blood rushed to his groin. His cock hardened. Lust burned like wildfire. The Egyptian silk of his Roman costume, a white mid-thigh toga, only made his balls tighten as the soft material slid across his groin. He rolled his hips, shifting his sandaled feet, trying to relieve the sudden discomfort.

Twisting, the woman swung around, took several steps, hesitated, before taking several more steps, and then finally drawing again to a complete halt. Her gaze darted around her.

Something about the way she moved gave Shawn pause. She looked lost, even frightened. He shook his head and released a discouraged breath.

Man, he was a sucker for helpless women. It had been the same with Chastity, or the now Mrs. Seth Allen. The woman had been assaulted by one of Ecstasy Island's guests, Morris Dawson, an influential businessman who had been barred from ever returning to Zygoman. And then the poor woman had been kidnapped and nearly killed by another man.

Shawn had acted the hero in both incidents and still lost the girl.

A deep throaty grumble rose as he remembered how he had fawned over Chastity. With a harrumph, he pushed aside his disgust. There would be more time later to berate himself. For now — he had a job to do.

He was a Dom. He educated women and men alike to their station in sexual pleasure. Whether it was domination or a submissive role, he taught people how to listen to and enjoy the darker side of their nature. He taught them to be free, to openly fantasize and to live their dreams.

As he moved to intercept the woman, Passion Flower appeared beside her.

Ahhh, so the new arrival was a slave. Shawn's pulse sped with the knowledge.

The petite Asian woman with long black hair standing next to the new arrival was his eldest brother's wife. It was her duty to instruct the inexperienced slaves in their duties in pleasuring their Masters. Appreciation filled his eyes as he watched his sister-in-law introduce herself. Shawn enjoyed looking at Passion Flower's full breasts since she wore nothing but a short skirt to cover her mons. The lotus flowers tattooed across her globes drew men like bees to honey, and he was no different. This was a world of freedom where fantasies and desires were cultivated and tended. But it was also a world of respect—Passion Flower was his brother's wife, so he referred to her as a look-don't-touch female.

Passion Flower greeted the redhead with a graceful bow, and then waved her forward. The woman hesitated. A look of panic skewed her pretty features as her gaze once again darted around the platform. Her body visibly flinched and Shawn had the strangest feeling she was going to run right back into the transport. But before he took two more steps, the redhead inhaled and released it slowly, turning toward Passion Flower.

Resignation was written on her face.

Shawn's breath caught. He choked. Was that a rosy nipple peeking out from the woman's tight outfit? He shifted his hips, easing the pain that gripped his balls.

Her chin rose. He could almost see her resolve rise, hardening as she straightened her backbone and squared her shoulders. Passion Flower again waved her forward and this time she followed.

Shawn's feet began to move of their own accord. There was something about the woman that drew him like a lodestone. Normally he would assist the Masters arriving on the bondage planet, but today he thought observing the slaves might prove entertaining and more to his liking.

As he entered the Preparation Room, a sterile white room with several tables containing static bands and carryalls for the slaves' clothing and personal effects, his presence created a stir. All chatter stopped. Passion Flower as well as the staff of Ecstasy Island who had been stripping the new arrivals and helping to prepare the slaves ceased their actions. Quickly they took a submissive stance. Legs shoulder-width apart, hands behind their backs, eyes cast toward the floor awaiting his commands.

Several new arrivals gave nervous giggles at their state of undress, throwing their arms around their bare chests. Others stood proudly unashamed of their bodies and respectfully took their position. One penetrating glare from Shawn and the inexperienced fell silent. One by one he raked his gaze over them before narrowing in on the woman who had drawn him there as if he wore the collar and she held the leash.

"Master Shawn," Passion Flower spoke in a hushed tone, "permission to speak."

The redhead trembled beneath his open scrutiny. "Permission granted," he responded, refusing to take his eyes off her.

"What may I do to pleasure you?" Passion Flower asked.

The woman's widened stare snapped to Passion Flower and then back to him. The moment their eyes met, fire licked Shawn's cock. He didn't hide his desire for her as it proudly tented his toga.

Impossibly, the new slave's eyes gaped more. Those big beautiful blue eyes pinned right on his member made the thing jerk and grow firmer yet. The most delightful blush rolled across her face as she recognized his body's hunger.

Beneath feathered lashes, Passion Flower glanced at him, and then the redhead. Her head rose. "Master Shawn, may I introduce slave Kitty?"

The redhead's chin dipped sharply, her brows furrowed with disapproval, but she remained silent.

He could not restrain the extreme sense of satisfaction that filtered through him. Kitty? If she was Kitty Carmichael, the woman had made special arrangements, arrangements that he would enjoy complying with. But then he remembered that Terrance, his middle brother, had been assigned Miss Carmichael.

Perhaps a switch in duties was in order. He openly scanned her delectable body, relishing the thought of his hands roaming over all that velvety skin. "Slave Kitty—Kitty Carmichael?"

"Yes." Her soft voice could melt chocolate. It certainly did a job on him.

The image of spreading her long legs, of thrusting between her parted thighs, sent the room spinning, nearly throwing Shawn off balance.

Damn it! He was not going to fall head over heels just because this woman reminded him of Chastity. He grinded his teeth and remembered his role, remembered what Kitty had paid a lot of money to experience — pleasure and bondage.

"Take that outfit off her," he demanded. His voice was harsher than he had intended. Kitty visibly flinched.

Damn. If the woman pried her eyes any wider, she'd be all pupils.

"Wa-wait one minute." Her stutter was a mixture of disbelief and the beginnings of anger. Anger that stiffened her backbone forcing two more inches of height out of her already tall frame. A red-hot flame flickered in her eyes.

He inwardly beamed. She had fire in her soul. He loved a woman with spirit. Still, he firmed his features. His chin dipped. His eyes narrowed as he began a slow walk circling her. She nearly tripped over her feet trying to keep her heated glare on his.

"You are new to Ecstasy Island, so I will allow this one indiscretion to be forgiven. Any future ones will be punished." Kitty had ordered that she be dominated, to be taken in any fashion deemed, and Shawn intended to give her exactly what she paid for and more.

Frustration flickered across her face. Still she snapped her mouth closed, and then yanked her gaze away.

"On second thought, I will remove the offensive clothing myself." Shawn couldn't wait to reveal what all that fabric hid. He couldn't wait to feel her soft skin beneath his hands. Visions of tangled sheets, entwined bodies, only made his desire burn hotter.

She was tall, close to five-ten, a perfect match to his six-five. Or, on her knees just the right height to take his cock deep within her mouth. The image jerked his staff alive. Blood rushed to the tip and he had the uncontrollable need to push her to her knees and feel her lips surrounding him this very minute as he thrust in and out of her warm cove.

When his fingers slid beneath the material at the top of her shoulder, she trembled, but held steady. Slowly, he pushed the cloth down her arm, feeling the silkiness of her skin, breathing in the fresh scent of sunflowers that clung to her flesh. A breast sprang forth, eliciting a gasp from her full luscious lips. His gaze narrowed on her rosy nipple hardening beneath his regard. He wet his mouth, hunger raging through his veins. He reached out, unable to stop himself from touching her.

Cradling her breast, he took pleasure in her reaction as the globe grew full and heavy in his palm. Their eyes trapped in a sexual trance, he bent and captured the taut bud in his mouth. A wonderful tremor shook her. He licked around her areola, feeling the rise of goose bumps across her heated skin. Then he flicked his tongue several times, teasing her. She whimpered, the light airy sound throwing him into a maelstrom of emotions. He suckled harder then scraped his teeth over her extended nipple, loving the catch in her breathing as her hands gripped his shoulders. Her chest arched, her body swayed, head lolling backwards.

With a *pop*, he broke the suction. Her head rose, again she met his gaze, hers soft with desire. Then she blinked several times and frowned, vision clearing as if a gale passed, blowing the softness away. He heard her sharp inhale. She licked her lips. Determination sparked in the depths of her blue eyes.

There *was* a fire in this woman, burning hot and alive.

Shawn wanted to strip her of all clothing, ravish her body, before taking her down on the marble floor and fucking her long and hard. Just imagining how slick and wet she would be as he entered her made him release a growl of anticipation.

She countered it with a frown, looking beyond him to the interested stares of those in the room.

Kitty was right. Now was not the time to let his passions run amok.

Never looking away, Shawn said, "Passion Flower, continue with the other slaves' preparation. I will see to slave Kitty."

Immediately movement sounded as people began to continue their duties, but no one spoke.

Kitty drew her attention back to Shawn, denouncing him with the briefest raise of her chin. A chuckle rumbled from his lips. She might not want to admit it, but she had enjoyed his touch.

Shawn sensed her inner struggle, her resistance to release herself to another—to him. But that was why many came to Ecstasy Island—freedom to explore, to discover. Was that why she had insisted on a contract, an agreement that would have her at the mercy of the Thorenson brothers' whims?

Still, it was obvious she would fight him and her own body's needs. As did many people who repudiated their dark side. To transcend the light and delve deep into the shadows of desire could be frightening—but extremely self-fulfilling, satisfying.

The corner of his lips rose with anticipation. He was a Master of Seduction—she would acquiesce and revel in her surrender as he unleashed her passion.

When he slipped her other arm from the pantsuit, baring both breasts, she parted her legs, steadied her stance. A brow rose, her chin inched a little higher.

With the slightest of challenge this woman brought the basic animal need out in Shawn. He wanted to fuck her, fuck her now. But she wasn't ready, she had not earned the right to feel his cock buried deep inside her warm body.

A provision from the contract made him tense. She had personally asked for Terrance as her Master. Unreasonable jealousy stung. Irrational. His attraction was based on another woman—not the one before him whose eyes appeared oddly distant through her determination.

Screw it. He needed release—to free the sexual tension building as this woman intentionally or unintentionally continued to place fuel, timber by timber, on his smoldering fire.

Shawn's fingers curled into the fabric gathered just below her breasts. With one quick pull in opposite directions, the material gave. She startled. He wasn't sure if it was from the sudden ripping sound, or the cool air that caressed her ivory skin sending goose bumps across her flesh. The fiery curls peeking beyond the cloth at the apex of her thighs was a propellant, exploding, and sending his body into meltdown.

He crushed his mouth to hers. There was a fury to their connection. No gentle kiss, just a meshing of lips, teeth and tongues. She gave as good as he did—surrendering nothing and taking all.

When he tasted blood, hers—his, he pulled away and took several steps back.

Shallow, ragged breaths raised her chest, shook her body. Her nostrils flared. Her lips were swollen, reddened from his assault. Moisture pooled in her cerulean eyes. There was a sadness—a weariness that lingered on the edge of desperation.

Had he hurt her? Had he misread her signals? If the eyes were truly the window to one's soul, this woman was hurting, deeply. Something told him that he was the catalyst in releasing the emotion she had previously held firmly beneath the surface.

Still he could not help himself. He reached for her. Her shoulders swung away to dodge him, but he moved with her until he had her in his arms. She felt wonderful, thigh to thigh, hips to hips, chest to chest, until wetness touched his shoulder. She was crying.

His large hand cupped the back of her head, holding her close. "Hush, angel, don't cry." Soft hands slid across his back, before gripping him tightly. He turned so that his body shielded her from the onlooking crowd.

Fuck. What had she done? Here she was supposed to be some ball-buster from California and the first chance she got she burst into childish tears.

Ciarra squeezed her eyes closed, moisture seeping past her lids as memories flooded her head. A room, a dead man, blood...so much blood, and the knife still in her purse next to her feet. *Damn*. Why hadn't she disposed of it while she was on the transport? So tired she had fallen asleep. Then the next thing she'd known it was time to depart. Ciarra opened her eyes, trying to close the door on the memories, lock them away. But they continued much like her tears.

For a moment she was disoriented, staring through misty eyes and grappling with what was real — what wasn't. Strong arms surrounding her brought her back, pulled her from the engulfing despair. She attempted to push from the man's embrace, but he held tight.

"Hush, angel." His soothing voice wrapped around her as comforting as his arms. She inhaled his male scent, a pleasing mixture of heat and masculinity. He was tall, her face pressed into a chest she swore no normal man possessed. His arousal was steel, hard and needy against her belly. When he had entered the Preparation Room he had sported a wild, untamed look with his shoulder-length blond hair and penetrating green eyes that had revealed his desire and had instantly immobilized her.

No one had ever looked at her that way, like he could gobble her up with one bite. For a moment she had forgotten her plight. Frightened at first, then surprised by the man's presence and the subservient attitude of everyone around him. There was authority in his voice when he spoke. Clearly by the way people reacted to his mere presence, the way he moved and carried himself, he was a man used to getting his way.

But his touch was gentle.

When his hand had slid beneath her outfit, fire licked her skin. When he bared her breast—his hot mouth, suckling, pulling and biting—desire sang through her veins and pooled between her thighs. She wanted him. And the hardness pressed to her belly revealed he wanted her too.

Gentle, yes, but there was that scorching kiss. That soul-riveting mating of their tongues that had her toes curling in her boots. Never had she been kissed so thoroughly. Just the thought of a night spent in his arms released sharp needles through her nipples that coursed straight to her womb. She was wet with desire and the need to feel him between her thighs. She couldn't resist leaning closer, wanting to be surrounded and sheltered by his massive form. He held her as if any minute she might shatter into a million pieces. He held her like she was special.

A frustrated breath squeezed through her kiss-swollen lips. God, she was pitiful. Even if it were true, what man would have her once she confessed her sins? The shame she felt dried up her tears. She didn't deserve to be comforted. She didn't deserve kindness or sympathy.

But did I really kill that man?

The evidence…

"Please release me." Her voice sounded small, fragile even to her own ears.

There was a moment of regret when his arms fell from around her and he took a step back. In silence he studied her face as if he searched for something.

The truth rang in her mind and she bowed her head, suddenly feeling unworthy, insignificant standing in his dignified shadow. She couldn't help the tightness in her chest or the unease that slithered across her body.

"This is not what I expected," she confessed.

His backbone stiffened with her comment. "Of course. You expected Master Terrance."

Did she catch a little acrimony in his tone?

"Excuse me." He pivoted, heavy steps carrying him toward the door.

She opened her mouth to explain, but nothing came out. Instead she simply stood and watched him leave.

Disappointment hung heavy around her. Then she released another breath of frustration. She didn't come here to enjoy herself, nor experience a lifetime fantasy she had never revealed to anyone. In the darkest recesses of her mind she had dreamed of being dominated, the thrill of releasing control to another, shedding responsibility, of handing over her wellbeing and sexual needs. Relying on a man to decide what was best for her would be comforting and exciting. Then there was the darkest of her fantasies — an orgy — taken by multiple partners, fucked every which way possible.

Again moisture dampened her thighs. Her breasts ached with the need to be stroked, caressed and suckled. She reached to cup her globes when a light touch on her elbow brought her back to the fact she wasn't alone. She glanced over her shoulder to meet Passion Flower's knowing gaze and about thirty others.

"Slave Kitty, we must hurry if we are to meet Master Terrance. He is not one to keep waiting," warned the Asian woman.

And hurry they did. Stripped naked, Ciarra was hardly aware as another dark-haired slave by the name of Tatiana slipped thin transparent bracelets over her wrists and ankles. Immediately the bangles adjusted to fit snuggly.

"What are these for?" Ciarra asked, tugging on the scraps of what looked like rubber or plastic that didn't give a millimeter. She looked down at the innocent wristband while Tatiana escorted her naked form quickly through another door. Ciarra didn't realize they had left the room, much less that the woman had not answered her question, until she looked up, her gaze darting around. Thankfully there was no one who stood before her in the garden.

The outdoor garden was exquisite. Flowers perfumed the air. Greenery spotted the scenery. She barely had time to notice the colorful birds perched high in the trees as she received a little push on the back.

"You must bathe with haste." The petite women with short dark hair and eyes to match guided Ciarra toward a beautiful pool of water. "Welcome to Zygoman," Tatiana said as if it were an afterthought.

The first thing Ciarra experienced was white sand so soft and light it felt like whipped cream squishing between her toes. She wanted to stop and enjoy the erotic sensation, run her feet through the stuff over and over again, but the woman prodded her forward.

The second was the pleasing sound of water spilling into the pond as it cascaded from a picturesque rock waterfall. Ciarra tilted her head to the blue-green sky and listened to the birds singing as they sat on the willowy branches of the *quinta* tree. She'd seen a picture once of the foreign tree with long narrow leaves that sprang from its limbs and pink balls of fur sprinkled throughout its branches. The tree blended with the other vegetation to assist in creating a tranquil and romantic aura. Even the crystal-clear water presented a sense of tranquility. She could actually see her toes as Tatiana pulled her deeper into its depths until she was submerged to her chest.

The coolness was invigorating, but something was in the water. It moved around her, stroking and making her body hum like a vibrator as it slipped across her labia, her breasts, little fingers massaging and teasing. The experience was a little unsettling. Still she was definitely enjoying the invisible caress as her nipples grew taut. She even spread her legs wider encouraging the water's touch.

"The water contains synthetic amoebas for cleansing. We use no soaps, no shampoos—the creatures in the water break down and dispose of impurities." Tatiana offered the explanation without question.

Perhaps this is just what I need…

Ciarra watched little whirlpools appear in and around white moth orchids with large, flat green leaves. Every few minutes the broad petals would close, and when they reopened a fountain of water sprang from their center.

A diversion until I can think of a plan and find a safe place to hide.

Maybe this is a safe place to hide.

Her thighs drifted further apart, a coil winding tighter and tighter in her belly as the amoebas slid back and forth across her swollen lips, circling her clit that was now beginning to throb.

But before Ciarra could reach fulfillment, Tatiana grabbed her hand and pulled. "We must hurry. Master Terrance will not be happy if you are late."

"Who the hell is this Master Terrance?" Ciarra asked wondering exactly what that nasty blonde in California had arranged.

Chapter Three

❧

What was that antiquated aphorism—out of the frying pan into the fire? It really shouldn't have surprised Ciarra, but this time she had outdone herself. Surpassed all the meaningless wrong steps she had taken throughout her twenty-six years on Earth. God should have kept her on her knees. Lord knew the mammoth giant with feral hazel eyes, Master Terrance, kneeling before her, intended to do just that.

Wrists bound to a St. Andrews Cross, she gasped as the man's strong hands pried her legs apart at the ankles, spreading her wide, exposing her naked body to intense scrutiny. His dark gaze burned into her calf, slowly up her knee to her thigh, pausing at the small patch of curls that matched her flaming red hair.

"Excuse me." She attempted to sound indignant, but came off somewhat feeble.

His pupils dilated.

A bottomless rumble surfaced from deep in his throat. For a moment the man sounded inhuman—wild, dangerous. When he pulled his gaze to hers, she swore his irises shimmered.

And oh, God, she was his bound prey. There was no escape, no freedom in sight.

Damn Tatiana for not explaining what was going to happen to her. The room had looked so innocent, clean with sky blue walls and a large X-shaped cross placed in the middle of the wooden floor. She hadn't fought the woman when she bound Ciarra's wrists to the crucifix, only asking why. Again the woman refused to answer. Soft steps echoed off the wooden floor as she'd moved away, pushing a button on the controller she held. The scraping of metal and wood sounded as the east wall rotated, revealing what looked strangely like an invitation into hell. Whips, chains, ropes, and other menacing-looking devices were hanging from the wall. Before Ciarra could speak, Tatiana disappeared, leaving her alone— that was, until the three Thorenson brothers entered.

Ciarra's body reacted immediately to Master Shawn's presence. Her nipples beaded into tight nubs, her pussy grew hot and wet. She needed him to touch her, take her into his safe embrace. Indifferent, he had stood like a statue, refusing to look her way.

The oldest of the brothers, Master Tor, had explained, "Per your request, Master Terrance will be your Master." Who happened to be the hulking monster between her legs, she discovered with displeasure. "However, rest assured that all three of us will service you one way or another." His grin was one of confidence and delight.

Now how was a girl supposed to take that?

Ciarra attempted to jerk her leg away, stop Master Terrace, but his iron grip never wavered.

Desperately, she tried to quell the tremors, the way her voice broke on each breath when he fastened her foot to the cool wood behind her. But damn it, she was scared. Way over her head. It was one thing to fantasize about bondage, another to actually take part in the flight of fancy.

As the final silk rope slithered across her ankle, Ciarra's last free limb, a sliver of fear iced her veins. This latest misjudgment was minutes away from the biggest mistake of her lifetime. Or perhaps the second biggest mistake, the first being the event that delivered her to this point.

I never should have run. But would the outcome have been any better? No—no, surely it would not have. No one would have believed her innocent of murder. Hell, given the facts, she'd convict herself.

Ciarra pressed her eyelids tightly together. For a moment darkness embraced her. The warm sensation of being alone, of being miles away from this place, this man, surfaced. Then sharp lights splintered as visions of dark red blood, so much blood, and the dagger in her hand slipping slowly from her palm, falling and crashing to the floor. The loud *clunk* of metal against marble shook her.

Nausea struck with a vengeance. Acids churned, rolling like an angry sea. Her back arched, revolting against her bindings, forcing her eyes to pop open only to meet the predatory gleam of her captor.

Perfectly sculpted lips curled into a snarl revealing perfect white teeth just like his brothers'. A bright light flickered in his hungry eyes. He was enjoying her fear.

The knowledge was a cold shower shocking Ciarra's system, awakening her anger, which reminded her who she was — or who she was supposed to be anyway.

She felt some of her bravado peek from beneath the curtain it had hightailed to when all this crap had begun. She was a high-powered copyeditor. She knew how to maneuver around shark-infested waters. She could handle these men. Her gaze darted to Master Shawn. His face was etched in stone, but her heart still jumped. There was something about him. Something her body recognized, but her mind refused to acknowledge.

No. There was no time for romantic entanglements. She was in a shitload of trouble and a man would only be a complication. She pushed thoughts of the gorgeous hunk across the room aside and focused on the one before her.

In fact, someone should tell these arrogant men that the little white skirt and sash of material thrown over one shoulder was outdated. If her memory served her it was called a toga. They weren't in Rome and it was the twenty-second century after all. But damn if it didn't give her a good look at their bronze chests, biceps and strong, powerfully built calves laced with brown leather from their toes to their knees.

Yeow! Another time, another place she would have loved to discover what was hidden beneath all that white and gold trim material. Now that was an idea that would merit blowing their skirts up.

"Release me, you son of a bitch!" she demand firmly, but her tone lacked conviction. Nevertheless, that is exactly how the rich-bitch from California would have reacted toward this man dressed like a Greek god from the pages of a history book. Not to mention Master Shawn and Master Tor stood across the dungeon, voyeurs and carbon copies of the man resting at her feet.

A bulging vein ticked in Master Terrance's neck. Slowly, the blond Adonis rose to his feet. A thumb and forefinger stroked his chin once. His warm breath fanned Ciarra's face. "You have earned your first punishment." The low tenor of his voice promised retribution.

A gust of disbelief pushed from her tight lungs. "Punishment?" It was hard taking control of the situation naked, bound, spread-eagled, but she had to do something. "Have you forgotten who I am? Who is paying the bill? You work for me, *buddy*."

Hey, that sounded pretty good. Confidence burst throughout Ciarra, raising her chin sharply. She would show this man who was boss. "I've had enough." Her eyes narrowed and met his steely gaze. "This isn't what I anticipated."

"All the better, slave Kitty." The look of satisfaction on the man's chiseled face made fire lick up her throat and flare across her cheeks. But it was his next words that made Ciarra want to gnaw through the ropes with her bare teeth. "You're a fine piece of ass. I will enjoy bringing you to your knees," he cupped his firm erection, "and feeling your lips around this."

Her jaw dropped. Her eyes widened. The man was a bastard. Her mouth finally snapped shut. If he came any closer she would give him a sample of the *Silence of the Lambs*. Even in the year 2106, twentieth-century movies were still being shown. Not quite the realistic quality of today's 3D digital cinemax displays, but entertaining nonetheless. And the thought of chewing his face off was sounding better by the minute.

And Kitty! Could the woman have chosen a flakier name? Unbelievable, because the woman Ciarra saw at the LA Transport Station was more lion than kitten. It was only after Ciarra arrived on Zygoman, Ecstasy Island, the well-known pleasure planet of the galaxy, that she discovered the woman had intended her vacation to be a crash course in BDSM 101.

Ciarra hadn't yet reviewed the contract, but from what Tatiana had said earlier, she would be receiving the ultimate package. And how fortunate she was to be trained by no others hands than the three Thorenson brothers, the proprietors of this planet.

Yippee! Oh, be still, my restless heart.

Kitty Carmichael had way too much money if all she could think about was being bound, tortured and fucked by three Grecian gods. Okay, so the last point wasn't too bad. By the looks of these men, a woman would not leave their beds unsatisfied, especially if she took them all on at once.

Still she couldn't help but wonder what it would feel like to be loved and cherished by Master Shawn. Where Master Terrance had almost a cruel air about him, Master Shawn was still waters, deep and mysterious. He made a woman lust for the unknown, made her want to discover what he alone could offer.

Shawn couldn't turn his eyes away from Kitty any longer. Myriad emotions swam in the bound woman's bright blue eyes. Prominent within their depths was fear that had immediately turned to stubbornness, strength and determination. Her porcelain features were frozen. The supple lines of her curves and mounds defined a masterpiece of womanhood. She was beautiful in her fury. So different from what he saw earlier. The insecurity that she had displayed was now gone. Instead she was preparing herself for battle.

Shawn watched as Terrence reached out and tweaked her nipple, hard. She wrenched, screaming at the unexpected pain. The high-pitched wail subdued when Terrence caressed his palm across the woman's other breast, fondling its nub. A light hue of embarrassment flashed pink across her shapely body, and then reddened with anger as she flung herself forward as if lunging at her tormentor.

"You sadistic bastard," she spewed, tossing her head. Fiery ringlets bounced in the air, ebbed around her face and shoulders, then gently at her waist.

Terrance had that effect on women. They either loved what he did to them, or wanted to scratch his eyes out. Clearly, Miss Carmichael was going for the eyes.

Terrence continued to familiarize himself with the bound woman's body. His brother's large hands caressed her thighs, hips, waist and breasts. Contempt flared in her stormy glare and Shawn had to admit he felt the same. Given half the chance he would tear Terrance into pieces.

She is mine.

He was startled, taken unaware by the irrational feelings. Tense fingers curled into fists as Shawn's jaws clenched. *She isn't Chastity.*

No, this woman was nothing like Chastity. She seemed somehow…different. Special.

"Terrence is a pro in stimulating the fuck/fight syndrome in a woman," murmured Tor, the eldest of his brothers. His knowing gaze skimmed up and down Shawn's face. Shawn fought to relax, hide the emotion that was surfacing like transports on the fast track. Last thing he needed was big brother's interference. "Look at him. The angrier she gets the more excited he becomes." The proof tented Terrence's toga and Shawn wasn't too happy about it either. Tor's eagle eyes once again gathered information that Shawn would rather keep unknown. "Yet it looks like she could use a softer hand. Eh, baby brother?" He paused. "She reminds me of someone. How about you?"

Tor waited for Shawn's response that was long in coming. "No." His reply was short with more heat behind it than he had hoped for.

Tor grinned as he gripped Shawn's shoulder and squeezed, then he released a chuckle. The gleam in his brother's eyes told Shawn his secret was out. Tor knew he wanted this woman. Not just because she reminded him of Chastity, but there was something more, some element that called to him. "We don't want Terrence having all the fun." He released Shawn. "Master Terrance, may I speak with you?"

Terrance pivoted on a dime, and by the frown he pinned them both with he didn't look happy. Heavy footsteps brought him to stand before the brothers. "What? I'm working here." His throaty growl revealed the lust that burned hot inside him.

"Perhaps our little brother should try his hand," suggested Tor.

Terrance's brows furrowed as Tor raised one of his. Then unspoken words transferred between the two brothers by a mere look and an exchange of understanding. They were less than a year apart. Their mother said the pair held a special bond being born so close. Hell yeah, the demons had learned how to tie knots and bind people by practicing on Shawn when they were little.

Damn. Shawn hated when they spoke without words. He hated it even more when they made him feel like their baby brother. Even their sister, Taryn, could make him feel young at his current age of twenty-seven. Still he'd take what Tor was offering. A chance to teach Kitty about herself, her sexual desires, her needs. But he would keep his desires in tight control. She wasn't Chastity and never would be. Kitty Carmichael was just another client. She was Terrance's responsibility.

"Fine," Terrance grumbled. Then a spark lit his eyes. "Hey, baby brother, wanna share her? You fuck her mouth. I'll take her fiery curls." When Shawn's fists tightened, the heat of anger blazing across his face, Terrance laughed. Shawn shouldn't have let his brother prod him. He knew Terrance hadn't fucked a woman's pussy since his divorce. "Too intimate," Terrance had explained. But Shawn knew it was Terrance's way of keeping women at an arm's length. But that was a whole story in itself.

Shawn's reaction to this woman was abnormal. He knew it, his brothers knew it. He was the quiet one, not easily moved and always under control. Tor was the studious and meticulous brother. Terrance was the short fuse. Yet when Chastity had been in danger several months past, Shawn had discovered a different side of himself, one that unwisely came out with the bound woman before him as well. Control was something he taught and practiced and prided himself on. He would *not* lose it, especially with this woman.

"If it is your pleasure, my brother. She is plenty enough woman for all of us." Shawn's temperate voice was back, his self-assurance followed on quick heels. This was just a job and Kitty Carmichael was just a client. The brothers had shared women before—well, except for Passion Flower—it was their job. The woman before them would be no different than any other woman who had sought their instruction.

"Shall we?" Shawn held on to his control, all the while tensing inside and praying that Terrance wouldn't take this opportunity to shed his oath of refusing pussy and actually fuck the woman.

When Terrance issued a, "Fuck you," Shawn knew the situation had not changed.

"Aw, now that is one thing we haven't tried." Tor's laughter brought Shawn and Terrance's glares upon him. "Go, Shawn. Soften her up so that she is ready when our grizzly brother takes over."

Terrance huffed and swelled up just like a grizzly bear or an *akmour-bull* found on the planet Baccarac. "She doesn't need to be softened. She needs to learn submission, and if she fails, she should be whipped, tortured and fucked thoroughly."

Shawn pushed aside his immediate reaction to strangle Terrance. Instead he bowed to his brother. "It will be as you wish. However, our methods are simply different." He turned and approached the woman on the cross.

She was gorgeous. Her long length stretched helplessly. Her beaded nipples and the light sheen of desire glistening on her mons gave away her arousal. Unconsciously, her tongue made a slow path along her bottom lip. Or was it deliberate?

Big blue eyes followed his every movement as he took from the wall of instruments two nipple rings that were connected by a chain. He turned to face Kitty. Her gaze flickered to the items on the wall—whips, paddles, chains, and leathers—then back to him. Her muscles and tendons strained tight against her smooth skin, anxiety revealed in her taut flesh. Delicious blue veins surfaced beneath the tender skin of her breasts. Man, he wanted to trace each and every one of them with his tongue.

She swallowed hard beneath his scrutiny.

There was always excitement, an adrenaline rush due to the unknown. The way her breath deepened as she prepared herself, her chest rising and falling, was heady and sent blood rushing to his groin. Her fingers curled into fists, but he wanted her relaxed, open to the experiences he had to offer.

Shawn's own breathing began to quicken. He couldn't wait to touch her, to feel the heat of her skin, the moisture of her arousal. Several steps had him standing before her. He raised a hand and brushed the air before her breast, but didn't touch her nipple. Still she shivered and thrust her chest outward toward his palm seeking skin to skin—heat.

Suggestion was heady. The human mind was a wonderful instrument, but easily manipulated. Just the thought of his touch had her reacting, as he knew it would.

When she realized what she had done, she frowned. "Release me." Her breathless demand made him ache with desire. Oh, how he wanted to release her. He wanted to do much more than that. Even now he could feel those long legs wrapped around his waist, his cock buried deep inside her hot channel, the sensation of her breasts skimming his chest as she rode him.

He twirled the nipple rings between his fingers. "No." It was taking an act of God to resist touching her.

She breathed more heavily, lifting her breasts, teasing him with her rosy nipples that were hard and pointing directly at him. "I thought that big oaf over there was my Master." Her gaze cut to his brothers across the room.

"No man can serve two Masters, but a woman...she can have many," he whispered leaning close, smelling the clean scent of almond and vanilla massage oils and woman.

"Chauvinistic?" The air leaving her mouth was warm on his cheek. He wondered for a moment what the warmth would feel like on his cock. His member responded with a jerk that rubbed against her hip. She gasped, the tiny sound encouraging him to continue.

He stepped back and met her dark gaze. "Fact," he said with conviction. "Should I demonstrate?"

She sucked the corner of her bottom lip into her mouth and her small white teeth bit down. "No. Just let me go."

His resistance faltered and he reached for a wavy tendril that lay upon her chest. "Angel, you know I cannot." The cool strand slid through his fingers. He closed his eyes, imagining her thick tresses covering his thighs, his legs, moving across his body as she slid against him, took him deep within her mouth.

"Why?" Her voice broke and she sounded almost childlike. But she gave a very womanly gasp as he brushed her hair across her sensitive breast. Tiny bumps rose across her satin skin.

"It was your desire to learn what we offer at Ecstasy Island." As Shawn spoke, a grumble came from Terrance. His brother was a man of action. Patience was not a virtue he possessed. Shawn glanced over his shoulder, receiving a quick brush from Terrance's hand to "get on with it", while Tor casually leaned against the wall, arms crossed over his chest, a smirk on his face.

Shawn ignored Terrance's prodding and Tor's quiet teasing.

Pleasure was not to be rushed. More enjoyment could be achieved with seductive words, a sensual touch and time—plenty of time.

Shawn placed his back squarely to his brothers and focused on the beautiful woman before him. "I'll start by placing a ring on your lovely nipple."

Her body tensed. Fingernails bit into the palms of her hands as she flexed and uncurled her fingers, leaving sharp impressions in her skin.

"Relax," he whispered just before capturing her nub in his mouth. She whimpered, the sound a desperate cry of longing. His tongue rolled the peak around and around, flicked the tip several times. Then he latched onto her nipple and drew hard, forcing yet another moan. She arched into him.

He couldn't help the smile that creased his lips. And he couldn't help needing to caress her as he slipped the rings in the pocket of his toga. While he suckled her, one hand remained at her breast softly kneading the under swell as the other followed the curve of her waist, the flare of her hip, the smoothness of her thigh. When he skimmed across her knee to the inside of her thigh she trembled.

Slowly his palm moved up her inner-leg. He released her nipple and feathered kisses along her throat, nipping at her chin before he pressed his mouth to hers.

The kiss was a gentle exploration, probing her full lips lightly for entrance. There was little fight in her before she opened and allowed him to taste her. She must have eaten a mint recently because her breath was fresh, a hint of evergreen against his taste buds.

When his hand neared her core he paused, waiting for her to give him a sign that she wanted, desired his touch. Her eyes closed, hips pushing against his palm. It was subtle, but all he needed to continue as he slipped a finger into her wet, hot chamber.

His body was a composition of taut muscles and raw nerves as he fought for control. She was slick and welcoming, her inner muscles contracting around his finger. He wanted to possess this woman. Wanted to tie her to his bed, spread her wide and memorize every curve, every mound, learn every erogenous zone that would make her squirm, scream in ecstasy. His finger steadily pumped in and out, her hips meeting each thrust. He wanted to fuck her pussy, her ass, her mouth, hour after hour until they both were sated and exhausted. Then he would lie with her in his arms and for the first time in a long time he would sleep peacefully, complete, waking to her lovely face. And then he would fuck her again.

Drawing the rings from his pocket, he slipped one over her erect bud. Her eyes sprang wide as if she had never felt the pleasure-pain of the jewelry. She whimpered a light cry of distress. But her eyes were bright with excitement.

She was ready.

Chapter Four

ะา

Ciarra could not believe how her body responded to this man. Just a touch from Master Shawn had her breasts swelling with need. Her nipples were tight aching buds screaming to be suckled, pinched, and even bitten. Her sex continued to hug his finger, weeping with anticipation of his cock, so large and thick pressed against her hip. She could just image how it would stretch and fill her.

Still the harmless-looking jewelry circling her nipple gave her pause. There was no pressure, no discomfort, yet she knew it was coming. She had heard of these contraptions, along with a few more she hoped she would never be introduced to.

Attached to the ring was a long gold chain sporting another round ring that dangled cool down her stomach. As she trembled, it slid across her skin almost tauntingly.

Inserting another finger deep inside her, Master Shawn slowed his thrusts as he reached for the gold circling her nipple. "The spirit is willing—the flesh weak. Pain is only weakness leaving the body. Breathe... Release your weakness... Cleanse your body... Embrace your strength."

Shawn tightened the binding one turn and she whimpered at the first sign of pressure.

"Breathing," his warm breath fanned across her face, "is the key. Deep..." He twisted the binding and red-hot agony burned through her breast. His fingers began to move faster, working in and out of her wet core, deeper and harder. "Cleansing..." Another twist and her breath halted. "Breathe."

He flicked her nipple and rays of fire shot through her globe. But this time it was white-hot and it was indeed pleasurable. The sensation headed south, straight to her womb. The combination of pain and the desire growing between her thighs blended. She was on the verge of climax as he finger-fucked her and tormented her nipple unmercifully.

Ciarra focused inwardly on the blood rushing through her body, the heat building, the tendons and muscles clenching and unclenching, and the heaviness between her thighs. She was almost there, almost to a point where time stood still and the world exploded in and out and around her. Then in the briefest of movements he withdrew his fingers from her pussy leaving her clit throbbing to the tune of unfulfilled desire.

"Do not come without my permission." The authority in his voice was disconcerting, as well as the intensity of the furrows lining his forehead. "I will place the other ring on and you will not make a sound. If you do you will be punished."

Ciarra had no doubt he meant every word. But even the knowledge of punishment by this man sent rays of excitement through her body.

How weird was that?

The ring was cool against her nipple as he slipped it on. He tightened it one turn.

Her breath hitched.

He frowned, his displeasure only softening when she focused her heightened gaze on him and began to breathe— in—out. Her lips twisted in a tight *O*. Her eyes wide open.

Then he tightened the ring two more turns.

On an inhale she choked and trapped air inside her lungs. Oh God, she was going to faint. Her chin dropped to her chest. She squeezed her eyelids tight together.

With his finger and thumb he pinched her chin and raised her head. "Open your eyes." It was a struggle, but she complied. "You will breathe. Deep, cleansing breaths. Enjoy the pressure. Enjoy the pain." The intensity of his fingers grew firmer. "Focus on my eyes."

It was as if she had no control. Her vision snapped to his. She stared hard into his bewitching green eyes. When he inhaled, she inhaled. When he released his breath in a slow, steady stream she followed. Amazingly, he held all the power. He was directing the flow of air through her lungs. He was in command of her body, willing pain to blur into pleasure.

Everything except the man before her and the strange new sensations overtaking her vanished from her consciousness. Even the other two men in the room.

Her sex called to Master Shawn, releasing another wave of desire. She was moist, hot, and horny as hell. She needed him to fill her and she needed to fuck him over and over, until she couldn't walk straight for a week. And she needed him now.

As if by magic her bindings released, freeing her wrists and ankles. As her arms fell to her sides, she tried to draw her feet together, tried to steady herself with no success. Her body felt weak, pliable, as Master Shawn assisted her so that she was standing—for a second. In the next moment he was pushing her to her knees, his large hands on her shoulders driving her to the wooden floor.

His eyes were dark, almost frightening as he stared down at her with something that looked like hunger, a lust so strong it bordered on starvation. Fear stimulated her excitement as he loosened his toga and it slid down powerful thighs, over taut calves to lie at his feet. Her gaze traversed his body, coming to rest on his magnificent cock.

He was long and thick, thrusting upward in an arch that almost touched his bellybutton. She had never had a man this large. But she would have this man. It was in his eyes, in the way he threaded his fingers through her hair and then wrenched her gaze to his.

"Fuck me with your mouth, angel." The words pushing through his thin lips were coarse and scratchy. Salivating, she could not wait to taste him. Her mouth opened, but he held her inches away. "Keep your eyes open and on mine," he growled as he thrust his hips. At the same time pain splintered her scalp as he jerked her closer by yanking on her hair. Without hesitation she licked along his length. He was salty and tasted of male, hot and ready.

She could not hold back the smile as a shudder raked him. His chest rose as if he held his breath.

Now who was the Master? Who was in control? Inwardly gloating, she wrapped her lips around his engorged cock and began to stroke while her hands cradled his sac. With soft kneading movements, her fingers massaged his scrotum, rolling his balls around, relishing the feel of the two large glands sliding through her fingers.

A gust of air pushed from his lungs in a hiss. He wedged his legs further apart. His grip on her hair tightened, the sweet pain urging her onward as her other hand gripped the base of his member. His hips began a gentle thrust, meeting her movements as she worked him in and out of her mouth. Her tongue circled his crown in slow, enticing swirls then slid along the length of him while she allowed her teeth to gently scrape his erection.

For a moment he broke their gaze, turned his head and nodded. But then his eyes returned to hers as he pushed the back of her head with his large hand, forcing her to take all of him, deeper, faster, harder.

When two strong palms gripped her hips, she cried out. The sound muffled around Master Shawn's cock.

"Hush, angel, we are just taking your training to a different level. If you refuse Master Terrance's touch you will be punished." It was a warning that Master Shawn made clearer when he urged her head up further, the arch in her neck straining as he pumped in and out of her mouth.

Ciarra tried to focus on the green eyes holding her gaze. But she couldn't help startling as the palms around her hips lifted her and she felt firm, muscled thighs enclose hers.

Master Terrance knelt behind her, the top of his thighs resting against the back of hers.

But that was nothing to the warm hard object that nudged her anus. The smell of something foreign rent the air and then that hard object felt cool and slick. Fingertips burned into her skin as the man raised her high and then slowly entered her, stretching, filling her with a burn that had tears moistening her eyes.

"Breathe," Master Shawn commanded. Yet the sensation of having her ass and mouth filled by two large men was too much. *"Breathe, damn it."*

Choking, Ciarra managed to inhale around the large cock in her mouth. Master Terrance remained still, his rapid pulse throbbing through his fingertips against her warm flesh.

Shawn smiled, his hold on her hair lessened. "Now enjoy, my angel. But do not forget. You must not come without my permission." As he finished the sentence, Master Terrance raised her hips and began to thrust in and out of her tight rosebud. It was an unusual sensation, both wicked and exciting as he invaded her ass, stretching and filling, while another man fucked her mouth, and a third one watched from across the room. In fact, she liked it. She had dreamed of being taken by multiple men—not exactly like this, but it was exciting nonetheless.

When Master Terrance cradled her breasts, then took her nipples between his fingers and began to squeeze, fire coiled in her belly. One hand slipped from her breast, smoothed down her belly, weaving through the tight curls at her apex before finding her clit. A single finger caressed her bud and then pressed, holding firmly.

"Do you like being fucked by two men?" asked Master Shawn. She could almost imagine bright orange-red flames flickering in his lustful eyes.

She managed a nod.

The smell of sex filled the air, mingling with the warmth of their bodies and the different cologne worn by each man. She loved the earthy scent of Master Shawn that reminded her of a warm summer breeze. Master Terrance's scent was spicy — it even had a bite to it — like the man.

As the men fucked her, Ciarra's body responded. A mass of shooting tingles splintered through her breasts. Her pussy convulsed — spasms that grew in intensity. Her empty pussy needed to be filled like her mouth and ass. Still the beginnings of a wild climax twisted and turned, building into a raging need for release.

Remembering Master Shawn's warning to not come without his permission, Ciarra focused on sliding her tongue over Shawn's cock, the texture of his skin, the veins protruding beneath the surface, and the slickness as he moved in and out of her mouth.

A growl sounded behind her. Master Terrance's fingers closed hard on her nipple at the same time he pinched her clit. She cried out around Master Shawn's cock and flames licked her womb. Desperately, she fought her oncoming climax as the man behind her groaned his release and filled her ass with his seed. Master Shawn was quick to follow, ejecting his fluid into her mouth.

"Drink," he commanded, but he sounded as if he had to force himself to speak through the haze of his own orgasm.

She did his bidding as she drank his essence. Swallowing, doing her best to fight back the fire that was slowing burning away her restraint.

Then both men moved in unison, easing out of her body leaving her empty and unfulfilled. Confused, she settled back on her haunches, while several parts of her anatomy screamed for what these two men had promised and abruptly ripped away.

Cold, angry tremors shook her. *How dare they?*

And then Master Shawn repeated, "No man can serve two Masters, but a woman…she can have many." His tone was cool and distant. He had been in control this entire time—not her. He brushed a hand toward his eldest brother. Master Tor crossed the room to join his brothers. "We are your Masters, slave Kitty. You will serve each of us as we desire."

Shawn turned and walked out of the room, but not before she saw him exchange looks with Master Terrance. For the first time the big oaf smiled and a brother's pride brightened his eyes.

Well, bully-bully.

Then again, perhaps these three men were exactly what she needed, a welcome break from reality and her unknown future.

As the cool night air caressed his heated body, Shawn bent at the waist, his palms resting on his thighs as he pulled in a ragged breath. No woman had ever tied him into knots like this woman had just done, not even Chastity.

It was only head, a blowjob, nothing more, he reminded himself. Still his heart thrashed against his chest. He wanted more of her. He wanted to fuck her pussy and her ass. Hear her scream of ecstasy surround him like a veil. Hear her whisper his name on a sigh and whimper for him to take her over and over again.

Tension dissipated on the breeze, soothing him and cooling the fire inside. It had taken a will of steel to signal Terrance and to allow his brother to fuck Kitty's precious ass.

"Mine," he growled and then shook with self-reproach. She was only a woman. A client who had paid a lot of money to experience all Ecstasy Island had to offer. *A client who has specifically asked for Terrance*. The reminder was bitter on Shawn's tongue. Even now he wondered what his brothers were doing to his woman.

My woman.

Shawn's fist tightened. She wasn't his. Resolve straightened his backbone. She *wasn't* his woman. Then his shoulders fell. But what if she could be?

He didn't have time to ponder the thought as Passion Flower appeared out of thin air, like always. How did she do that? When his sister-in-law was needed she materialized, as if by magic.

The Asian woman bowed. A silky emerald robe hung in the bend of one arm. "I am needed." It wasn't a question.

Shawn nodded. She rose and pushed through the door he had just exited. A moment passed and then Tor and Terrance came through the same exit. Both glanced his way, smiling.

"You did good, little brother," Tor praised.

He slapped Terrance on the back. Terrance's toga was thrown over his shoulder and he was still as naked as Shawn was. In one hand he held Shawn's toga, which he proceeded to toss, hitting Shawn square in the face.

"He took too long," grumbled Terrance.

Anger sparked inside Shawn, but he snuffed it out and steeled his frame. He bowed quietly. "Tortoise and the Hare," he offered. The ancient childhood story was one of Shawn's favorites. He believed that a slow hand was more adept than a bull in a china shop. Different approaches as different as the brothers standing before him.

Tor chuckled. "Passion Flower will prepare our delectable client for dinner." He raised a brow, mischief twinkling in his eyes. "Are you going to join us?" he asked Shawn.

Fuck. There was no telling what Tor and Terrance had planned for the woman. All he could do was go along with them.

"No." He feigned indifference, pausing as his brothers shared an expression of disbelief. Then he yawned, hand over mouth, before casually adding, "On the other hand perhaps I will." *You bet I will*, he mumbled to himself.

Shawn's constraint was well under control. If his brothers thought he would let a woman take away years and years of training they were wrong—dead wrong.

Shawn was definitely under control...until Passion Flower exited with Kitty Carmichael following. The woman's long red hair showed rich against the emerald green robe. He had the desire to run his fingers through her tresses. A shapely leg peeked through the folds of the robe and his cock hardened. His hand holding his toga slid in front of his groin to hide her effect on him from his brothers. But by the grins on the two bastards' faces he had not moved fast enough.

Then he raised a brow, nodding to Terrance's hard-on. The damn man wore it proudly. It appeared that the woman had the same effect on his brothers, because Tor's toga had lifted as well. A realization that did not set well with Shawn, as his attention returned to the two women.

Kitty was frowning. Her face was drawn. Her eyes look weary, tired, as her gaze darted away from his. The blush on her face revealed her embarrassment, an emotion that he would drive out of her before she left this island. She would leave this planet confident in her sexuality, attuned to her dark side and open to new experiences. And he could not wait to get started.

Chapter Five

ଯ

Laughter and various sounds of dinner being served, glasses clinking and dishes set upon the tables met Shawn as he entered the communal dining hall. Already slaves and Masters alike were enjoying the fare before them in the room designed to give an outdoor atmosphere. It was a jungle environment of trees, vines and colorful flowers along the walls. A full-figured woman sat upon a man's lap feeding him *vitia,* a rare fruit from Ardorian, another pleasure planet in the galaxy. Several erotic planets existed in the solar system, but Zygomen outranked them all.

Large, round, stone tables dotted the room, each with a natural champagne fountain surrounded by edible exotic flowers floating on the surface. Among them pineapple guava blooms were sprinkled. Their light pink petals were sweet and melted on the tongue. The *cunnilingus orchid* from Ardorian was a favorite among the men. Appropriately named because its flesh-colored petals were gathered tight in the center to form a pocket filled with sweet tasting pollen.

Several guests had already gravitated to their seats, while others hovered around the hors d'oeuvres table sampling the multitude of offerings. A number of people mingled holding glasses of champagne and wine offered by the slaves moving about the room.

Although Shawn scanned the room indifferently, he was anything but. Every muscle, every tendon was rigid beneath his skin. An internal struggle waged to take what was his against what he knew was not. Kitty Carmichael was only here on vacation — nothing more.

Off to the side of the dining hall were four alcoves which allowed privacy for certain events and those individuals who had prior reservations. Each had a different theme. Shawn had been told earlier that the Snack Chamber had been reserved for his brothers and Kitty.

The woman who had consistently invaded his mind the last hour or so had not arrived. But already the thought of her made his cock rise with anticipation.

Damn this outfit, he thought as his toga rose.

Shawn's attire was again a toga made of white Egyptian linen, and a gold medallion and chain hung around his waist. Brown sandals with black straps wound around each powerful leg to mid-calf, where the strings of leather were tied.

The Thorensons had modeled their island to resemble a Roman palace, the same place where sexual discovery evolved so many years ago on Earth.

A spicy scent filled the air as a roasted pig on a wooden slab, carried by two slaves, passed by. Steam rose from the delectable cuisine, the smell making his mouth salivate and his stomach growl. Had he eaten today? He couldn't remember as his only thoughts had been of Kitty since her arrival.

The woman was becoming a nuisance in his head, crowding his thoughts with memories of the way her mouth had felt against his lips and around his cock. His member jerked beneath his toga. Tatiana, the dark-haired slave who had graced his bed more than once smiled, her eyes glued to his groin. Her come-and-get-me look was dismissed as Kitty entered the room.

Just the sight of the woman made Shawn short-winded. She looked refreshed as if a shower had breathed new life into her. Shoulders back, head held high, a river of hair flamed around her shoulders as she stood quietly beside Passion Flower. But the pink tinting her cheeks gave her away. It was only a pretentious show on her part. Several times her fists clenched and unclenched. She visibly attempted to restrain herself from drawing back and shielding her body from the appreciative eyes that lingered on her. And how could they help but look?

The woman wore a lacy white bustier that lifted and presented her full breasts, but covered nothing, leaving her luscious nipples free. She wore a matching garter belt that held up white stockings which caressed her shapely legs, yet she wore no underwear. Her fiery curls were bare for all to enjoy. The stilettos gave her an extra three inches that almost made her eye level with him.

Several Masters eyed her and then their own slaves, their gazes moving back to the redhead. One Master in particular rose from the table and headed in her direction. No woman could even come close to Kitty in looks or sensuality, and if Shawn had his way no man would be allowed near her.

A stalwart man with brown hair stood before her. "I don't believe we've met. I'm Matthew Collins, Master Collins."

As Shawn approached he heard her say, "Ci—uh—Kitty Carmichael."

Collins' grin nearly undid Shawn as recognition brightened the man's eyes. "Ah, yes, Kitty Carmichael, I've heard of you. You work for the Kohler Advertising Agency. I didn't realize you would be here."

Kitty visibly flinched at his words. Something close to panic filled her eyes. Her tongue swiped a path between her lips and she swallowed, hard. Her chest rose, catching the man's attention as she pulled in a deep breath then released it slowly. Her nipples tightened under the man's scrutiny sending red-hot jealousy through Shawn.

"Yes, I can see this is going to be a very profitable vacation." Collins' smiling brown eyes finally focused on her face and away from her full breasts. "Since I have an account with Kohler, perhaps we could mix business with pleasure."

Before Shawn could speak, Terrance was beside him. What did his brother do—run across the damn room?

"That may be possible as Slave Kitty will be auctioned off three nights from now," Terrance said.

Both Kitty's and Shawn's glares met Terrance's nonchalant expression.

Laughter broke out, loud and rambunctious at a table across the room. Two men had chosen to sample their slaves' offerings between their thighs instead of the food spread generously across the table. One brawny man in particular insisted that the young man to his left taste both women to break the contest as to whose slave was the tastiest.

Shawn figured by Kitty's deep frown she wanted, as much as he did, to knock the lingering grin from Terrance's face.

She took a deep breath. "I don't think...I—"

Terrance interrupted, "That's right, you don't think. You will do exactly what I tell you to do and you will not speak again unless I grant you permission. All infractions will be dealt with immediately."

Master Collins retreated a short distance. Terrance's warning was obviously taken seriously as Kitty held her tongue. But the fury reddening her eyes was enough to incite Terrance further. "Take the stance. Cast your eyes down," he demanded.

A flicker of confusion flashed across her face. Before she could react, Terrance gripped her arm and turned her about. Without hesitation he activated her static ankle and wristbands.

The clear bands placed around her wrists and ankles in the Preparation Room upon her arrival would allow Terrance to position Kitty's body any way he desired. Evidently, their use had not been explained to Kitty as she looked helpless while an invisible force jerked her hands high above her head, both welded together at the wrists. The heels of her stilettos scraped the floor as her legs spread a shoulder-width apart.

When she attempted to move her legs back together she stumbled. Shawn caught her to him before she fell.

Damn his brother. Terrance had not activated the energy source that would keep her entire body stationary, only her ankles and wrists. And since Kitty had no previous training she had no idea what was happening or expected of her.

Shawn held her close, mouth pressed to her ear. "It's a force field that allows Master Terrance to restrain and position you. You cannot fight it. Fighting will only arouse him further," he warned before releasing her and taking a couple of steps back.

The gleam in Terrance's eyes revealed the enjoyment he was having at both Kitty's and Shawn's expense. Even Master Collins was smiling.

Terrance pulled a small whip with eight leather thongs from his waistband. He struck the long handle against one of his palms repetitively as he circled her. "You have but four basic duties—to serve your Master's needs, to obey his orders, to accept his domination and to please his desires."

"I—"

"Again, you speak without permission," Terrance scowled, but excitement raised his toga a little higher. "Hold her steady, Master Shawn. Our slave has earned a punishment."

Shawn gritted his teeth. His brother could be a sadistic bastard when he wanted to be and tonight he was definitely in the mood. Shawn moved in front of Kitty. In one hand he grasped her bound wrists held above her head, the other he held at the back of her head as he drew her against his length. Immediately he felt the peaks of her nipples brush against his bare chest. His cock grew firm as he relished her softness while he pressed against her belly. The contact made his balls swell and ache.

Her breath came in nervous pants, her warmth spreading across his chest. She trembled from head to toe. When she leaned into him to quiet the tremors, he wanted to whisper assurances in her ear.

The scent of sunflowers. Her silky hair teasingly wrapped around him as static electricity zapped them both, raising some of her tendrils and sending a shock wave through him. It was like everything came alive on this woman at once. She was a hundred volts of raw power and he couldn't wait to feel her sparks flowing through him.

Terrance pried the whip between Kitty's and Shawn's bodies, the prongs dangling so that their tips feathered across her mons and whisked over Shawn's dick. Through the thin linen, the leather teased. He snapped his jaw tight. He was going to kill Terrance when they were alone. Another wiggle of Terrance's hand and another brush of the thongs gliding between them had Shawn praying for control.

When the whip was dislodged, the woman pressed into Shawn again, thigh to thigh, hips to hips, chest to chest. "I don't know what to do," she admitted. Her voice sounded small, scared.

"Breathe." He ran his tongue along the shell of her ear, felt the tremor in her hands held high above her. "Breathe and envision me between your legs, entering you, spreading you wide."

The whip cracked and Kitty arched into him as a cry left her lips. Her knees gave a little and he tightened his hold on the back of her head.

He nibbled lightly on her earlobe, before circling it and slipping his tongue into her ear. She moaned, the sound airy and delightful.

"Do you want me to fuck you?" he murmured between strokes.

This time when the whip cracked, her cry was, "Yes."

The pressure between his legs was becoming unbearable. He knew the two whippings Terrance had given her landed on each ass cheek. He wanted to see her pink flesh, feel the warmth of her angry skin beneath his palm. And he wanted to hold the whip. In his mind's eye she would beg to be whipped, her body branded by him, knowing that he would make love to her afterward like she had never been loved before.

When the whip cut through the air again, Kitty arched into him, but this time her body slid seductively against his length. Her movements inched his toga up, baring his cock as another movement had her gripping his member between her thighs.

It was heaven. He had died and gone to heaven. Her folds were wet, hot, and eager to accept him. He ground his hips against hers, wanting to enter her, but not positioned to do so. It was frustrating—more than frustrating—as he thrust his cock along her swollen folds.

Another crack of the whip and she bent, widening her thighs so that the head of his erection inched into her warmth. One thrust and he would be buried deep inside her, feel her heat surround him, cradling him.

"That is enough. Release her, Master Shawn." The sound of Terrance's voice was like fingernails across a smooth surface. It made Shawn's skin crawl. He had forgotten that anyone existed beyond this woman pressed against him. He had forgotten about his brother and the room full of onlookers.

His cock was positioned and ready. The woman was ready. Her quick, shallow pants were proof, not to mention her hips still undulated, urging him onward. Her moist cove called to him, begged him to finish what had begun.

Instead he stepped away, still holding her wrists above her head. The disappointment on her face humbled him. Twice he had brought her to the precipice and twice he had left her longing.

Her chagrin quickly twisted into anger. Kitty jerked her hands away from him, bringing them sharply in front of her. Evidently, Terrance had released the force field on her arms. Feet still parted and rooted to the floor, she snapped her head around, glaring at Terrance over her shoulder following his movements as he walked off to her side.

Terrance chuckled. She was playing right into his brother's hands.

Ciarra had reached her limits. She was so horny, so hot that even the flogger the big oaf had in his hands looked inviting. Given half the chance she'd fuck the whip. But what she wanted was Master Shawn. The gentleness of his touch made her ache, while his kisses promised a night in heaven. Unlike his brother who was the epitome of the devil reincarnated.

Master Collins moved beside Master Terrance and Ciarra's heart leaped remembering his words. He insinuated that he knew Kitty Carmichael, or least knew of her. Ciarra had almost swallowed her tongue when the man said that Kitty worked at the same ad agency that she did. Ciarra had never seen the nasty blonde at a meeting, nor had she seen her name plastered on any door.

"Would you consider selling or trading her?" The man in black leather reached into his pants pocket and extracted a blank money voucher. "Name your price." He winked at Ciarra and she looked away, head bowed in frustration.

Sold or traded—like an animal? Surely the man jested. Still Ciarra's heart leaped and her pulse sped. Then she felt a tear form. She didn't deserve anything better. She had murdered a man. Perhaps this was her just desserts. Maybe it was fate's way of retribution. At least she didn't have to worry about birth control. The shot she had taken at the beginning of the year was still in effect.

A growl surfaced from Shawn sending goose bumps across her skin as her gaze snapped up to met his. Strong fingers closed around her biceps as he moved to her side, placing his firm body between her and Collins, not to mention his brother. She glanced askance at the men, her feet still immobilized, an ache beginning to develop in her neck, afraid to let them out of her sight.

A champion was just what she needed at this moment. She welcomed his support, as well as the delicious view of his backside. He had a body made to touch, caress and to make love to. Her arousal, that had subsided when the cruel memories flooded her, was heating back up.

Through muffled voices, angry words were exchanged between brothers. Terrance took a long look at the voucher Collins held in his hand, but remained silent.

The breadth of her protector's shoulders and back seemed to expand before her eyes. He looked wild against the tropical backdrop. Primitive and unrestrained and strangely right in this motif.

"She is not for sale." Master Shawn's low menacing voice left no room for negotiation as he addressed Master Collins, but glared at his brother. No one attempted what was clearly indisputable, not even Master Terrance. He frowned in return and slowly stroked the handle of the flogger, returning Master Shawn's scowl.

There was more to the calm exterior than Master Shawn displayed. Barely leashed strength tightened his body. He balled his fists, his tense veins bulged beneath his tanned skin, and he clenched his jaw. He was a power to be reckoned with. And he guarded her like a lion protecting his lioness, or a man his woman.

Emotion squeezed her chest. She had searched high and low for a man like him. Wouldn't you know he would appear at a time when she didn't deserve even the lowest of men? That is if she really did kill Stan Mayhem. Something just wasn't right, her loss of memory for one thing. She had the memory of an elephant. And she would never hurt someone, much less commit murder.

She twisted at the waist, could not stop her bound hands from touching Master Shawn's arm, a light touch of her fingertips.

He pivoted and faced her. For a moment his expression softened, then turned cold.

"Master Terrance, take your slave in hand. Dinner is about to begin." Without another word Shawn turned his back to her and headed toward the alcove where Tor awaited them.

Master Collins bowed to Master Terrance and returned to his table. A woman with the same fiery red hair as her own cuddled up to him. The shapely woman cut a devilish grin toward Ciarra that she ignored.

Ciarra was shattered. The so-called lion that had protected her now threw her to the wolf—or troll was more like it. She was confused and disappointed. One minute her hero was gentle, caring. The next he was like a northern breeze, cold and distant. *And they say women are fickle.*

Master Terrance grumbled something beneath his breath. She leaned forward, struggling to hear him as he repeated the single word. At the same time he extracted a handheld controller from the pocket of his toga, pushed a button and released the force field locking her feet. Electricity shimmered through her ankles and she almost fell forward, stumbling to maintain her footing.

Did the bastard just say, "Heel?" Her backbone went ramrod straight. She was not a dog and she would not be treated like one. She didn't move. Her feet rooted to the ground by her anger. Her fists buried into her hips.

"Did you not hear me, slave Kitty?" the obnoxious man murmured. A smile gleamed in his eyes that said he knew damn well she'd heard him. "Is another punishment warranted?"

Okay, now she was in a quandary. If she held her ground she'd be punished. If she conceded she would all but agree to let this man treat her poorly. Then she thought of her last punishment, a punishment that had morphed into sensual foreplay. The flogger had stung, but Master Shawn's sexy voice and dirty talk, not to mention his hot body pressed to hers had turned the whipping into something pleasurable. And she had been so close to feeling the man's cock deep inside her.

Moisture dampened her thighs. Her nipples stung. Shit. She'd screw the big oaf if she could only assuage the ache between her legs.

As Ciarra struggled with her decision, Master Shawn caught her attention from where he sat. With a jerk of his head he called her toward one of the private alcoves along the wall. A strange triangular table sat in the center of the small dining room. Each of the three sides had what appeared like a bite taken from the middle. There were three throne-like chairs. Master Shawn reclined in one, and his eldest brother Tor in another.

She went willingly, much to the big oaf Terrance's disappointment and her surprise. What was it about Master Shawn that made her trust him, a mere stranger? But she did. There was no logical explanation, just the need to be near him.

As Ciarra approached, she noted the walls in the cove were stone. Water glistened over them and disappeared into a slit in the floor. Out of small crevices in the wall, colorful flowers grew. Their scent was light and sweet, mingling with the delicious smells of the food arranged in the center of the table and along the sides of each indentation. Some of the food was familiar, others piqued her curiosity.

"Take a seat," barked Master Terrance. When she began to sit in the remaining chair, he said, "On the table."

Her eyes widened in disbelief. What was this man up to?

Ciarra had never been ashamed of nudity, but she felt self-conscious as she climbed onto the table, careful not to bump any of the food dishes. Her dilemma reminded her to go along with this man until she could find a way off this planet.

She still hadn't decided where she would go or how she would get there.

Master Terrance took the chair in front of her. He frowned. "Spread your legs."

Ciarra hesitated only a moment before she complied. Her thighs parted slowly, their lengths aligning with the food placed at the corners of the table. More food was to her back, as well as the two other Thorenson brothers. Heat spread across her face as Master Terrance ogled her moist folds.

Damn the man. His chair legs scraped against the stone floor as he moved closer into the groove in the wood allowing him to move freely between her thighs.

Master Tor cleared his throat. "Shall we eat?"

The table began to shake. Terrance lurched backwards almost tipping his chair as the table rotated. Ciarra braced her palms on the table as she moved away from Terrance so that she was situated in front of Tor.

Ohmygod. She was sitting on a revolving platter, like a Lazy Susan, and she was the main course.

Nice," Tor murmured stroking her chest and exposed sex with his gaze. "I believe I'll have the baked chicken." He bent forward, his tongue skimming across her slit sending a shiver through her body. Then he looked up at her expectantly.

Startled at the man's actions, her hips rose and her eyes widened further.

"Beside you, slave Kitty, the platter next to your right knee. Feed me," Tor commanded as he leaned back in his chair and relaxed. He placed one foot beside her thigh on the table's edge, watching her every movement and giving her a clear view of what lay beneath his toga. Damn. Were all the men on this planet hung like a horse?

She reached for the dish of chicken sliced in three-inch strips with lemon sauce drizzled upon the golden fowl as his foot came off the table. The plate was warm to the touch, the smell made her stomach rumble. She hadn't eaten anything since last night. At first she couldn't, nor wanted to. Now hunger gnawed at the lining of her stomach. Using a fork she stabbed a piece of chicken and placed it before the man's mouth, which he refused to open.

"Place an end in your mouth. You will feed Master Tor in this manner," instructed Master Shawn. She turned at the sound of his voice and glanced over her shoulder. No emotion graced his features.

Ciarra straightened. She could do this, she had to.

Tor scooted his chair closer as the tabletop descended and brought them to eye level. She held the fork before her mouth and placed the chicken between her lips and waited. The succulent chicken oozed juices down her throat and made her stomach growl again. Before she could think of devouring the food, Tor's lips met hers. Their gazes met, held. She could feel his smile against her mouth and wanted to lash out at him. Instead she raised a brow, causing a chuckle to bubble from the man's throat. He bit, chewed.

"Eat," Master Tor ordered. She chewed and swallowed. In a surprise move the man leaned forward and licked a path around her lips. "Delicious... More."

Again she fed him a slice of chicken. Each time he would follow it by licking her lips with his tongue and kissing her.

"I'm thirsty," barked Master Terrance. And with that, the table rotated so fast that Tor almost fell out of his chair trying to move away as the surface spun. Ciarra felt dizzy, forcing her eyelids closed. Damn this game between brothers. When she opened them she faced the menacing man with hazel eyes.

Without being told, Ciarra looked behind her to find a crystal glass with a red substance. She retrieved the drink and extended her hand toward the man. He laughed, the sound ominous.

"Take the drink into your mouth and feed it to him, slowly." This time Ciarra could have sworn she heard a growl in Master Shawn's voice.

As she raised the glass to her lips, the legs of the devil's chair scratched across the floor as he drew closer. She leaned forward, cheeks inflated with the sweet wine, and for a moment she thought of spewing the substance in the man's smug face.

"Don't do it," he warned.

Damn. Was the man a mind reader? Or, she grinned inwardly, had some woman already spit in his face? She was tempted, Lord, knew she was tempted. Yet Ciarra was tired and her stamina was becoming a dry well. There was something about this man that told her he could get real nasty and she just didn't have the energy to find out.

Instead Ciarra leaned forward and placed her mouth to his, slowly releasing the wine and letting it flow into his mouth and down his throat. Finished, she started to draw back, but not before Master Terrance assaulted her mouth.

His kiss was firm, demanding, as his tongue pushed past her lips, invading her depths. He took what he wanted, unlike his brother. He pulled her into his arms, a grip that felt like chains closing around her.

Although appalled, her body reacted—the traitor. Her breasts filled with desire, heavy and needy. Her nipples were tight aching buds as she threaded her fingers through his blond hair and kissed him with the fury inside her. His response was aggressive. Their teeth clinked together. A battle ensued between their tongues. It was all-out war.

If Ciarra didn't know better she would have thought Master Terrance was fighting his own demons.

Then the table began to move, jerking her. It was either slide off the table face first, or let go of the man whose arms had already released her. Ciarra let go and found herself eye to eye with Master Shawn. His jaw was a tight line. A vein bulged in his forehead. If she didn't know better, she would have thought the man was jealous. But this was just a job for these three men. The nasty blonde from California had arranged this experience. Until Ciarra found a way out of the mess she might as well enjoy herself, because right now she could use a good fuck.

Ciarra waited for Master Shawn to ask for his pleasure when Master Terrance stood up and walked around the table. Man, she hated the twinkle in the man's eyes. If it was a sign of what was to come, she was in trouble.

"Master Shawn, I believe that you are hungry for dessert. Perhaps junket."

Ciarra looked over her shoulder for the sweetmeat—milk sweetened, flavored and thickened into curd with rennet. Nowhere could she find the custard.

"Here." Master Terrance reached behind her and then handed her a small bowl. She looked around for a spoon, but found none. "Use your fingers and spread it thick over your breasts."

What did she have to lose? Perhaps this would lead to what her body was screaming for. She needed to get laid. Needed to forget about what she'd done and what her future held—or didn't hold.

Fuck me, she prayed, looking into Master Shawn's intense green eyes. *Fuck me and make me forget.*

Ciarra took the bowl and looked into it, frowning. Junket was usually a cream color. The substance in the bowl had a pinkish tint to it. There was something else added to it and by what she'd seen so far on this planet she was better off not asking.

Nevertheless she dipped two fingers into the pudding and began to smooth it over her naked breast raised by the bustier she wore. Immediately her nipples puckered. Warmth penetrated her breast, her blood. The sensation was heady and she could not help adding more pudding on her globe. The swirls created the most wonderful sensations. She circled her nipple more than once, loving the tingles that pulled and drew like tethers connected to her pussy. The scent of cinnamon and cloves rose as she began to cover her other breast with the junket.

Ciarra blinked hard. The room was getting hotter and the man before her unbelievably more appealing than he already was. She remembered how his cock tasted, how he felt sliding in and out of her mouth. Her tongue traced her bottom lip as her gaze fell to his crotch. She squirmed, needing to feel his long length thrusting between her thighs. Her knees parted further as a wave of desire flowed through her. She was wet, so wet.

When her gaze finally rose it was to meet Master Shawn's and his was cold enough to freeze water. Ciarra refused to let his mood detour the path her body was taking her down. She slipped one finger into her mouth, tasting. *Ahhh.* She closed her eyes savoring the hot flavor that melted upon her tongue. Her eyelids rose, feeling heavy.

She giggled and Master Shawn frowned. What hit her as so funny, she didn't know — didn't care. She only knew one thing and that was she could and would thaw the chilly demeanor of the man in front of her. Before the night ended he would be in her bed — his bed — oh, who cared which bed.

With a custard-covered finger she generously spread the substance across Master Shawn's thin lips. Intense eyes pinned hers as his tongue slid across his lips. He frowned, tasting the dessert again.

"What did you add to the junket?" Accusation hung heavy in Master Shawn's question. He braced his palms on the arms of his chair as he made to stand.

Ciarra didn't know what was happening to her. But she giggled again, placing her feet on Shawn's thighs, holding him down.

Master Terrance shrugged. "*Philter.*"

"*Philter!*" Master Shawn growled. His body stiffened as he used the back of his arm to wipe the remaining pudding from his mouth.

From his reaction Ciarra should have been concerned, but the heat in her body was growing. She arched her back, offering herself to the man, needing to feel his hot mouth on her breasts, between her thighs.

It was like someone had taken sandpaper to her nerve endings—they were raw, excited and hungry.

Chapter Six

ஐ

The anger Shawn felt toward his brother faded as Kitty moaned. Her body moved seductively toward him. Her custard-laden breasts were inches away from his mouth, her thighs parted, the pink flesh of her pussy begging to be eaten. When he raised his gaze, her blue eyes were dark with desire. The aphrodisiac from *Gamu* Terrance had added to the junket was already taking effect. She would be aware of what she did, but she would have no control. Her body would dictate her needs.

He too, felt the warmth of the drug igniting inside like tiny bombs exploding. Blood rushed to his groin, filling his cock and testicles. The tempting woman closed her eyes as she leaned back on the palms of her hands. Every movement was sensual, a temptress calling to her mate.

Shawn brushed aside her feet resting on his thighs and stood. He wanted to chastise his brothers, but he was drawn to the siren calling his name beneath her breath.

"Shawn," she murmured. Her eyes slid open and a moment of confusion crossed her face. Then her heavy lids drifted halfway, her breathing laden. She peered through feathery lashes. "Shawn, I want you." The sexy plea nearly undid him.

Through the pull of the aphrodisiac, Shawn faced his brothers. "You have created this situation. Therefore, she will stay with me tonight."

Mine, whispered through his mind. *All mine*.

"But—"

"No, Terrance. In fact, this changes things. I'm taking the lead from this point on. Fuck the contract." Perhaps it was the determination in his voice or the conviction in his eyes he knew was there—he felt it. Neither brother dared to defy him. It would not have mattered if they had. Shawn had made up his mind—this woman was his while she was on Ecstasy Island. He only had to make her believe it.

"Shawn." The sound of his name on her sexy lips drew his attention. She had raised a leg, spreading herself wider. "I need you." Her tongue caressed her bottom lip. The action drew his balls tight, making him ache to the point of pain. But he would be damned if he lost control under *Philter's* influence in front of his brothers. He knew how the drug worked. Just the small taste he had was heating his body like a furnace. He could only imagine what it was doing to her.

The body absorbed the drug through the pores of the skin. It didn't have to be ingested to take effect, which was obvious as Kitty moved like her namesake, a cat in heat needing to mate.

Shawn's control was slipping and it wasn't just the aphrodisiac. He needed to fuck this woman and he needed to do it now.

A sound of surprise squeezed from her puckered lips as he scooped her up and cradled her in his arms. She snuggled closer, setting off every nerve ending in his body, especially those in his cock. She rubbed against him, covering him in the aphrodisiac, stoking the flame inside both of them, and making his control even harder to hold on to. He half expected to hear her purr, and then sink her claws into him. The thought put him in motion.

As Shawn hurried through the dining hall past curious stares, she began to nibble on his neck. Tiny kisses followed as she made her way to his ear, sucking his earlobe into her mouth as he pushed through the last door and entered the gardens outside the main building.

The pressure between his legs was growing to a point he thought walking would be nearly impossible if she didn't stop. Then she slipped her tongue into his ear and his knees buckled. He barely caught himself before taking them both to the ground.

As they lay next to each other in the soft grass, she moaned, "*Now*. I need you now." Her hand found his cock beneath his toga and her slender fingers curled around him. She stroked from base to tip, a steady rhythm that made his hips undulate. The woman had a magical touch, or had she bewitched him? His breath hissed through clenched teeth as she fondled his balls. She was going to drive him mad if he didn't stop her.

Shawn eased out of her grasp and pushed to his knees. No use in spilling good seed on the ground. What he wanted lay between her thighs. She watched, eyes transfixed on him as he began to disrobe. Hunger flared in her dark blue depths as he cast his toga aside.

Releasing a soft whimper, she reached for him. "You are so beautiful."

"Beautiful?" A grin creased his mouth as his gaze caressed her length. Her long red hair fanned out around her, her skin almost white against the green grass as she writhed against its cool surface. Dual moons hanging high in the sky cast a blue-gray glow, giving her an ethereal appearance.

And she was his angel tonight.

Her palm was warm, soft to the touch as she accepted his outstretched hand. She looked so innocent, so trusting as she rose to her knees. For a moment they simply gazed into each other eyes.

"Now." She pressed herself against him rubbing *Philter* into both of their chests. The friction of their bodies coupled with the drug was volcanic, raging through him like a violent storm. Her hands were everywhere at once, touching, kneading and seeking. If he didn't bind her wrists, this loving would be over in seconds.

Taking the medallion and chain from around his waist he clamped her hands behind her back so quickly she didn't have time to react. Immediately, she began to fight against her bindings.

"No. I have to touch you." Her small cries and struggle heated his blood.

Shawn needed to be in control. But control was illusive — too much *Philter* and too much Kitty was in his system. She was driving him mad with lust. He was barely hanging by a thread as he secured her wrists with his chain. Then he relaxed on his haunches and took a deep calming breath. He paused to admire her body bound for his pleasure, while he fought the effects of the drug. When he took this woman for the first time he wanted it slow.

Still on their knees, her body swayed into him. "Shawn," she moaned.

He knew what she wanted — needed. But he had to taste her. He leaned forward and took her nipple into his mouth. The taste of cinnamon and cloves exploded on his tongue. But it was the soft mewling sound Kitty made that really turned him on.

His engorged cock beat against his belly. His testicles ached with anticipation. *Take her now*, screamed in his head. Blindly he reached for the fasteners holding her bustier in place. With a couple of twists of his fingers the material popped open and completely freed her breasts. He took the garment and wiped the custard from his chest and then hers. When he finished he tossed the scrap of material aside.

The effects of *Philter* would last for about an hour. He had just ingested enough to put him at the same level as Kitty.

Damn. He needed to fuck her. Was it the drug? Was it the woman?

"I need to taste you." He lowered her and then rolled her on her side, the soft grass a cushion as he pressed his length opposite hers so that his head was positioned between her thighs and they lay in the sixty-nine position. Moisture glistened on her swollen folds. The womanly scent of passion caressed his nose. He breathed deeply and slid his tongue over her warm slit.

"More," she moaned, pressing her fiery curls against him. "Eat me. Oh, yes, eat me." As she spoke, Ciarra raised her upper leg, draping it across his shoulder to give him access to her aching flesh.

With his fingers, he spread her wide. Her pussy was the most delicious shade of pink begging to be licked, sucked and eaten. She writhed, as his tongue thrust deep into her hot core. She tasted so sweet, so womanly. Like a fine wine he savored her juices.

When her mouth found and closed around his erection, the ground moved beneath him. She took him to the back of her throat and then slowly moved down his member. She sucked, stroked and caressed. Their position and the fact that her wrists were bound was a little awkward for her as she struggled to keep contact. He bent his knee, tucking it behind his other leg, his palm pressed to her back securing her to him, as his tongue circled her clit again and again.

Someone cried out. Shawn wasn't sure whether it was her or him. All he knew was what she was doing felt wonderful. There were no words for the ecstasy that built and pulled forcefully through his body and straight through his cock.

"My hands, release my hands. I need to touch you," she murmured before licking the length of his member and then taking it deep again. The muscles of her throat squeezed and for a moment he thought he'd fill her mouth with his cream.

But he too, needed to feel her hands, her embrace. As he lapped at her moist folds he reached behind her and tried to release the chain. It was awkward fucking and being fucked and focusing on chains he had haphazardly wound around her wrists. This wasn't working.

"Kitty." Shawn attempted to ease out of her mouth, but she sucked harder, drawing him further down her throat. The pressure was so great he almost lost it. She had a strong grip.

He had to use his hand to break her hold. It took all his strength to withhold his climax.

"More," she whimpered, smacking her lips.

He chuckled. "First, let me undo the chain." She rolled to her stomach, giving him a good look at her firm ass. Drawn to the smooth, rounded globes, he forgot about the chains and began to knead her softness. Her back arched, raising her butt into the air and giving him an eyeful of her swollen, drenched pussy. He smoothed his tongue over each cheek and then kissed one and then the other.

She moaned. The soft sound sent fire shooting through his engorged cock. He had to feel her warmth surrounding him.

Grass stained her nylons and garter belt, and somewhere along the way she had lost both stilettos. He pulled and tugged at the chain once again, giving up when the ache between his thighs was too much to bear. Instead, he parted her legs and moved between them. Placing his hands beneath her abdomen, he raised her ass higher, opening her wider.

"Yes," she murmured. Her face was pressed against the soft grass. Her legs sprawled, ass waist high—the perfect height.

On his knees, he positioned himself at her entrance, his engorged cock throbbing against her swollen flesh. He paused, steadying his breathing, holding on to what control remained. If he thrust into her now he would lose it. But the *Philter* was playing havoc with his senses, waging war against his mind.

It was a wicked image to have her bound, helpless and lying on her stomach, while he dominated and fucked her. He was a Dom used to conquering, but this was different, this was new and exciting—something he hadn't felt in a long, long time—passion so wild, so raw, it bordered on obsession.

"*Shawn.*" His name was a desperate plea on her lips. He reached for her breasts, rolled her taut nipples in his fingers.

Her soft mewl met his groan as he nudged his erection in about an inch and felt her warmth surround him.

"Now." She rocked backwards, but he grasped her hips, staying her, wanting to prolong the blissful torture. He ached beyond reason as he pushed a little deeper. "Please fuck me now," she cried.

Still he took his time, a tribute to his control—or stupidity.

Shawn stroked her abdomen, while his other hand griped his erection and eased it out of her. She gasped with displeasure. But then her cry was one of delight when his cock caressed her pussy, and he slid back and forth against her clit.

As her body began to tremble, Shawn could wait no more. He thrust, pushing beyond her swollen folds, and as he buried his cock deep inside her, she screamed. Her channel was hot, wet, and more than he could have ever dreamed.

Holy Christ! She was tight.

It was pleasure-pain watching his erection slide in and out of her pussy. He moved slowly, reveling in their bodies coming together, the sounds of their flesh meeting. Soft mewling rose from her lips. He allowed one finger to find her clit and she groaned deep and low. While he stroked her, he moved the other hand to her ass. Her tight rosebud was too inviting to ignore as he slipped his thumb inside and began to pump.

Everything shattered into a rainbow of colors. Ciarra convulsed as her climax fractured her, sending waves and waves of pleasure to every part of her body. She jerked, raked by another climax that followed at the speed of light. She barely had time to catch her breath as another struck without mercy. Her body was a conduit for electricity ricocheting off the walls of her sex. Small tremors followed as if they rode a swell crashing against the rocks. She had never felt anything so powerful—it was frightening. For a moment she couldn't breathe. She couldn't think. Her face was pressed into soft grass that was becoming firmer with each second that passed. The chains around her wrists were biting into her flesh. An ache had developed in her shoulders. But the best part was that her pussy was stretched wide by his thick cock, her ass invaded by his thumb, and her clit was having the time of its life.

Then the man behind her gave one last thrust. His painful groan sounded like it was torn from the very depths of his diaphragm. She could feel his thick cock pulsating, filling her with his seed as his hands stilled and then he collapsed atop her, squeezing the last of the air from her lungs.

Grass tickled her nose, filled her mouth. "Shawn." Her voice was muffled against the ground. "I can't...breathe."

Then the heaviness atop her disappeared.

What was wrong with her? Ciarra raised her head and looked around, taking in the starry night, the fresh scent of flowers and the gentle flow of water in the distance. Surprise registered at the two moons high above.

She had just had wild sex with a stranger and it wasn't the first time. Not to mention she felt like going at it again and again and again.

"*Ahhhh*," Ciarra moaned, trying to shift her weight, feeling the effects of being bound. She rolled to her side and made several attempts to rise, each ending in failure as she lay on her stomach. She strained her neck to watch Shawn stand, and then drift away from her.

This wasn't who she was. She didn't give herself to anyone. Something wasn't right. Hell, she had begged Shawn to fuck her—but it hadn't been her.

She recalled the dinner. Oh God, did she remember the dinner—the men, reaching the garden, the exquisite sense of her body being filled by Shawn who now had his back to her. She gave thanks that at least he was still breathing. The last one who had spent the night with her had not been so fortunate.

True, she had wanted this man—still wanted him with an irrational passion. Yet she would never be so forward and she would have never begged to be fucked.

Ciarra had the uncontrollable urge to wrap her arms around the man staring off into the night. But that wasn't going to happen with her wrists bound together. Actually, she had a powerful desire to roll him on his back and ride him hard. Her body felt used, delightfully so, but it wasn't enough. She wanted more. He was like a craving, something that crawled beneath the surface of her skin, something that couldn't be restrained.

Tears filled her eyes as she rested her face on the ground. She was losing it again. *No! I didn't kill Mayhem. I couldn't. It had to be a setup. But why?* Who would benefit from framing her and killing Mayhem? And how would she ever clear her name?

Ciarra was so absorbed in her thoughts she didn't hear Shawn approach. Strong, gentle hands startled her as he reached for her wrists. She wrenched her neck to watch him.

"Did I hurt you?" Concern filled his green eyes as he began to fumble with the chain.

"No." She attempted to blow a strand of hair out of her face, but it refused to comply.

Shawn stopped his deliberations and brushed her hair aside. Just the contact of his hand against her cheek kindled the passion inside her. Before he pulled away she rubbed her face against his hand, her eyes closed. She savored his touch, wanting those big, strong hands on her body.

"I want you again." The man's straightforwardness caused her to open her eyes. She met his gaze that was dark with desire. His breathing had elevated to match hers. Heat waves shimmered between them.

"Yes," she responded without thought. What was it about him that made her shun her inhibitions? Forget about her dilemma?

Shawn smoothed his knuckles once more over her cheek and then began to unravel the chains binding her.

The man was magnificent. Tendons and muscles flexed in his broad chest, his sinewy arms, even his thighs bulged with strength. And his hands...she could not wait to feel them upon her breasts, kneading, teasing and plucking at her nipples. Even now the coil in her belly was growing tighter and tighter. She knew her short hairs were moist with excitement. Several times his eyes had wandered toward her taut nipples, ready for his wet, hot mouth to devour.

"There." The chain slipped from her wrists. She tried to rise, but her body was stiff, making it difficult to move much less stand. "Let me help you." Shawn stood then took her hand and pulled her to her feet and straight into his arms. Their eyes met, locked.

He released her and took one of her wrists between his palms. He massaged where the chain had bitten into her skin. The sensation of his touch was soothing and arousing all at once. Passion stirred within her, coupled with the warmth of the caring she witnessed in his expression.

He released her hand and sought the other. Gentle, he was so gentle. He raised her wrist and frowned as he looked at the angry red indentations on her skin. "I should have taken more care." Shawn pressed his warm lips to the inside of her wrist. His tongue flicked against her pulse point, sending a shiver throughout her body.

She quivered as he released the snap holding her garter belt in place and then slipped his fingers into the elastic of her stocking, torn and grass stained. Slowly he slipped the hose off. Then he did the same thing to her other one until she was completely naked.

"Shawn." Her cry was a whimper of need. She saw the same need in his thick erection arcing proudly against his belly. Ciarra ran a fingernail down the length of him. What drove her she didn't know, what she did know was she loved the way his member jerked, eager for her caress.

When she folded her fingers tight around him, Shawn growled, "*Philter*." The disgust in his voice was confusing.

"What?"

"Nothing," he said peeling her fingers away. "Not here. My place." He grabbed her hand and took off.

Ciarra had long legs, but she still had to hasten her steps to keep up. It wasn't all bad being dragged behind Shawn. She had the most delightful view of his taut ass, the strength in his shoulder blades. Each step was an act of power. It was frightening and exciting all at once.

When they stood before the magnificent main structure, rounded arches, a tall vaulted roof with all the grandeur of a palace, she stopped to gawk, but only for a moment as he led her to one of the several smaller replicas of the statuesque building.

"You live here, in this monument?"

He brushed aside her comment as they slipped through the front door and into the massive house. "It's home. I would show you around, but I need to be inside you." The truth darkened his eyes and made his cock lengthen.

Touring the mansion could wait. Her body seemed foreign, controlling her. All she could think about was having this man thrusting in and out of her pussy. As if to attest to her arousal, moisture slid down her thighs.

Then she stilled.

What if the authorities found her? Would they think Shawn was involved? Or worse, what if the person who framed her was looking for her? A tremor assaulted her.

She couldn't put another in danger.

She had to get out of there—now.

Chapter Seven

෨

The desperate tug of Kitty's hand folded in Shawn's was the first clue something was wrong. The next was moisture gathering in her big blue eyes as he glanced over his shoulder.

She swallowed hard as if she fought some inner demon. "I-I've got to get out of here." She looked back toward the entrance of his home. The large oak door seemed to call to her.

"Kitty, what's wrong?"

"I've got to get out of here," she repeated with more urgency. Then she squared her shoulders, placing a warm palm on his chest. "Please, I left something unfinished on Earth. Something I need to deal with before it gets out of hand."

Something was wrong, definitely wrong. She was even able to push aside the effects of the drugs and that was no simple feat. His free hand caressed her arm as he tried to comfort her.

"Please," she choked, her stance planted firmly on the marble floor beneath her feet. "Help me to leave this planet." She held tight to her tears, never allowing one to fall.

There was something about her, something that called to him on a deeper level. He wanted to be her protector, to discover and solve whatever was frightening her, because it was definitely fear that made her eyes desolate and desperate as she stared up at him. What had happened on Earth that had turned the chic, sophisticated woman known to have brass ovaries into the vulnerable woman before him?

"A transport to Earth is not expected for another week."

His words seemed to deflate her as her body went limp. She buried her face against his chest.

"Hold me." There were tears in her voice—none on her face.

He wrapped his arms around her trembling body. Soft hands slid up his back with a grip that bordered on desperation. "Talk to me, Kitty."

Anger in a woman he could handle—even tears, but her silence left him feeling helpless. Her anguish felt like it was tethered to his chest, pulling at his heartstrings. She was an enigma, strong one moment and childlike the next. It was as if she were two different people. Or she was running away from something or someone.

The instant jealousy he felt was illogical. The possessiveness he felt was illogical. What was it about Kitty that made him think and act irrationally?

His hand swooped beneath the bend of her knees. The sudden movement forced her arms around his neck as he swept her off her feet and padded across the marble floor.

"Shawn?"

"*Shhh*. You can't leave right now, so we might as well continue where we left off." His footsteps padded down the long hallway that was aligned with multiple doors, to a series of rooms for his personal use and occasional guests. He climbed a flight of stairs at the end of the hallway. The entire upper flat was his bedroom, along with several suites and a dungeon. Rarely did a woman grace his domain, and never through the entire night.

What was this woman doing to him?

Shawn was perplexed. He had acted out of character from the moment she stepped off the transport. Yes, it was true that he was first attracted to her due to her resemblance to Chastity, but there was something more. He had defied his brothers, something he rarely ever did. He'd insisted on taking control of Kitty, damn the contract. But so far he had given her nothing of what she had described and paid for. Hell, Kitty had declared even if she demanded contract modifications after her arrival that her commands should be ignored.

Shawn pushed open his bedroom door and entered. She made no sound as he approached the bed, pulling back the heavy comforter and slipping her onto the silky red sheets.

Kitty Carmichael was a domineering woman who knew herself well. He had personally reviewed her contract. Used to power and influence, she wanted to experience the strictest sense of submission. The woman had spared no expense to see that her requests were adhered to. Or was she hurting and in need of self-punishment to fulfill that ache?

Indecision immobilized him. Should he attempt to soothe the woman before him, or ignore her obvious grief in strict accordance to her contract?

A warm fire burned in the large marble fireplace just as it always did at this time of night. The flames threw shadows across the dimly lit room catching the colors in the imported *albutra* rug lying before the stone hearth. Gray images flickered and bounced off the table and chairs to his right and the dark wood wall unit to his left.

"Brighter by fifteen percent." Shawn took a moment to raise the lighting using the voice-activated system. "Reduce flame by twenty percent." The temperature was just right for his comfort, but he knew the two of them would soon be creating their own heat.

Kitty lay on her back staring up at him. She looked young and vulnerable. The bed moaned beneath him as he sat. He scooted closer, needing to touch her. He spooned her body with his length, wrapping one arm around her slender waist and pulling her onto her side.

Damn, but she made him want to be her defender, to protect her from whatever it was she was running away from.

The heavy sigh she released felt like she held the weight of the world on her shoulders. There was definitely something wrong. Could it be a bad deal gone awry? A break up with a boyfriend? The last one had Shawn cringing.

She was his woman. He wanted Kitty, and not for just a one-nighter or the length of her vacation.

Now where had that come from?

She placed a warm palm against his chest. Could she feel his heart pounding beneath her touch? Did she know how much he desired her?

Then she leaned forward, her mouth finding his. She moved her lips over his in a soft and sensuous kiss that stole every bit of his remaining breath. She tasted of the future, bright and promising. Her kiss deepened and he reached for her.

"Hold me," she whispered against his cheek, before sliding her lips across his in a kiss that said, "forever."

Damn, if his control wasn't slipping again. It actually felt like this woman was mentally and physically winding him around her finger.

And what was she hiding? Did he dare get involved?

"Make love to me." Her words said one thing, her strained voice said, "Chase the demons out of my life." She rolled onto her back, encouraging him to follow, which he did willingly.

She felt good beneath him. Somehow right. Yet when he looked into her eyes he saw pain so raw, so consuming, that he hesitated. Was this what she really wanted?

"Please." It was impossible to resist her profound plea. He wanted to be her champion. He wanted to drive her demons away and he wanted to free her from whatever held her mind and body captive.

Soon she was kissing him again and all honorable thoughts disappeared. All he wanted was to be her lover, to cherish her body as it should be.

Their lips parted, allowing him to feather attention down her neck to the swell of a breast. He flicked his tongue over her nipple then gently pulled at it with his teeth. She released a taut cry and arched into him. "Yes," he thought he heard her say as her fingernails bit into his back. Her thighs parted and he eased between her legs, before moving to the other breast.

"*Shawn.*" She raised her hips, inviting him in. Her core was wet, sliding along his erection, anointing him with her juices. His balls drew up and his groin tightened. "Shawn," she whispered his name again, pleading, before she added, "tie me up."

For a moment Shawn was stunned. He released her breast, resting his head on her rising chest. The rapid beat of her heart pounded in his ear. The scent of her heated skin rose up to tease him. She threaded her fingers through his hair, pulling gently.

Had he misinterpreted Kitty's needs?

Disappointment was a strange bedfellow. Shawn thought she wanted a gentle loving, to be held, their bodies intertwined, coming together as one.

He almost flinched with the realization that this feeling was something he had desired — not Kitty.

The desperation in her voice, the sadness in her eyes was a need to be dominated, to be punished — not the deep and tender expression of two people's affection. The discovery made him pause. Is that why she came to Ecstasy Island — to find release and to exorcise the nightmares from her mind?

He almost laughed. He was such an idiot. The woman lying beneath him did not come to his planet to find love, especially his love.

Shawn nearly choked on the word. Love — marriage. Were these the things missing from his life? He fought the awkwardness of the moment. But it was true. He envied Tor. His eldest brother never hesitated to do his job well, no matter what woman he might instruct. But when Tor was with

Passion Flower he was different. The man's features softened when he looked at his wife. Tenderness was in his touch, pride and love shone in his eyes for his Asian beauty.

Even Terrance had been a different man when he had been married, no matter how briefly. Now there was a lesson to be learned in choosing the wrong woman. His brother had been burned so badly that he fought desire with anger—God help the woman in his path. But Shawn knew the truth—it was more hurt than anything else. His brother was a good man—regardless of what some individuals might think.

Kitty stirred, her luscious body sliding and arousing him, heating his blood. Then it happened.

Like the many skins of an onion, Shawn felt his soul bared one layer at a time. A kaleidoscope of emotions bombarded him, exploding and throwing him off guard. Was he unconsciously searching for his mate?

Was Kitty Carmichael the woman?

His woman?

Her supple form matched his perfectly. She incited feelings within him that he had never before felt, desires that lingered on the edge of obsession. Once was not enough. Even now her body called to him and his responded with an insatiable hunger to taste her, bury his cock deep inside her warmth.

Mine.

Ciarra had to have Shawn one more time before finding a way off this planet. Never had any man treated her with such sensitivity, made her feel special and cared for. And never had her body demanded a man's touch like it did Shawn's.

You idiot, she chastised herself. But she loved the feel of his hot mouth and teeth on her breasts. Even his weight pinning her to the bed felt like a cover of seduction as he feathered kisses across her abdomen. Her thighs parted of their own accord. She arched, needing him inside her now.

He was an expert, and his expertise was sexual. He knew what a woman liked, wanted. Her hips rose, undulated, spreading her juices along his thick cock. Man, he was hard. Anticipation was another wave of desire flowing between her thighs.

Yes, she would make love to him at least one more time before she found away off the planet. She asked to be tied up because she wanted this time with him to last. As hot as she was she'd lose it if she touched him and she feared that she'd never let him go.

When Shawn moved from atop her, a sense of loss invaded her. When he returned he held a small device in his hands. He held the three-inch box up so that she could see it.

"This will activate the static bands around your wrists and ankles, unless you would like me to use silk." A rapid shake of her head answered him. He crawled between her legs, kneeling. "Are you sure you want to be restrained?"

Ciarra was startled by his question and the look of disappointment that flickered across his face and then disappeared as quickly as it had appeared. *Couldn't be…it was just my imagination…wishful thinking.*

No. "Yes," she responded. Yet it was true, she would rather stroke him and learn the nuances of the taut muscles beneath his firm skin. She wanted to hold him so tight that he could never get away from her.

"Wrap your fingers around the bars of the headboard."

When Ciarra did, electricity shimmered through her wrists. She released her hold and attempted to pull away, but the bands held her fast in place. Anxiety from being bound again made her grow rigid. Still she recalled how it had felt to have her hands chained behind her as Shawn fucked her in the garden. It had been thrilling and had added to the experience of being taken by this man beneath the stars.

Fear and excitement made strange companions, but somehow they belonged together—fed off each other. Helpless and not knowing what Shawn might do to her next was heady. Her breasts were heavy and the sting in her nipples was becoming unbearable. She needed this man's cock thrusting in and out of her pussy.

When he bent her knees, widening her, placing the soles of her feet firmly on the bed, she felt that familiar radiation spread through her ankles. She tried to lift her feet, tried to draw her knees together, but her body was frozen as he had positioned her. Part of her panicked, while the other part reveled in what was to come — and hopefully it would be her.

A flash of memory dampened her excitement as she recalled the times today Shawn had brought her near the apex only to let her die along with the embers of lust. Surely, he wouldn't do it to her again.

"What do you want me to do to you?" His sexy voice was a caress down her naked body.

Anything — everything. "Fuck me." She wet her lips. His eyes darkened and for a moment she let fear override excitement. She could sense his strength as muscles rippled across his broad chest. Veins bulged in his powerful biceps. There was a mysterious, almost dangerous mien to him as he stared down upon her as if he were the hunter, she his prey. Would he unleash his might upon her?

It was amazing how gentle his large hands were as they smoothed up the inside of her thighs, beginning at her knees and moving slowly toward her sex. His thumbs stopped on each side of her slit then he began to massage. His touch was tender, arousing.

She closed her eyes, enjoying the sensation. Yet anxiety was building within her for what was to come next.

"I want you to watch me. I want to see your expression as I fuck you." He paused before adding, "If you close them you will be punished." Ciarra felt her brows furrow with his last words.

Punished. He was playing a game with her. They weren't two people caring about each other and enjoying sex. The man had slipped into his Dom role and he was giving *Kitty* what she had paid for. Ciarra could not help the disappointment that consumed her. And, God, she hated being called Kitty. She wanted this man to whisper her name, *Ciarra*. Just the thought made her eyes close on a sigh.

Damn.

Before her lids flickered open, Shawn was off the bed and retrieving a small box from the nightstand by his bed. He turned and looked at her, frowning. Apprehension prickled her skin. She held back a cry as he crawled back upon the bed and between her legs.

She flinched at the cool metal as he laid the box on her stomach. The hinges creaked as he opened the lid.

"Sexual fantasies are gateways to greater enlightenment, self-actualization and fulfillment." His voice lacked enthusiasm. It was as if he had recited these words many times before. "Our bodies hold both positive and negative energies. When sexual fantasies are acted upon a release is experienced." He reached into the box, and then met her gaze. "What are your sexual fantasies, Kitty?"

Ciarra felt her eyes widen. "I-I don't have any."

What was he up to?

He grinned, the smile slipping across his handsome face. "Liar." He took out a small yellow jar and set it beside her hip. "Remember I saw your face when Terrance fucked your beautiful ass and I your mouth." He unscrewed the lid. The scraping of metal against glass slithered up her spine.

He was right. She had liked being fucked by two men. It had felt wicked. And it had been a fantasy... One she would never forget.

Shawn reached again into the box. "Whether it is to gain self-acceptance through multiple partners, the need for attention or the search for karma, we seek balance." He paused a little longer than was comfortable. "Even exorcising anger through giving or receiving punishment is a way to center oneself." He pulled a thin, tubular object about three inches long from the container. Its width was no bigger than a pen or pencil. He held the silvery rod up so she could take a good look at it. "Are you searching for balance? Are you seeking to forget?" he asked, catching her off guard.

Ciarra could do nothing but shake her head. What was he going to do with that thing? Her spread legs made her feel vulnerable, exposed. And how did he know she needed to forget? The question slithered across her skin.

He dipped the metallic object into what look like cream from the yellow jar. A menthol scent arose, hot and minty. "Most are taught to be ashamed or embarrassed by their sexual feelings. To be healthy, a complete person must learn to experience her sexuality without fear and accept it as a beautiful part of life." Again he held the object up, allowing her anxiety to grow. "Is this why you came to Ecstasy Island? Or is there something more?"

Oh God, he knew. Not what she had done—possibly murdered a man—but he knew she was hiding, running from something.

Nooo…

She could see what he was doing. He was stringing out the anticipation of the unknown. He wanted her on the edge. He wanted to pique her fear and interest. And he succeeded.

Ciarra's heart fluttered then picked up the beat raging against her chest. She had tried several times to draw her knees together, unsuccessfully.

Just exactly where was he going to stick that thing?

She didn't have to wait long when he slipped it into her tight anus. The object was cool, the cream hot. "*Ahhh…*" The two sensations exploding in her body made her back bow. It was like fire and ice warring against one another.

"Relax." He stroked her slit with his knuckles. "While you are here on Ecstasy Island you must obey your Master's commands. That is me, Kitty, not Terrance. I have made an adjustment to the contract." She heard the determination in his lowered voice. "Do you agree?"

Her head wagged in agreement. But the thing crammed up her ass had the bulk of her attention as it began to move.

"The wand will help you to conform."

Her asshole felt like it was twisting, morphing from the inside out. "What?"

"The Nourishing Wand contains energy in the forms of rays of light, heat, atoms and molecules adjusting and undergoing internal change created by your body's reactions. Relax and enjoy the sensation." He continued to caress her folds, but her mind was focused on a different orifice.

What was he doing to her?

It was like hell and heaven had been let loose to run rampant up her ass. The object shifted and probed, released heat then cold, it touched areas in her body she never knew existed. One minute was painful—the next she was experiencing such ecstasy that she had to catch her breath.

"Relax?" she hissed through clenched teeth. "Bend over and let me cram this thing up your ass." She jerked against her invisible bindings as anger built with the speed of light.

He chuckled. The damn man laughed as she continued to fight her bonds. What had come over her to once again beg this man to fuck her? How had she ever found him attractive? Caring?

"Kitty." He pinched her chin drawing her attention to him. "This is a training tool. When you comply with my requests you will receive great enjoyment. If you don't the wand will punish you. Now relax." The last two words were a command.

She tried to breathe, but each inhale was a shaky, trembling experience. Then the box disappeared from atop her belly. Instead Shawn's massive body draped over her, closing in as he pressed his lips to hers. And then she was lost.

His kiss was masterful, strong and demanding. He took what he wanted, leaving her breathless. She could do nothing but surrender.

Chapter Eight

෧෨

Shawn was holding on by a thread. His cock ached to a point of pleasure — pain. She was so responsive, so receptive to his kiss, his touch. He had never had a woman melt in his arms, but she melted like a bright falling star in the heavens cutting through the sky and then disappearing into the dark. She felt like a lump of clay ready and willing for his hands to mold, to create. The power in the knowledge was an aphrodisiac. It was like pure energy rushing through his veins, strengthening him and lighting his body aflame.

His balls drew up and his groin tightened. All he could think of was delving into the soft pink flesh between her thighs, her sweet taste upon his tongue and how it would feel to wake with her in his arms come morning.

She was gorgeous lying on his bed. Her hands gripped around the bars of the headboard, knees bent and spread wide. The red silk sheets added to her allure.

But he had a job to do. Regretfully, he broke their connection, holding her gaze as he slid his body up and down hers. The friction between them was hot. Lust made her eyelids heavy. Her lips were swollen from his caress. Her breathing labored.

"Fuck me, Shawn, now." Her low, sexy voice might as well have been fingers curled around his cock and pumping for the effect it had. He hardened even more.

Wrists and ankles bound, she wanted him. A halo of silky red hair framed her face. The blue in her eyes had darkened to almost a pitch black. She was beautiful in the throes of passion as her chest rose invitingly, her nipples tight beads.

Shawn cleared his throat, struggling with his own desire. "Master. You must remember to refer to me as Master, especially when others are present." Shawn had to make sure both brothers were satisfied with Kitty's training. If not, either one wouldn't hesitate to take over. And he would not allow that. A growl rumbled in his throat at the thought. She was his and no one, brother or not, would interfere with what he had planned for the weeks to come.

She frowned. The small defiance triggered the Nourishing Wand. Her body flinched, then tensed on a gasp that slipped from her lips.

"Breathe," he coached. Inhaling and exhaling, he encouraged her to follow suit. The distress on her face was disconcerting. "The wand reads your body's emotions. Disobedience or rebellion activates a negative response. Obedience and submission give a positive one. It is your choice, slave Kitty. Now breathe."

Her brows furrowed at his reference to slave. Her back bowed as another sensation shot up her ass. "*Shawn.*" Her high-pitched wail elevated on a desperate cry.

"Master," he corrected, knowing the intensity of the wand, because he had experienced it first hand. Never did he employ any instrument or form of torture that he hadn't undergone himself. He also was alert to an individuals' pain threshold, watching for any true signs of distress. Beads of perspiration formed above her lips. She was uncomfortable, but wasn't under any undue stress—yet.

"Master," she said breathlessly. With her capitulation the wand eased. Immediate relief filled her eyes.

"Good girl. Now shall we continue?" He almost laughed as she struggled briefly with the question then quickly nodded her agreement. "Earlier Terrance recited your four basic duties—to serve your Master's needs, to obey his orders, to accept his domination and to please his desires. My pleasure should be at the forefront at all times. Your pleasure is only secondary and an award for obedience."

"*Ahhh.*" A sudden cry tore from her thin lips as the wand activated. Her back shot off the bed, her bound wrists and ankles the only thing keeping her in place. He tensed, remembering the sting of fire shooting up his ass when he had activated the learning tool with just a damning thought.

"Evidently, you do not agree with these duties. Breathe," he reminded her, "and yield."

"Fuck you," she said on a ragged breath, her body trembling. Wrong response. Another fire-bolt ripped through her by the way she trembled.

Again he used his lips to calm her. Again she melted in his arms. This was going to be harder than he had expected, because Kitty had spunk. Buried beneath all the mental baggage she carried around was a confident woman with courage and a strong constitution. She might want to experience the submissive side of life, but he would bet his soul that what she truly wanted was an equal partner in life.

Damn. He was doing it again. Was he seeing only what he wanted? He could not mold this woman into what he wanted her to be.

Shawn ran his fingers through his shoulder-length blond hair. This wasn't working. It was getting late and he still had not instructed her in the various positions expected of a slave. He had no doubt that Terrance would drill him first thing tomorrow on her progress.

Weariness weighted her eyelids this time more than desire. Her face was pale. A rumble from her stomach confirmed she had not eaten much at dinner. Actually, she had not been given the chance, which he was going to rectify.

"If I remove the wand, will you obey me? We have a lot to go through tonight before the morning. You must be ready for Master Terrance and Master Tor's inspection tomorrow."

"Yes-yes." There was no hesitation in her reply.

"Then relax." As he knelt between her legs he couldn't help but touch her. She moaned as his finger circled her clit once, twice. "You're so beautiful." The words tumbled from his mouth. "I need to taste you." He leaned forward, stopping inches away from her sex. The scent of her arousal was sweet. Blood rushed into his cock, the pressure creating a blessed ache between his thighs. "Do not come until I grant permission."

"Shit—" Her curse and the way she twisted her body, fighting the effects of the wand, told him that she wasn't happy with his command.

"Must I leave the wand in place?"

"No, please… *Arghhh…* Master." With her acquiescence he dipped his head and pressed his lips to her swollen folds while extracting the wand and tossing it aside. He heard it clatter as it hit the floor and then rolled. Hot, wet and slick, she tasted of heaven as his tongue swirled around her button, and then delved into her heat. She groaned and raised her hips to meet his thrusts. One palm slipped beneath her ass holding her close, while his other sought out a nipple. He rolled the tender nub between his thumb and forefinger. She whimpered, the sound making him thrust his tongue faster, harder, deeper.

"Oh-oh, Master, I'm going to come." Her shrill cry was a breathless admission.

"Do not—not until I tell you to." Shawn blew a stream of air across her moist pussy sending a shiver through her body that he felt against his palms. "Do not make me punish you."

The intensity in her eyes as she released a breath to gain composure made his cock grow harder. He wanted those lips wrapped around his throbbing erection. Instead he moved atop and with one thrust he buried himself deep inside her pussy. The feeling was so exquisite. A sudden quiver shook him as his balls drew up and his groin tightened. The sensation shoved him over the edge and straight into an explosive orgasm.

"Now, angel. Come for me now," he groaned as he pumped his hips again and again.

Ciarra's attempt to hold back the inevitable had unbelievably increased the fervor of the moment. She was so sensitive—aroused.

On his command, a throaty moan left her lips and her climax washed over her like a wave capsizing a ship. Swallowed up in swirling passion, their bodies convulsed together—and then it happened. It sounded like a cliché, but they became one. His heartbeat echoed through her body.

It couldn't be, but she swore she was experiencing his climax. She felt the warmth of her body, the tightness convulsing around his cock, the pull of gravity that rushed through his erection and bursting through the small slit with such pleasure it bordered on pain. It was so unreal. Something she wanted to deny—something she knew was impossible. By the strange look twisting his features she knew he felt it too— he felt her orgasm. The electricity that flowed between them was unmistakable and too powerful to deny.

She'd never experienced such an earthshaking summit. It was like together they had traversed the boundaries of heaven to slowly drift back to reality. It made no sense. Yet a veil of rightness surrounded her, leaving an intrinsic sense of peace and tranquility.

Or was it her terrifying situation? Was Ciarra so scared, so insecure that she was reaching for anything or anyone to ground her? Was she allowing this man to inadvertently take advantage of her vulnerability?

In the afterglow, he lay quietly atop her, nuzzling her neck and feathering light kisses upon her heated flesh. It was so tender, so exquisite. Her skin was so alive that his touch tickled. A giggle slipped from her mouth as she hunched her shoulders and writhed beneath him.

Shawn raised his head. "You're ticklish?" Laughter sparked in the depths of his emerald eyes.

"No." Her quick response was met with a big grin that softened the hard angles of his jaws.

"Hmmm." Ciarra didn't like the humming sound that left Shawn's—uh—her Master's gorgeous mouth. Like Terrance he had perfectly sculpted lips, lips meant for kissing.

Master. There was something wicked and exciting just imagining this man in control of her body… And he *was* in control. Every time he touched her she responded. All thoughts left her mind as if they had wings and she was but his slave.

"Are you hungry?" he whispered before taking her earlobe into his warm, wet mouth.

She squirmed. "Uh…I-I can't think when you do that, Master."

His semihard cock was still buried inside her body as he propped himself on his palms and stared down at her. "How ticklish are you?"

"I'm not ticklish. Did you ask if I was hungry? Ummm…Master." She was ticklish, but it wasn't something she cared to share, especially to this man with a devilish look in his eyes. "Yes, as a matter of fact, I am. Hungry, that is, Master."

An arched brow expressed his skepticism. She wasn't fooling him—not in the least little bit.

Smiling, he ground his hips to hers hard, before he pulled from her body, leaving her feeling empty and incomplete. It was strange. She had never felt a loss after sex. This man was doing something to her. He even made her forget why she had fled Earth.

Well, almost. Despair hit suddenly and with such a vengeance that she gasped.

Slowly Shawn's smile disintegrated. "What? Did I hurt you?" He shifted his weight.

"Just a little," she lied as heat flooded her face. He frowned. This man read her too easily. If she was going to make it through the two weeks, or until she could find a way off this planet, she would have to do better disguising her feelings. "But I like you atop me, Master."

An inner light brightened his face. "You do?" He looked so young, innocent—the male vanity in his voice encouraged her on.

"Yes. But I like you inside me better," she purred the truth, because it was. He did things to her, eliciting feelings that no man had ever done. He made her forget and she needed that.

He puffed up like a proud peacock. It took everything Ciarra had not to laugh. *Men.* Who knew that this big brawny man could be conquered by a little sweet talk? Stroking his ego was almost as effective as stroking his cock.

With a quick movement he rolled off the bed and stood before her. His thick, rock-hard member drew her attention. The man was magnificent. He had the physique of a bodybuilder, a cock a porn star would envy and a smile that made her insides flutter. With a quick movement he snatched the little remote control off the end table. With a press of a button he released her bound wrists and ankles.

"Oh," she moaned when she attempted to move. Damn. She hadn't known it was going to be so uncomfortable being restrained. Guess it was a taste one needed to become accustomed to—like tequila.

It was the first opportunity Ciarra had to see her surroundings. She rubbed her wrists and stretched her legs as she scanned the room. Elegance encircled her. Marble graced the floor, so shiny she swore she could see herself lounging on the bed. His four-poster bed had railings crossing from one post to the other. A crystal chandelier hung like raindrops from the ceiling, matching sconces dotted the walls, as well as several explicit pieces of artwork.

One picture was a close-up of a woman's breast, the artist capturing the fullness and rapture of the woman in heated passion. The next was the curve of a female's hip, another was the lithe lines of her back. Every part of the woman's body was displayed skillfully. Each done so vividly that Ciarra felt like a voyeur—and she liked it. She'd never known that another woman's body could be so arousing, so beautiful.

"A woman's body is a masterpiece." Shawn's deep tone was a sensual caress tightening her nipples. "I see that you agree with me." He pinched his chin and rubbed. "Hmmm…" Again that hum that made her wonder what he was thinking. Irresistible malachite eyes captivated her, drawing her off the bed. She stood and began to walk toward him, drawn by his energy.

Silly, but Ciarra would lay a bet that his sexy voice and words alone could incite a woman's orgasm. It was simply amazing how in such a short time he had done something she thought impossible. He made her feel special.

Did he have the same effect on all women? She stopped a foot away from him. The thought didn't sit well with her. Neither did the flicker of jealousy she experienced. This was ridiculous. Shawn was a stranger, a means to her return to Earth, because that was what she had decided. She needed to return and clear up this mess. She didn't kill Stan Mayhem. She knew she couldn't have.

With just one step he closed the distance between them. His knuckles skimmed along her cheek.

"The bathroom is to the right if you want to freshen up. But no clothes." That boyish grin surfaced and she felt it straight to her toes. "I want you naked all night long." Then he planted a quick kiss on her lips, turned and walked out of the room, leaving her alone.

Ciarra inhaled, dragging in his essence that lingered around her. There was an earthy, nature aroma about him. It made everything seem pure and innocent, which she was not.

How did you get into such a mess? Her question went without answer as she entered the bathroom. She truly didn't know how it could have happened. Palms resting on the counter, she leaned forward and stared at herself in the mirror. She looked like hell. Her eyes were weary, skin color washed out and her hair was a disaster. But she didn't look like a murderer.

She didn't kill that man. She wasn't like her father.

Then who did?

It had to be a setup. But who would want to pin a murder on her?

Of course, everyone had enemies. Hadn't she left all of hers back in New York? Morris immediately came to mind.

At Kohler Advertising Agency she hadn't been there long enough to offend anyone. Hell, how many people could you offend in fourteen days? And who hated her enough to want her convicted of murder?

Ciarra swiped her hand beneath the faucet, activating the water. She bent and splashed cold water on her face and scrubbed, hard, as if she could wash away the previous night.

Was it only a night ago? God, it seemed like forever.

There had to be a way out of this mess. There just had to be.

She grabbed a towel off the rack and patted her face. Folding and straightening the towel, she returned it to the rack before reaching for a brush. Running the brush through her hair she wondered if she should confide in Shawn. Then she laughed at her naïveté. The man was a stranger. Yes, she had just fucked him, but that was sex — nothing more, nothing less.

"Kitty." Shawn's deep voice pushed past the closed door and released a ripple of pleasure through her body. At least in his arms she could forget, pretend she was someone else — Kitty Carmichael — innocent of murder. Ciarra set the brush back on the counter and exited the bathroom.

Silver tray in hand Shawn had entered his empty bedroom. A moment of unease had slithered across him before he called out to Kitty. The bathroom door creaked. His heart stuttered as she appeared. Her red hair covered her breasts, hiding the luscious nipples from his sight. The small patch of curly red hair at the apex of her thighs looked good enough to eat. She reminded him of a woodland nymph.

She had brushed her hair, but she looked weary, bone-tired.

Just before the event that took place in the dining hall, while Kitty had showered, Shawn had met briefly with his brothers regarding her training. Actually the two had drilled him, reminding him of the contract and pointing out one specific requirement—to experience multiple partners.

Damn that contract.

He walked toward the fireplace and set the tray down upon the marble floor. "As your Master it would please me to feed you. Come." He curled his fingers, calling her to where he stood next to the *albutra* rug.

There was no hesitation to her steps as she complied. He remained as naked as she and he couldn't help the smile when her eyes widened at his already hard cock. "He's insatiable."

She laughed, the sound warming him like a cup of java on a cold, cold night. When she wet her lips his teeth clenched. Man what he'd give to fuck her mouth, at this very moment. He hissed a breath into his tight lungs. There was too much to do and the night was waning. Still there were ways to accomplish both—her training and his need to be inside her.

The rug that once looked so enticing took second place to the armless chair. "Over here." He retrieved the tray and sauntered to the chair, setting the food upon an end table as he took a seat. "Straddle me." Her gaze darted to his stiff erection and he chuckled. "It won't bite."

Her hands went to her hips. She gave him a *duh* look. "I know that." She approached and threw one leg over his thigh and then another, wrapping her arms around his neck. Her moist heat was pressed against his member, but it wasn't enough. She released a tight squeal as he grasped her hips, raised, and then impaled her core with one thrust.

"Ohhh…" Her gasp sent chills up his spine.

"Now," his throaty voice was like sandpaper, "here's the plan. You eat. I talk. Then we fuck."

Chapter Nine

໕ၥ

It was a dream. The night of sex was just a figment of her imagination as was the hand between her thighs lightly stroking her. Ciarra's body felt used and abused and she could not remember when she felt so alive. Her hips rose, shifted so that the finger slid across her throbbing clit. Man, she hoped she never woke up.

"Morning, angel." The deep voice next to her ear made her eyes open wide. Not a dream. Real. The hunky man with penetrating green eyes was real. The night had been real and his hand drawing her closer to climax was real.

She reached for him, remembering his words from last night. "I want to wake in your arms," he had said before kissing her and then drifting into a deep slumber. It had been a stressful night, her fighting sleep, him snoring softly, his arms locked around her making escape impossible. Finally, exhaustion won and she slept.

And what a way to wake up. She was moments away from sexual fulfillment. Yes, she had died and gone to heaven and she owed it to the man nibbling lightly on her ear and causing goose bumps to rise across her skin with his caress.

Wham! Bam! The walls of her sex convulsed. It was like an earthquake shaking her body as her orgasm ripped throughout. Her hips rose off the bed, slamming back down hard. She squirmed beneath the relentless finger that continued to stroke her clit over and over.

"No more." Her cry elicited the opposite response as he moved with such speed between her legs.

"I need to taste you." His tongue took over where his finger had left off. He sucked hard and long, drawing her sensitive nub into his mouth. Pulling and flicking her clit with his tongue, he teased and tormented. Then he bit down. She screamed as another climax shook her with a force so great she could have sworn she heard her brains rattling around in her head. Small spasms rippled through her core, her belly, and straight to her heart. Damn, he was good.

"Now it's my turn." He mounted her and in a single thrust drove deep inside, stretching and filling her pussy. Her mouth opened and air pushed from her lungs. The sensation of his thick, hard cock pumping in and out, the sound of his balls slapping against her ass was too much.

Lights and colors crashed behind Ciarra's eyelids. Shawn groaned long and deep, joining her as their bodies tumbled over the summit and straight into ecstasy. Again, it was as though their souls had united, traveling the same blissful path. So intimate, so self-defining that she felt part of him—his other half. Locked in each other's arms, joined at the hips, she felt the overpowering joy of belonging to someone for the first time. Even if it were only for a week or two—only make-believe.

As the tremors subsided, Shawn eased out her core and rolled off the bed. Sated, she placed her hands behind her head. Three, count them, three orgasms within thirty minutes. Her body was sensitive, alive. Her nerve endings were raw, all her senses were intensified. She smelled his wild musk and the unique scent of their loving surrounding her. She wet her lips, tasting his kiss. How she wanted to touch the man who was now fumbling through his armoire like he was on a mission. She wanted to give back to him the pleasure he had given.

When he turned, he had a handful of black satin ropes clutched in his fist. She gaped. Now what exactly did he have in store for the day?

"It's time to begin." His tongue slid between his lips almost as if he was nervous. "Get up and put this on." There was authority and a hint of anxiety in his voice this time.

She eased into a sitting position then threw her legs over the side of the bed and rose. "But it's nothing but rope."

He frowned. "Do not question me." She startled at his gruffness. It appeared it was time to play this Master/slave game. "It's for the first test."

Her knees suddenly turned to jelly. "Test?"

"Your contract states that Master Terrance would perform the position of Master. If you concede to the modification of me as your Master, then both Master Terrance and Master Tor must approve." A flicker of doubt appeared and disappeared in the green depths of his eyes. "This is what you wish, is it not?"

Okay—the choice of the big growling bear or the magnificent man standing before her? No contest. "Yes, I wish the change of Masters. But—"

"Then you must comply with all my demands—do not hesitate. You must remember to refer to me as Master at all times. And you must remember all that I taught you last night."

All that he taught her last night? Oh, Lord, there was no way that she could remember the commands he taught her. "I'll try."

Concern furrowed his brows. "Kitty, you must do more than try or punishment will follow."

"Punishment?" She hated that word.

"Punishment," he repeated firmly. "There are specifications in your contract, as you are aware of, that will dictate your day."

"Meaning?" Panic slithered across her body. She hadn't had the time to review the damn contract. How did she get into this mess?

"Meaning that you requested several specific scenes, a few that I've made some slight modifications to. There will be no auction."

Holy shit! Did he say auction? "Auction?" Yes. She remembered Master Terrance telling Master Collins that she would be auctioned off.

He slanted a worried look in her direction. "Are you insisting on the auction? You know you'll not be able to choose who purchases you for the night. Or what they might demand you to do."

"No!" She nearly screamed the single word. "No," she said a little calmer. "Whatever you have in mind instead is fine with me." For some silly reason she felt like she could trust Shawn.

His gentleness, his caring and their night of loving had given her hope. Hope that life was worth living and that running wasn't the answer. When her time at Ecstasy Island was up she would return to Earth and pray that the authorities believed she was innocent, because she hadn't killed Stan Mayhem. She couldn't have.

She owed the man standing before her, ropes in hand, so much, because somehow he had given her back her self-confidence, made her feel like there was something to fight for. If it was the last thing she did, she would make him proud of her. She would endure whatever was necessary.

With her chin held high, her shoulders squared, she approached Shawn. "Please help me put this on...Master."

A grin crept across his face. "Good girl."

The ropes tickled as he slid the harness-like outfit across her sensitive skin, especially the ones that parted her labia majora. Her pussy was spread wide, she felt exposed, vulnerable.

But there was something sexy, something untamed that made her blood course through her veins like wildfire.

A strong hand circled her foot as Shawn slipped a three-inch stiletto strappy thing to her foot and wound the leather over her instep and around her ankle. She balanced on the damn thing as he placed its mate on her other foot. Then he took a step back and a look of appreciation curled his lips.

"Beautiful. Just one more thing." He reached for her mons and fluffed her red curls with the tips of his fingers. Then he leaned forward and gave her a quick kiss. "Make me proud." He slapped her ass and she jumped. "Let's go."

Ciarra's feet jerked to a stop as she caught her reflection in the hallway mirror. Shawn moved behind her, drawing his length against hers. "Beautiful," he whispered.

Beautiful wasn't the quite the word she had in mind. It was more like "Kitty-cat, wanton slut, does Ecstasy Island". Her red hair flared around her shoulders while the crisscross of shiny satin ropes lifted her breasts and exposed her—it was downright wicked. Her gaze slid from her legs to the decadent heels she wore. She looked feisty, naughty in a playful way.

"I need a whip," she spoke out loud of what she felt was missing from her ensemble. Heat flared across her cheeks.

Shawn chuckled. "That you do." He turned and when he returned he held a short flogger of soft satin ropes to match her outfit. "For effect only." He handed it to her. "Or maybe I'll let you run that across my body tonight." He had donned a pair of black leather pants, and by the bulge between his thighs the man was as aroused as she was. Tonight couldn't come too soon.

A thrill fluttered in her belly. Her juices dampened the ropes baring her pussy and her breasts filled with desire. How had she let this man mean so much to her in one day? Was she that lonely? That frightened?

He jerked her into his strong embrace. His tongue ran softly along her lips. So enticing that she welcomed him inside, savoring his taste. When they parted she found the promise of another night spent with Shawn and the flogger intoxicating.

"Let's go, slave Kitty."

So it was to begin.

Shawn didn't know who was more nervous, he or Kitty. Her gaze darted around the courtyard beyond the citadel, taking in the multiple couples in different positions of copulation. The air smelled fresh and the sun warm upon his back. Ecstasy Island was a pleasure planet and pleasurable events were happening all around them.

A group from Pandorvia had arrived. There were special rules for the vampires. With their extraordinary abilities, which included mesmerizing their prey and then sexually enslaving them, law stated that they could only mate with their own kind. Their unusual diets included many rare and exquisite foods, including blood. Their sexual appetites were insatiable as evidenced by the two men devouring the woman between them. One fed from her neck as he fucked her pussy, the other's teeth sank deep into the woman's shoulder as he thrust in and out of her ass. She too, was Pandorvian and it wasn't only obvious by the deep blue-black hair they were known for. It was her pearly white fangs visible from her lips that parted on a scream, before she pressed her mouth to one man's neck.

"Ohmygod," Kitty gasped. "I've heard about this race." Curiosity overrode her shock. "Are there werewolves here too?"

"The Lycanians are not due until next month. We try to schedule them months apart." Kitty looked confused as Shawn continued, "The two races are not compatible. Both have a dominating culture." Shawn folded his fingers around hers and pulled as he began to walk.

Before she could ask another question, he ushered her toward the beautiful pool she had bathed in upon her arrival. The gentle sound of water cascading into the pond was relaxing —

That was until he saw his brothers approaching. He knew neither would make this day easy for him, or Kitty for that matter.

Shawn squeezed Kitty's hand and then promptly released it and took a step away from her.

Like Shawn, each brother wore black leather pants instead of their normal togas. Two sets of eyes, one blue and one hazel, made a demeaning sweep across Kitty's rope-laden body. Out of fear or excitement her nipples hardened into tight nubs. A spark flittered in Master Terrance's eyes, the *thing* locked away in his tight pants jerked alive. Evidently, he liked what he saw.

Had Shawn made her don this revealing outfit for his brothers' pleasure? The thought made her stomach churn. She connected gazes with Shawn's. His was one of indifference — an act, of which she was the main character in the play.

"Take your stance," Shawn ordered. The firmness in his voice as she complied, hurt. Her legs drifted a shoulder's width apart. She placed her hands holding the flogger behind her back and cast her eyes downward.

"Well, what do we have here?" Master Terrance's question made her skin crawl. He was a handsome man, as was Master Tor. Hell, all three could almost pass as triplets, but there were subtle differences, eye color being one, height another. Terrance was the tallest of the three. But their real differences were obvious in their expressions. Terrance was mischief with a hint of cruelty. Tor was the intellect, studious and thorough — one might describe him as cunning. And Shawn was a book that had yet to be finished. He held mystery, adventure and romance between every page.

Terrance reached behind her, grasped the flogger, and took it from her. "Does the woman require punishment?" Slowly he patted the whip in the palm of his hand. Was the man salivating? Because he sure had the air of a rabid dog.

Before she could scream *no*, Shawn beat her to it. "No. I believe you will find *my* slave obedient." Ciarra didn't miss the emphasis placed on *my* and neither did his brothers as their eyes met and each one cocked a brow in unison.

"We'll see." Terrance's grumble sent a shiver through Ciarra. From the corner of her eye she watched Shawn tense. "May I take control, Master Shawn?"

Shawn nodded. His palm was damp with perspiration as he cupped Ciarra's chin, raising her eyes to meet his. "You will obey Master Terrance and Master Tor."

"Yes, Master, if it will please you." A flicker of pride lit his green eyes and Ciarra felt his warmth fill her. She would not fail him.

"Kneel," the arrogant man with hazel eyes barked.

Ciarra cringed at Terrance's command. Still she slid down to her knees, her buttocks resting on her heels. Glancing at her thighs, she ensured that the distance between her knees was correct—two fists-width apart as Shawn had taught her. She had paid close attention to everything he did and said last night. With a slight adjustment, she straightened her back, pelvis tilted slightly forward. *Damn, there was so much to remember.* Head erect, except for the very tip of her spine, she bowed slightly forward.

"Adjust right." She hesitated only briefly beginning to slide left, then quickly switched. *Other right,* she blew out a breath of relief at catching her mistake. Placing her right hand on ground, she gracefully shifted her body so her right buttock rested on the grass. She half expected Master Terrance's next command to be adjusted left just to watch her twist awkwardly. Instead he growled. The deep, gritty sound revealed his dissatisfaction.

The fluttering of wings and the soft chirping of birds as they landed high above her in the trees followed Terrance's next command. "Kneel forward."

For a moment she smiled, wondering what the arrogant man would do if one of the birds shit on his head?

Ciarra placed her right hand palm-down about a foot in front of her knees. Left hand followed, her thumbs touching each other as her index fingers formed a triangle directly in front of her body. Her heart was pounding, lunging against her chest as she pressed her forehead to the ground, raising her ass into the air. A cool breeze stroked her pussy and then Terrance's knuckles followed.

"Very nice, Master Shawn. Have you tasted her honey pot?"

Anger and embarrassment sparked in Ciarra but she reined it in. That was exactly the reaction Master Terrance expected and she was not going to deliver—not today.

"Yes, I have. It is very sweet," Shawn responded a little surly.

"Mmmm…" hummed Master Terrance, "Master Tor, shall we?"

Ciarra wanted to die. Both of these men were going to eat her pussy and Shawn would just stand by and watch?

Fury and hurt stung, one energizing, one zapping the other away. Humiliation and surrender were only part of the game. And it was just a game, Ciarra reminded herself. She might as well get used to it and perhaps even try to enjoy it. Besides it was Kitty Carmichael's dollar being spent. Who knew when Ciarra would ever get an opportunity to shun her inhibitions and be free of all her restraints again?

Shawn knew his brothers were baiting him. This little *bon appétit* was for his benefit as much as for Kitty's, including the position. The position Terrance demanded was a very submissive, penitent position exposing her back, buttocks, anus and genitals. Everything about her was bared for his brothers' pleasures.

As both of the men knelt behind Kitty, Shawn clenched and unclenched his fists. Kitty deserved to experience what she came here for. But it was hard, damn hard to let another man touch his woman. But touching would not be all they would do by the end of the day. In order to ensure that Kitty would not be sold at auction as specified in her contract, Shawn had agreed to a foursome with his brothers. The woman would get a taste of multiple partners, all three brothers, at once.

A gasp brought Shawn's attention back to what his brothers were doing. Terrance lay on his back, head directly between Kitty's thighs, making slurping sounds as his tongue and mouth fucked the woman.

She arched her back. Whimpered. Her shoulders and back expanded in deep breaths, falling on slow exhales. She was a fighter and he couldn't be prouder.

Shawn knew how wet she became when aroused. Now Terrance knew, which turned up the burner beneath Shawn's temper.

"Do not come without permission, wench," Terrance warned between licks. From where Shawn stood, he saw the corner of his damn brother's mouth rise. He planned to tease Kitty into a sexual frenzy.

Tor's knowing gaze captured Shawn's heated one. Both knew what Terrance was up to. He'd aroused Kitty to where there was no way in hell she could hold back her climax, and then he'd punish her.

Too much stimulation. Shawn's fists tightened. The woman sobbed, moving her ass helplessly to each of Terrance's thrusts. Her mind should be as aroused as her body. Only then would she understand the nature of submission.

But teaching was not Terrance's intent.

The undercurrents seething inside Shawn were building to the strength of a massive tidal wave. He was going to kill Terrance.

Tor stood, nudging Terrance's hip with his booted foot. "Move aside, Master Terrance. It is my turn to taste her nectar." Leave it up to big brother to ease the tides.

As Terrance moved aside, Tor hesitated. "Master Shawn, are we in agreement for tonight?"

Shawn didn't need any reminders of tonight. "Yes."

Tor drifted to his knees behind Kitty's uplifted ass. He laid one hand on her hip. "Have you arranged the dungeon as agreed upon?"

Shawn knew his brother was introducing the woman to his touch, slowly. "It is being done as we speak."

"Good." With a finger, Tor smoothed the length of Kitty's spine stopping just above the cleft of her ass.

Terrance frowned. He looked to the submissive woman and then to each of his brothers who were now deep in conversation.

Watching from the corner of his eye, Shawn almost chuckled. All Terrance's hard work was going to waste. Shawn knew Tor was giving Kitty much needed time to descend the peak Terrance had taken her to.

Terrance knew it too, by the low menacing growl he released.

All too soon it was time for Tor to take action. Shawn tensed as his brother turned his full attention to the woman before him. With both palms the man caressed Kitty's rounded ass. She swallowed hard, the movements of her throat hard to miss. The small muscles in her arms and legs were tight beneath her soft skin.

"Nice, Master Shawn." Tor's finger circled her puckered rosebud. "Real nice." Then he dipped his head and sampled her juices.

"Enough," Shawn growled. Heavy footsteps brought him in front of her. Her eyes were closed. She panted in small quick breaths. "She has been in this position too long. Blood is rushing to her head." Tor did not hesitate to rise and move away.

Terrance made a snide comment about blood rushing to another part of her anatomy, but Shawn ignored him.

"Rise, slave Kitty." She attempted to comply with Shawn's command, but she stumbled in the process. He linked his arms beneath hers and helped her to her feet. "You did well," he whispered. "I am proud."

Kitty's face was indeed red. Whether or not it was from blood, embarrassment or anger he wasn't sure. Before he could determine the cause she bowed her head, a flow of silky auburn hair hiding her emotions.

"I believe we should adjourn to the gardens," Terrance suggested, a hint of mischief again raising the corners of his mouth. Tor turned to him. They locked glares and one of those silent conversations that Shawn hated so much transpired between the two.

Anger in Terrance's eyes revealed his displeasure.

Determination in Tor's said he would not back down.

"Fine," the one word spewed from Terrance's thin lips. "But I will have my fun." Heavy footsteps pounded the ground, halting as he looked over his shoulder. "Are you coming?" Then his frown diminished, replaced with a smirk as if the idea of the century came to him.

A knot formed in Shawn's stomach. There was no telling what Terrance had in mind.

Just remember that this is what Kitty had requested. What she wanted to experience. Shawn had to keep reminding himself of that fact over and over. Although it was all about a Master's pleasure, money had made this more about the woman's need for adventure. Control in check, he followed his brothers, Kitty walking silently beside him.

Still, by her troubled expression, Shawn would lay a bet that this wasn't exactly what Kitty Carmichael had expected.

Chapter Ten

ഔ

This was *not* what Ciarra had expected. Never in her wildest dreams—well maybe in her *wildest* dreams—would she be on her knees, head down—ass skyward, as two men ravished her pussy, while she wore an outfit made of ropes crisscrossing and accentuating certain body parts. And the most embarrassing part was that her body had enjoyed it. Hell, *she* had enjoyed it. She had been on the verge of losing it countless times.

As she walked beside Shawn, his brothers in the lead, she could not quite make eye contact with Shawn. He did not look happy. The searing glares he gave his brothers were hot enough to melt metal. Furthermore, it reinforced her opinion that this man was not one to trifle with.

Still waters and all that crap.

Ciarra Storm, who had been raised in a religious environment on Rhode Island, would never have gone through with such an escapade. And it was all because she had the hots for one big Greek god. She was beginning to think she'd do anything for him. And that was just dumb, really dumb.

Need she forget the trouble she was in? Playing this masquerade, impersonating someone else, was only going to get her into deeper trouble. And what about that poor man she'd left dead on Earth? Someone had killed Stan Mayhem. Someone needed to pay. And *dammit*! She didn't kill him.

The aroma of roasted chicken wafted through the air and her stomach growled. Both she and Shawn had risen too late for breakfast. The man next to her looked down, a softness easing his strained features.

It was approaching noon and the garden was empty as they entered through a flower archway. To Ciarra's surprise there was a large rectangular table on one side laden with food. Her first reaction was, "All right." Her second was, "Oh no, not again." The last time she attended a meal with these three men she became the meal.

"Relax," Shawn said as he gripped her arm and positioned her so that she was standing at the foodless end of the table.

"Easy for you to say," she muttered, receiving a chuckle and then a stern warning from Shawn not to speak without permission.

Ciarra's skin felt too tight for her body and her throat began to close as Terrance approached. She clenched her teeth, unconsciously moving closer to Shawn and away from his brother. She'd never allowed a man to get under her skin like this one. She was a professional who dealt daily with all types of people. Yet given half the chance she'd claw Master Terrance's eyes out. There was just something about him that rubbed her raw. Heat fanned her face remembering the last place he had rubbed her raw.

"I'll feed her," Terrance murmured. The intensity of his stare made the fine hairs across Ciarra's extremities stand on end.

"No." Shawn's response was firm.

Terrance's eyes widened with surprise. "What?"

Shawn's presence seemed to grow larger, more dangerous as he faced his older brother. "She is my slave and it would please me, as *her Master*, to feed her."

For a moment Terrance looked like he would argue with Shawn. The tension was so thick Ciarra could hardly breathe. Muscles rippled across Shawn's broad chest. Terrance's eyes flickered molten gold with slivers of the same unnerving green in Shawn's. Their fists were clenched.

Would these two mammoth men fight over her? The thought both scared and excited her.

"She's mine." The low rumble in Shawn's throat left no doubt that he meant exactly that. Chills slithered up Ciarra's exposed backside. There was possessiveness in his voice that frightened the shit out of her, as his brother conceded with a single nod. Shawn's nostrils flared in response.

Then Shawn's large hands circled her waist, lifting her up on the table. "Lay on your side facing me. You may prop your head up on your palm."

As she took the position, he seated himself in front of her. To her surprise Master Tor and Master Terrance took a seat behind her. Not exactly who she wanted at her backside, especially Terrance.

Shawn stroked her with his hot gaze, sending her body into meltdown.

How she wished it were just the two of them. She'd roll over on her back, spread her legs, and welcome him to the best buffet she had to offer. Yeah, she would fuck him senseless. Already her desire was preparing the crème de la crème. She was wet and ready for the man.

As her mind wandered, she was surprised when Shawn slipped a slice of what she thought tasted like papaya between her lips. The tropical fruit instantly dissolved on her tongue. She didn't even have to chew.

"It's *cucie* from Pandorvia," Shawn offered as he retrieved another piece from the side of the table containing the food. Pandorvia, she recalled, was the planet the vampire-like people came from that she'd seen fucking earlier. "Do you like it?" he asked.

Ciarra nodded, while listening to the sounds Tor and Terrance made filling their plates and then returning to sit behind her. Shawn smiled, pleased that she remembered not to speak. Why his approval meant so much to her she didn't know. It just did. She wanted to please him, wanted him proud of her.

As Shawn placed something that appeared to be a chunk of baked fish in her mouth, a strong hand circled her ankle. She startled as her foot was raised, knee bent, the sole of her foot touching the table so once again her pussy was exposed. The brush of cool air was a reminder that her rope outfit spread her labia lips. To reiterate the fact a single finger stroked between them making the muscles between her thighs clench. And she didn't have to wonder whose finger. No doubt it was Master Terrance.

Someone brushed aside her hair baring her back. Then something cool and wet slid down her spine followed by a swipe of warmth that sent goose bumps across her skin.

A man's tongue—Master Tor.

It was funny, but Ciarra felt she already knew each of the Thorenson brothers' touches. Terrance's teasing and cruel. Tor's firm, but sensual. And Shawn's was masterful. He knew how to take her body and turn it into a work of art. He was truly a Master.

When a hand cuffed her ankle tight, then smoothed up the inside of her calf to her thigh, she knew it was Terrance's handiwork. She wasn't even surprised when a long finger delved into her exposed heat. She was, however, startled by the growl easing through Shawn's gritted teeth. The tight lines of his forehead only softened when Terrance removed his finger, but not before he flicked her clit making her back arch and her hips to thrust forward.

Terrance's palms struck the table as he stood. At the same time Tor came to his feet. "Master Shawn, may I have a word with you?"

Shawn glared at Terrance as he followed Tor a small distance away.

From Shawn's ramrod-straight stance and the fury that looked permanently etched on his face, Ciarra knew he wasn't happy. As Tor spoke, Shawn threaded his fingers through his shoulder-length blond hair. Tight veins bulged in his biceps. And his thighs looked like they were going to tear through his tight black leather pants. Ciarra would have given anything to hear what Tor was saying. Shawn adjusted his stance to where she couldn't see his face, but when he finally turned around his expression might as well have been a wall of stone.

Emotionless. Cold.

She could almost feel a hard shell of ice forming around him. When he again sat in front of her this time it was as if he stared right through her.

What had his brother said to him?

"May I have permission to speak, Master?" Her question was hesitant at best. She swallowed hard.

Their eyes locked, held.

"You may," he finally said.

"Would it please you for me to feed you?" *Say yes, please say yes.* Ciarra hated to see Shawn like this. She had to do something to ease his troubled expression. She had to please him.

His rigid body relaxed. "Yes, it would be pleasurable, my slave."

Ciarra didn't know what came over her. She scooted her aching body toward him and gently crawled into his lap. The shock that registered on his face as she straddled his legs was priceless. Before he could respond she reached for a piece of *cucie*, placed it lightly between her teeth praying it would not dissolve, and leaned forward. He smiled and took a bite, brushing his lips across hers in the process. Her heart stuttered as she felt his cock jerk. Her nipples hardened at his touch. Warmth greeted her thighs with moisture. His leather pants rubbing against her pussy was erotic. Her juices acted as an accelerator enhancing the masculine scent of his pants. The smell of leather had always turned her on and she couldn't help moving her hips along the ridge of his erection.

His nostrils flared, but he made no sound, gave no other hint that she had aroused him. She would just have to work harder. Male voices murmured behind her. She had almost forgotten that Shawn's brothers were in attendance. Even when Master Collins and his redheaded slave approached the table, she refused to draw her attention from her goal. And her goal was pleasuring the man beneath her.

Next Ciarra retrieved a glass of wine. "A drink, Master?"

He nodded.

She sipped lightly from the crystal rim, holding his gaze as she threaded her hands through his silky hair. Then she slanted her head and leaned forward. He parted his lips as she pressed hers to his. In a slow stream she released the heady wine from her mouth, letting it flow into his. She felt him swallow. As she began to pull away his arms suddenly embraced her, crushing her breasts against his naked chest in a hold that stole her breath. His kiss was firm, demanding, and she surrendered.

Someone cleared his throat. Still Shawn devoured her mouth, his tongue thrusting in and out of her mouth as he ground his hips against her pussy. Her sensitive nipples slid across his chest, the tingles growing as she began to ride him.

"Master Shawn." Tor's voice broke through Ciarra's foggy mind as Shawn severed the connection between them.

She lost control of her breathing. She couldn't take her eyes off Shawn's lips. Her palms fell away from his head, smoothing across his broad chest. His hands caressed her back and settled on her hips, before forcing her down upon his large, hard erection.

"Master Shawn," Tor repeated. "We have guests."

Ciarra had almost forgotten that Master Collins, the man she met last night who had insinuated he had heard of Kitty Carmichael, had joined them. Kneeling at his feet was a beautiful redhead.

Had there been a sale on redheads? Or were they just in season?

Ciarra swore the woman's breasts were twice the size of her own and they were bared for all to see. In fact, the woman was completely naked, except for a collar she wore around her neck connected to a leather leash Master Collins held lightly in his hand.

Again, Master Collins stroked Ciarra's body with his hungry gaze. She couldn't put her finger on it, but there was something she didn't like about him. He wore a musky cologne that almost matched that of his slave's—his and hers. Although handsome enough, his brown eyes were shifty—his eye contact unsteady. She had learned to read people pretty well and something hid beneath the façade he presented. The man simply didn't belong among the wild tropical ambience. He was better suited for a jacket and tie and working behind a desk. A bird dived from the branches, swooping low, and made the man duck.

Ciarra wanted to laugh. Here she stood, metaphorically speaking, in the largest glass house pitching stones at another.

"Should your slave not return to her position at the table?" Ciarra looked over her shoulder catching the gleam in Terrance's eyes. The damn man was up to something, she just knew it.

Her heart sank when Shawn said, "Take your place upon the table."

Well, fine. She could get through this last little bit of humiliation and then she needed to search for a tele-commuter and the transport schedules for Earth. She still had Kitty Carmichael's travel voucher. She could exchange it for an earlier transport or perhaps a connecting flight from one of the other planets close by when the next transport was available, which was supposed to be in a week's time.

Ciarra took one last look at the hard angles on Shawn's face before she wiggled off his lap and crawled back upon the table. As she began to slide upon her side she was halted by Terrance's annoying hand upon her hip.

"On your back," he demanded. The man was standing, a glass of wine in his hand. When she looked to Shawn for confirmation, Terrance made a gravelly noise deep in his throat. Shawn nodded and Ciarra took her place.

Elegantly Terrance raised his glass. "A toast. To Master Collins for joining us." Everyone raised their glasses, bringing them to their lips, except for Terrance. Instead the man poured the glass of red rich wine across Ciarra's breasts, a path down her abdomen, over her mons, dribbling it between her thighs.

A gasp left her lips as the sticky substance covered her.

"Whoops." The damn man had the nerve to feign innocence, which was laughable given this big oaf's demeanor. "Master Collins, would your slave wish to clean Master Shawn's slave?" Terrance asked, taking his seat.

Ciarra's eyes widened. Surely she hadn't heard the man correctly.

"It would be her pleasure, as well as mine." Collins chuckled. "Cherry, please lick clean Master Shawn's slave."

Lick! Ciarra's breath caught on an inhale. She swung her head to the side, meeting Shawn's indifferent expression. "You will allow slave Cherry to see to your needs."

No! erupted in Ciarra's head. She'd never been touched by a woman in any intimate way.

Shawn leaned forward, his voice barely audible. "Relax." His hands folded in front of him on the table.

Relax? Man, was Ciarra getting tired of being told to relax.

"Spread your legs wide," ordered Terrance. He cocked a brow, looking toward Shawn as if he expected his brother to object. Ciarra swung her gaze to Terrance and then back to Shawn.

Object! her mind cried out to Shawn. When he nodded in agreement Ciarra died a little inside. When she didn't immediately comply, Shawn's brows furrowed.

"Spread your legs." Okay, what happened to the man she thought she knew? When he growled, "Now," her legs sprang wide like they were spring-loaded.

Immediately cool air wafted, caressing the folds of her pussy, and the resulting shiver made her buttocks clench tight.

Ciarra's mind was in a whirl of chaos.

An incredible rush of adrenaline pumped through her bloodstream at the apprehension of what was to come. She was completely and totally beside herself. How could she lie docilely on this table while another woman stroked her with her tongue? Not to mention there would be four men watching.

Damn if her nipples didn't peak with the thought. A wave of arousal dampened her sex.

"Raise your arms above your head and lace your fingers," Shawn ordered.

As she complied, he reached for that little black controller *thingy* she had seen him use in his house to activate the static wrist and ankle bands. She hadn't seen him take it out of his pocket, hadn't seen it lying on the table. Where had it come from?

Ciarra couldn't resist moving her arms to see if they were immobilized. Her heart jumped in her chest. He had bound her wrists and even her legs wouldn't move. She was helpless.

All-out panic rose as a scream in her throat. She could taste fear upon her tongue. Pleadingly, she looked to Shawn but he refused to meet her gaze.

And it was too late. Cherry climbed upon the table with lithe movements that emphasized the elegant line of her slender body. Her long red hair swayed seductively, brushing the tabletop. Her large breasts hung full, her nipples hard nubs. Lust radiated in her beautiful blue eyes pinned on the tender folds of Ciarra's pussy.

Ciarra struggled against her bindings. She opened her mouth to protest—

"Don't." The warning Shawn issued left no doubt she had no choice in the matter.

Cherry continued her examination as her heated gaze burned into Ciarra. When the woman's head came level with Ciarra's sex, she dipped low and inhaled deeply.

A tremor shook Ciarra. She sucked in her bottom lip and bit down hard to stop another cry building in her throat. *I can do this. I can do this. No, I can't.*

Resigned she closed her eyes and waited.

"Open your eyes, angel." Shawn's voice was low, sexy. "Open them." How could she refuse the sensual caress whispering in her ear? His emerald eyes were dark, so intense she couldn't look away. She couldn't speak. "Watch the woman as she devours your body." A coil began to wind within her belly. Shawn was aroused. It was in his deep breathing, the way he licked his lips, and soft way he was stroking her arm. "Feel the difference between a man and woman's touch." His warm breath brushed her cheek, slid down her neck. "Feel her soft skin slide across yours." He paused. "But think about me...my touch...me pleasuring you..."

Ciarra's pulse quickened and that coil wound a little tighter. To hell with this woman, she wanted Shawn's hard body atop hers. She wanted his mouth and tongue stroking her heated skin. She wanted his long, thick cock buried deep inside her wet pussy.

He smiled. The man knew what he was doing to her, and by the bulge between his thighs he wanted the same thing. Still he continued to heighten her desire as he stood and leaned over her body. "Compare her scent, her taste to mine." He licked a slow path from her chin, along her jawline to her ear. "Enjoy the experience."

Ohmygod, Ciarra gasped as he returned to his seat. Just his sensuous voice, his wicked words hardened her nipples to the point of pain. Wave after wave of energy surged through her breasts and the coil notched a little tighter.

Then Terrance's haughty voice shattered the moment. "Don't forget, slave Kitty. You must not climax without permission."

Okay, only moments ago Ciarra would have said *no problem*. But now—now that Shawn had worked her body and mind into a slow burning flame, she was no longer so sure. Especially when the woman dipped between Ciarra's thighs and released a long, warm gush of air on her exposed pussy that sent shivers up her spine.

A deep-throated groan pushed from Ciarra's trembling lips. This was going to be harder than she anticipated and perhaps not at all offensive.

"Cherry, your job is to clean, not to pleasure." The warning came from Master Collins. Disappointment wiped the smile off the woman's face.

From the top of Ciarra's mons the woman slid her tongue across Ciarra's skin, dipping into her bellybutton and drinking the excess wine that pooled there. The sensation was strange and different and not at all displeasing like Ciarra had expected. In fact, knowing this woman desired her was shamefully exciting. Cherry was beautiful.

When Cherry had ensured Ciarra's abdomen was sufficiently clean of wine she made a path to Ciarra's breasts. Long, drawn-out licks circled her globe sending fire shooting through her taut nipple.

Cherry was close enough that Ciarra could smell her perfume. The sweet musk was light, pleasing and feminine—not masculine and heavy like Master Collins' that clouded the senses. Ciarra tried to focus on the differences, ignore the sensations echoing through her body, but then Cherry latched onto Ciarra's nipple, sucking, pulling, and scraping her teeth across the sensitive bud.

Ciarra whimpered, her chest arching into the woman, pressing her nub deeper into Cherry's hot wet mouth. The difference between man and woman began to blur, the need for fulfillment came to the forefront.

While Cherry's hand stroked Ciarra from wrist to armpit on one side, Shawn teased her other arm. Calloused and strong versus soft and smooth, so different and each so delightful, except Shawn's touch tickled and sent her squirming.

Escape. Climax. The two feelings battled each other.

"Cherry, you have earned a punishment." Master Collins issued his gravelly reprimand. "Get on with it."

Ciarra couldn't see Master Collins from where she lay, but she could the Thorenson brothers. Each of their faces was riddled with lust. All three of them were getting off on what the woman was doing to Ciarra. No, make that four with Collins— No, five if Cherry was included— No, six if she included herself. Because Ciarra had to admit that this experience was indeed heady.

"I believe I saw a little drip between slave Kitty's thighs." Ciarra shuddered at Terrance's helpful observation. Did the man ever give up?

"Master?" Cherry asked, hesitant to move until instructed.

"Yes, Cherry, clean her good." Master Collins laughed. His voice was deep and hoarse as he repeated, "Clean her good."

A spasm rippled through Ciarra's core. She didn't think she would be able to withstand what she knew was coming next—which undoubtedly would be her by the excitement radiating through her body.

Like a serpent, the woman slid down Ciarra's body. She was soft, her large breasts and beaded nipples sliding against

Ciarra's skin. The sensation was different, pleasing. For a second, Ciarra wondered what the woman would taste like.

The first swipe of Cherry's tongue against Ciarra's exposed labia sent her hips thrusting toward the woman's mouth. The mass of red hair bobbing between her legs nearly threw Ciarra over the edge. She wasn't prepared for this or the excitement she felt ripping through her body.

She inhaled, slowly releasing it as she turned her head to focus on Shawn and not the woman between her thighs. His gaze was glued to Cherry's head. His eyes dark with lust, his knuckles white as he clenched his hands together and leaned forward.

The man was turned on. And the mere fact twisted the coil in Ciarra's belly tighter until she was a breath away from climaxing.

"Master?" It was all Ciarra could manage to say.

"Hold." A vein ticked in Shawn's neck. His knuckles were white, his fingers tightly woven together.

"Master?" Ciarra repeated with more urgency. She didn't know how much longer she could withstand.

"Hold." Shawn unfolded his hands and pressed his palms on the table before rising. The tendons in his arms bulged. "Now. Come for me now."

Ciarra's scream rent the air as her hips moved with the rhythm of Cherry's thrusts, faster, harder. The woman continued to suck, drawing out every last spasm from her body.

"Stop," Ciarra pleaded. Her clit was so sensitive that Cherry was pushing pleasure away, allowing pain to take over. "Stop."

"That's enough," Shawn bellowed, coming to her aid. He pushed a button releasing Ciarra's bindings. Nudging Cherry aside, he assisted Ciarra from the table.

Cherry was breathing rapidly. Lust raged in her wide blue eyes as she stared at Ciarra. Clearly, the woman needed release. For a moment unease slithered across Ciarra's skin. Would Shawn make her perform the same task on this woman?

It was one thing to be the recipient—another to be the giver of pleasure.

"Get off the table." Cherry scrambled, slipping once as she hurried to comply with Master Collins' demand. "On your knees." She drifted down as he approached. The wildness glowing in the woman's eyes, the way she trembled was frightening. "Take me into your mouth." Without hesitating, Cherry undid the man's pants. His hard cock sprang out and immediately disappeared between the woman's lips.

Collins' face distorted as he threw back his head, closing his eyes. He pumped once, twice and then he released a deep groan. Ciarra watched amazed as the woman swallowed the man's seed down her throat in front of everyone.

"Enough." Collins eased from the woman's mouth. He tucked his flaccid member into his pants not making any attempts to fasten them. "For your punishment, Cherry, you will pleasure Master Shawn."

"No!" Ciarra stiffened. Shawn was *her* Master.

Terrance burst into laughter—the asshole.

Shawn turned slowly and faced her with an expression of anger. "Your outburst has earned you a punishment. Now, take your stance and remain quiet."

Ciarra's legs parted, her hands locked behind her back, and she bowed her head.

Shawn cupped her chin jerking her head up. "No. Look at me. It would please me for you to watch."

A part of Ciarra's heart crumbled. She didn't know this man who glared down at her.

He was a stranger.

Then she remembered. This was a job—a game to him. She wasn't anyone special to him, just another client.

Ciarra narrowed her gaze on Shawn. Her resolve took form, hardened. It was time to find a way off this planet.

Chapter Eleven

ಬ

Excitement built with the speed of light. Shawn had not expected jealousy or possessiveness from Kitty. But it was there in every tight muscle, every wrinkle that creased her forehead. Her chin was raised slightly in defiance. If her eyes had been daggers, Collins would be dead by now.

He never felt more alive standing in the garden as life exploded around him. The colorful array of hibiscus, roses, gardenias and orchids dotted the scenery, their sweet scents mingling with Kitty's to create a sensual atmosphere. Vines wrapped around the tree trunks made Shawn wonder what she'd look like with the greenery wound around her delectable body.

As Master Collins' slave approached, he could swear the delicate hairs on Kitty's arms rose. Excitement built inside him. She was as prickly as a porcupine, but cuter than a kitten.

It had been hell on Earth when Tor had warned him about loss of control earlier. That his needs and desires were secondary to those specifications Kitty had outlined in that damn contract.

Problem was…his brother was right.

Ecstasy Island was a business. What he did reflected on all of the Thorenson brothers. Shawn was allowing his personal interest to cloud his professional responsibilities. It was his duty—his job to see that Kitty's experience at Ecstasy Island was fulfilling—that the contract's specifications were met.

The woman wanted sex and lots of it, and with multiple partners.

As Cherry unfastened his leather pants, Shawn inhaled sharply. The sound made Kitty clench her teeth together, a vein flickered in her throat. Shameful, yes, but he was enjoying her discomfort. Could she actually have feelings for him after only two days? He knew it was possible, because it was exactly what he felt.

The soft hand cradling his balls drew his attention downward. Cherry wet her lips, making a smacking noise as her gaze darted to Kitty. Cherry's intentional smirk made Kitty tremble. She looked like she was ready to spit fire.

Hope that something just might exist between the two of them had Shawn's cock lengthening, hardening. Kitty's eyes gaped. He loved that little trait in her when she was surprised—or in this case angry.

She was jealous.

Then Cherry took his cock into her mouth and for a moment Shawn's mind went blank, confirming that a man's brain was between his legs. He closed his eyes, enjoying the warmth slide up and down his erection. The woman was masterful as her tongue swirled around his crown, dipping into the small slit, wrenching out every sensation from his body.

But something was missing. Even in the throes of lust, something was missing.

Kitty.

Still his body reacted as any normal male's would. His erection hardened, pulsed as blood rushed into it. Nerves clenched, unclenched, raw and ready to explode. His pulse sped and his breathing labored. His fingers grasped handfuls of red hair as he thrust his hips, driving into her deeper, faster. Her head bobbing between his thighs made him wish it was Kitty's mouth that fucked him. Again, all thought disappeared as his climax rose and then ripped through his cock like acid, burning, sending white-hot pleasure to every extremity.

As the last of his cum filled her mouth, he released the hold he had on her hair. She continued to milk him, taking every last drop of his semen down her throat. When his eyes drifted open it was to meet Kitty's damning glare. She wasn't used to their life on Ecstasy Island. He could see how she might feel betrayed, where sex on Earth was viewed differently between partners. Here, on Zygoman, pleasure was all that mattered.

How absurd was that thought? Betrayal. You had to be in a relationship to feel betrayed. She was jealous, so there had to be something. Then he reminded himself that this was a job. And it was time for Kitty's punishment.

Shawn knew what his brothers expected. They both had to be rock hard watching Cherry perform oral sex on Ciarra, Collins and himself. He knew he couldn't be so lucky that each had jacked-off beneath the table. As his brothers rose, their cocks at attention, it was clear that they had not sought their own release.

With trepidation, Shawn ordered Ciarra to his side. A cool chill blew by as she approached and he was sure it wasn't the light breeze that had kicked up and feathered back her long red hair. A bird chirped high in the willowy branches of a *quinta* tree. Several pink blossoms broke loose and floated through the air, one landing on a red curl winding down her chest. He reached to pluck the petal as she jerked, brushing the flower away.

She was angry, but he had to continue — to perform his job.

"For your punishment you will pleasure Master Tor with your mouth." Shawn turned to Terrance. "Master Terrance it is your choice which of the lovely entrances of my slave's body you wish to fuck."

Both Terrance and Kitty shared the same wide-eyed expression that turned immediately sour. Kitty clearly did not care for Terrance. And Shawn knew what entrance Terrance would choose, saving Kitty's precious pussy for himself. This was one time Shawn would enjoy Terrance's hang-up about fucking a woman's core. Terrance's exwife had really done a job on his brother.

With a little grin, Tor lay upon the grass, his hands resting beneath his head. Tor was a man—a man needing release. This Shawn understood, but he didn't have to like the expression of anticipation that said his brother was looking forward to fucking Kitty's mouth.

"Kitty," Shawn growled, unable to hide his resentment.

A scowl on her face, she whipped her shoulders around, turning her back to Shawn as she approached his brother. She hesitated, glanced over her shoulder at Shawn, an expression of pure disdain, before she focused on Tor. Slowly she stroked him with her gaze.

"Kneel," Shawn commanded. She floated downward and without being told, reached for the waistband of Tor's leather pants. With a flick of her wrist, she bared his brother's cock.

Shawn realized that his heart was pounding. Perspiration beaded his brow. Fuck, this was difficult. He didn't want anyone touching Kitty, not even his brothers. He held his breath before releasing it in one gush.

"Take Master Tor into your mouth." Kitty was hesitant, but she complied with Shawn's demand. "Master Terrance."

Terrance turned to Shawn, and from behind his back he produced the flogger that Kitty had carried this morning. He extended the whip to Shawn. Shawn took a step forward then drew to a halt. This type of punishment the brothers had performed on many women. Both brothers would expect Kitty to be treated no differently. And they would be correct.

Shawn closed the distance between them and reached for the whip, which Terrance drew back suddenly.

"How about us exchanging parts? You fuck. I will administer punishment." Shawn didn't know what to say. Terrance placed his hand on Shawn's shoulder and squeezed. That was about as close to a sentiment of brotherly love that

Shawn was going to receive from his brother, and it said more than words could. Terrance understood his feelings for this woman.

As Kitty's head bobbed, Shawn couldn't keep his gaze off her lovely ass raised high in the air. That ass was his—all his.

Kneeling behind her, he admired her moist pink flesh calling to him. He took his cock in hand, gliding it along her slick folds, anointing his erection with her sweet juices.

Terrance moved in place. His wrist snapped and a light snap sounded just before it landed on Kitty's tender ass cheek.

She whimpered, the cry muffled around Tor's member. Several flushed marks rose on her tender flesh. Shawn caressed the angry flesh, sensitizing the area as another lash landed on her other cheek. Then he moved to the next area, stroking her as he wedged the head of his erection into her slit.

Her ass was a delightful rosy tint after two more snaps of Terrance's wrists, and heat warmed Shawn's palm as he caressed her skin. Then his brother took a step backwards and folded his arms over his broad chest. The tension in his face softened. *Take her, little brother*, he mouthed, standing aside.

Shawn was touched by his brother's actions, but the ache between his legs was bordering on pain. If he didn't sink his cock deep into Kitty soon he'd have a sure case of blue balls. With one thrust he pierced her tight, wet channel.

She moaned. Her body arched and moved against him, trembling. Small tremors quaked around his erection. She was close to climax. By the strained expression on Tor's face as he fucked Kitty's beautiful mouth, the same was true for him.

Faster. Harder. Deeper. The sound of Shawn's hips, his scrotum slapping against Ciarra's sex, was heady. One more thrust and he'd be joining her in ecstasy. His palm skimmed through her mons, found the button of her desire and he pushed.

The ground trembled beneath Kitty as he approached then disappeared behind her. His touch was like fire, hot and stimulating. Her climax all-consuming, swelled higher and higher, building, then shattered with the pressure of Shawn's finger. An exquisite thunderbolt ripped through her with the intensity of electricity discharging in the sky, heating her blood, setting her on fire. Her body drank greedily of both men fucking her as wave after wave of aftershocks shook her. Swallowing, she relished the warm masculine taste of Tor as he filled her mouth with his semen. But the most exhilarated feeling was Shawn's strong hands stroking her as his cock completed her.

Her anger with the man had dissipated. Although there was a thrill being taken by two men, she would have preferred being wrapped in Shawn's arms alone. Strange, but Shawn felt like an anchor keeping her grounded when her world was coming apart.

But heaven had to come to an end as it did when she heard Terrance's deep hoarse voice. "Slave Kitty, you have earned another punishment."

Shit. She had climaxed without permission. But damn, it was Shawn's fault. She had no willpower, no control when the man touched her.

As Shawn and his brother eased from her body, she collapsed in a sated heap upon the ground. The smell of grass mixed with rich dirt filled her nostrils. Her breathing was labored, the scent of both men lingered on her skin, and even the big oaf who stood arrogantly above her could not take the delicious sense of perfection away.

Damn, if all punishments were like this—bring 'em on. Even the lashes thrown from the beast's hands had been exciting. Before her pulse could subside, those said hands wrapped around her waist and jerked her to her feet, bringing her face-to-face with heated hazel eyes. Lust flickered hot in their depths. He had stripped his toga off, his cock thrusting fierce and hard before him.

The Charade

Okay, so Master Terrance was horny.

Let's see. He had witnessed sex between two women spread before him on the table like a feast, two men receiving head from a gorgeous redhead, and then his two brothers enjoying what Ciarra's body had to offer.

Impressive shoulders rose and fell sharply with his heavy breathing. Kitty half expected smoke to stream from his nose as he raked his gaze over her naked breasts.

She trembled at the ferocity. It was almost as if she could feel him stroking her, causing her nipples to draw into taut beads.

The grunting sounds Master Collins and Cherry made fucking in the distance added to the fire in the Master Terrance's glare. He reached for her, his touch surprisingly gentle as his palm caressed her breast. Kitty was absorbed in his hunger. She couldn't move, trapped by his desire.

"Master Shawn, may I wield your slave's punishment?" The request was said with authority, but Terrance's coarse voice was strained and held tightly under control, and it gave him away. He needed release.

Shawn's tone displayed the exact tension when he replied, "You may, but it will have to wait. There is a bondage clinic that requires our presence."

Amazingly, Ciarra swore she could see the muscles and tendons in Master Terrance's body tighten another notch and his cock twitch with disappointment. If ever she saw someone in need of sexual release it was this one. He was stretched so thin that she doubted he could walk. But the man of steel took a deep breath, released it slowly, then turned and strode away, Tor falling in behind him.

This was a helluva gimmick the Thorensons had going here on Ecstasy Island.

Sex and more sex.

Push a woman to the edges of insanity 'til there was no possible way to hold back her climax and then punish her with more sex. This would be a wonderful place to hide out if she hadn't decided earlier to return to Earth and face the consequences.

I'm innocent. The authorities have to believe me, because I did not kill Stan Mayhem.

Shawn disengaged her thoughts with a simple touch of his hand upon her shoulder. Warmth spread through her body, her nipples pebbling into nubs. Amazingly, she lost it when he touched her. Slowly she looked up into his green eyes. Ciarra hadn't just fallen off a skyglider, but if she didn't know better, he liked her, not just sexually, but truly liked her, possibly even cared about her.

"You have been assigned a bungalow for the down periods of your stay. Anything you wish will be at your fingertips. I will send Tatiana to assist you." His hand brushed up and down her arm. He gave her a gentle squeeze. "You will have the remainder of the afternoon off. Your training begins again at seven o'clock."

A quick peck on the cheek and then he was gone, moving with haste, his long strides taking him further down the cobble path until he disappeared from her sight.

Ciarra stood befuddled. There was almost a boyish shyness just now about Shawn. He was an enigma that she knew there was not enough time to figure out.

But in truth, Ciarra was ready for a little alone time. There was a murder to solve and she didn't yet know how to approach it.

As she sauntered down the path she couldn't help but feel a little self-conscious about her dress, or lack of. The little rope getup she wore hid nothing and attracted attention from several men walking past. One in particular stopped, blocking her way.

It was the Pandorvian, the vampire she'd seen earlier today. White teeth glistened between his parted lips that lifted into a seductive grin. Jet blue-black hair brushed his shoulders and matted his bare chest, narrowing to a line past his bellybutton and disappearing beyond his tight leather pants. And his eyes were so blue they were hypnotic, mesmerizing.

He reached for her hand, bowing over it before placing a light kiss upon it. "*Mio amore*, may I introduce myself. I am Paolo de Rimini." His voice was silk sliding over her body. "Will you join my friend André Moselle and me?" Her eyes followed the path of his gaze, which rested on the other Pandorvian leaning casually against a stone pillar. One leg bent, sole of foot resting on the column, he wore the most enticing smile and that was all.

Damn, but these men were gorgeous and dangerous. She had heard that their bite was an aphrodisiac—once bitten, a woman would never be satisfied by anyone else, at least not human. Since she planned to live a long time there was no way she was going to tempt the fates, no matter how yummy he and his friend appeared.

With a small jerk of her hand, Ciarra broke the man's grasp. "Thank you," she said. "It would definitely be a pleasure, but I have a prior engagement." She tried to break eye contact, but was unable, as if a force kept her glued to the spot where she stood.

He placed his fingertips lightly to each side of her head, touching her temples with his middle fingers as he began to massage. "Will you not reconsider?"

Flash! An image of these two men caressing her naked body sparked in her head. One was positioned between her thighs lapping at her pussy. Her head rested in the other's lap as he kneaded and stroked her breasts watching his friend devour her.

Ciarra flinched as the picture disappeared, realizing that the man had removed his fingers from her face.

Eyes that had once been sky-blue were dark. His smile had vanished, the tips of his canines pressed against his bottom lip. "Will you not reconsider, *mi amor*?"

Ciarra clenched her eyelids, breaking the trance. "No, I mustn't."

A soft, sensual laugh swirled around her, winding along her arms and her legs like he was casting a spell over her. Again she felt his fingertips against her temples, but this time the image had changed. Instead she stood sandwiched between the two Pandorvians, their muscled bodies sliding against hers, up and down—up and down, the friction so hot Ciarra half expected her body to self-destruct. Her breasts felt heavy, moisture dampened her thighs. Her nipples ached, pulling at the tethers connected to her pussy.

Ohmygod, she was going to climax.

"Slave Kitty." A female voice shattered the image in her mind. Ciarra opened her eyes to meet Tatiana's puzzled stare and both Pandorvian's were gone—vanished as in thin air.

A light perspiration filmed her body. Her knees felt weak. Her clit throbbed with need.

"Slave Kitty, are you all right?" the dark-haired woman asked.

Ciarra's gaze darted around the garden. "Where did they go?"

"Who?" Tatiana's brows dipped. She looked about.

"The Pandorvians."

Tatiana's brows shot up so fast that Ciarra thought they might touch her hairline. "You mustn't play with the Pandorvians, they are dangerous."

Irritated at Tatiana's insinuation, Ciarra murmured, "I wasn't *playing* with anyone."

"They are hard to resist, but you must," she warned, grasping Ciarra by the wrist and pulling her along the pathway.

Ciarra resisted, planting her feet firmly on the ground and jerking back her hand. "I didn't do anything wrong. And why all this heebie-jeebies stuff." She waved her hands about.

"Listen," exasperation raised Tatiana's voice, "I'm not your keeper, but know that this race is a dominant one. Once they have marked you as theirs—you are. You can't run fast enough, or go far enough to get away. And the bigger problem is you wouldn't want to escape. Now, may I show you to your bungalow?" With that Tatiana pivoted on a heel, her toga swishing, giving Ciarra the impression she didn't care whether Ciarra followed or not, which put her feet in motion. She had no idea where she was much less where she was going.

The bungalow was impressive. After Tatiana showed her about she left, leaving Ciarra to explore for herself. The room looked like one big playroom. An oversized bed was against one wall, a fireplace with a large white angora rug adorned the floor before it, and one wall was complete with every type of sex toy imaginable. Hell, by the vibrators and the horse—a bench-style chair that allowed interchangeable "heads"—self-satisfaction was at one's fingertips.

But what Ciarra needed was a tele-communicator. Her gaze scanned the room as she walked around searching for a wall unit or the small handheld type of device. She needed to get her life back on course. She needed to right the wrong she left on Earth.

When she came to a closed door she opened it and entered an elaborate bathroom, almost as big as the main room itself. A sunken whirlpool was surrounded by vegetation making the bubbling water even more enticing. Visions of wildcats stalking the area or colorful parrots and chattering monkeys appeared in her mind. How she longed to lounge in its warmth and forget about her problems. Instead she backed out of the room and continued her search.

Another door led her into a walk-in closet. All her clothes were hung neatly in a row. Her body continued forward, while her feet abruptly stopped, jarring her. Clothes—not Kitty Carmichael's, but her own from Earth. How did her clothes get here?

Her pulse sped. In disbelief she ran her fingertips over her favorite leather skirt, her green silk blouse. Her personal shoes, purses and other accessories were neatly placed beneath coordinating outfits, including the purse taken from Stan Mayhem's home that held the incriminating knife. Not to mention the pantsuit she had arrived in. The rip had been repaired as if Shawn had never torn it off her. Next to it was her briefcase. Trembling hands reached for the brown leather satchel that usually held her identification and emergency money.

A flicker of doubt touched her, and then quickly disappeared. *No. There was no way I could have arranged this without remembering.* Yet she had no recollection of the night before she left Earth, Stan's death, or how she came to be involved in his death.

In a state of denial she exited the closet, crossed the room and drifted onto the bed. The fine hairs on her neck bristled. She looked about the room, fighting the sense that she was trapped.

Was the room smaller? Were the walls closing in on her?

With a press of her thumbprint to the lock on her briefcase, she activated the identification code. A sharp *click* followed as the latch released and the lid popped open. Her palm covered her mouth, a strangled cry emerged.

A picture of her and Stan Mayhem in an intimate embrace lay before her in an intricately carved oak frame. She shook her head in disbelief. As she moved aside the frame, she found two tickets to Baccarac, one in her name, the other in Stan's. One after another she revealed her passport, receipts that she had closed out her banking accounts and several money vouchers totaling fifty million dollars. A spreadsheet showed each transaction. Funds being withdrawn from one account and deposited into an account in Liberty Dale Trust.

And everything was in her name.

No. The single word caught in her throat as she frantically moved more documents aside, each one more incriminating than the next. Lying before her in black and white was all the evidence needed to lock her away for life. Evidence that proved she and Stan had stolen monies from one of his partners.

Matthew Collins.

Chapter Twelve

ജ

The last silk rope in place, Shawn moved away from Passion Flower. Her gorgeous lotus tattooed breasts were bare for all eyes as her wrists were bound together and stretched tight above her head, her legs spread wide and shackled to the floor of the citadel. There were about twelve new Masters in attendance, their attention riveted on the beautiful Asian woman. Their eyes burned with lust in the dimly lit room, where a bright light shone on the woman in the middle of the stage in the Orientation Hall.

The actual instruction on positioning and tying knots had taken more time than Shawn had expected. Twilight had fallen. It was time to wrap up the session and get back to the real subject on his mind — Kitty.

"Even those not interested in other aspects of S&M, find beauty in bondage." Shawn was only a voice in the dark as Tor approached his wife and entered the spotlight. "The fantasy to be bound, rendered helpless, is a dream many have imagined at one time or another, whether Dom or sub." Shawn paused and then smiled, recalling this morning when he had teased Kitty that perhaps he'd let her use the flogger on him. His erection grew firm. The feel of soft leather thongs teased across his skin, the sting —

Terrance cleared his throat, urging Shawn onward. As Shawn complied, he inched his way closer to the exit. "Remember, a Dom uses bondage to enhance his slave's experience and tighten his control. On the other hand, bondage allows a submissive to escape — live for the moment — release her inhibitions and the stresses of the outside world."

Tor caressed both of Passion Flower's breasts, rolling each tight nipple between his fingers and forcing a soft moan from her lips.

Thoughts of Kitty were making Shawn restless. Tatiana had informed him of her brief encounter with the Pandorvians. Hell would freeze over before he let them take her. He should have known that they would be attracted to her. Obviously the woman needed a protector. He would speak to the Pandorvians, emphasize their contract regarding humans and ensure their compliance—one way or another.

Terrance issued one more throat-clearing warning, forcing Shawn back to the immediate situation—the final lesson.

"Love bondage is a scene created to heighten your slave's awareness of her body, her vulnerability, and emphasizes your control." Shawn envied Tor the relationship he had with his wife. When they looked at each other something special was there—an intimacy only they shared—like a secret.

Tor removed his hand from his wife's body and immediately a whimper left Passion Flower's lips as her chest thrust forward in search of his touch. Over and over, he'd stroke her into a heated frenzy, stepping away to allow her body to cool and savor the ebbing sensations, only to rekindle them and build the sexual tension once again.

The heat in the room soared as Shawn searched the faces of the audience. The air hung heavy with lust. Several men cupped their erections, others stroked. Their slaves were in for a night of play.

Shawn didn't know how many times Tor and Passion Flower had performed for this class and each time it was like the first for the two of them. His balls ached with thoughts of Kitty. Shawn wanted this type of passion in his life. He needed the unity. Except that he wouldn't want her bared for any eyes but his after they wed.

Now where had that come from?

"Tease her into arousal, then prolong it without giving her release," Shawn finished, as his brother knelt and immediately began cunnilingus, licking and sucking between his wife's spread thighs. The sweet smell of sex rose alongside Tor's growl as he devoured Passion Flower. When a tremor shook her, Tor stood and moved behind her to knead her breasts. The Asian woman squirmed. With one hand he continued the assault on one globe. The other slipped between her thighs and fondled the sensitive bud. All the while he whispered softly into her ear.

Passion Flower's breathing elevated. A light sheen of perspiration glistened on her dark skin. Black, feathered lashes slid closed, her lips slightly parted, an expression of anticipation on her face that quickly soured when Tor again withdrew both hands.

"If properly done, your slightest touch will send pleasure up your slave's spine, through every inch of her body— exploding in her mind and between her legs." As Shawn completed his sentence, Tor thrust two fingers deep inside his wife and she shattered. Her body shook. Her jaws clenched as she arched, pressing her sex into Tor's hand and undulating her hips as a throaty groan surfaced.

End of session—

Shawn headed for the exit, tossing over his shoulder. "Bondage and submission will be held tomorrow at noon. Bring your slaves along and we'll have a little hands-on practice." His words were clipped.

"Master Shawn." Terrance's raised voice was promptly ignored as the door slammed behind Shawn. He was in a hurry to get back to Kitty, feel her silky skin slide against his and finally to lose himself in her warm body.

As he turned the corner of the citadel, heading for the bungalows, he was surprised when Kitty slammed into his chest. She bounced. As she fell backwards, he reached out and grasped her by the arms before she could hit the ground. Still in her black satin rope harness, he pulled her to him.

Man, did she feel good in his arms. "Going somewhere?" He chuckled at the mass of red hair hiding her face. Gently, he brushed the unruly curls aside. Unease slithered across his skin as he took a good look at her.

Kitty was sheet-white and trembling. Fear widened her eyes and thinned her lips. If he didn't know better he would have sworn she'd seen a ghost. The beat of her heart against his chest made him wonder what exactly had happened since he left her.

"What's wrong?"

"Nothing." She breathed heavily.

"Kitty?"

"I need to get off this planet."

Anger surfaced and jealousy followed close on its heels. "The Pandorvians," he hissed. "Blood sucking—"

"No. I-I just need to leave." She placed a hand over her mouth. Moisture gathered in her eyes, but she didn't cry as she withdrew her palm. She nibbled on her bottom lip and blinked hard as she fought to gain composure.

Shawn adjusted his hold and snaked his arm around her tense shoulders, holding her close. He used his body to guide her in the opposite direction of her obvious destination, the transport platform. Truth was there wasn't a transport to Earth for a week, but there were shuttles to other planets that provided connections. "Let's go to my place. We can have something to eat, then you can tell me what this is all about."

She resisted, her feet dragging. "I shouldn't—"

He overpowered her with his strength, his will. "Yes, you should. Remember there isn't a flight leaving until next week."

She glanced up at him pleadingly. "I need a tele-communicator."

"We'll see." Shawn wasn't ready to let her go. He gazed into the starry night. If by chance it was an exboyfriend that kept Kitty in constant distress there was no way he was going to let her near a tele-communicator or tell her about the shuttle connections.

Sounds of the evening closed in around them. A cricket's chirp, the coo of a dove, the gentle flow of water in the distance blended together to provide a soft serenade. If she wasn't trembling so much the night would be ideal for seduction.

Seduction.

Yes. It was time to erase the demons or the man from her mind.

After ushering her through the large oak doors of his home, it took mere minutes to arrange the night. A button here, a button there and candles breathed life, lights dimmed, and dinner was on its way. Soft music played in the background as he led her up the stairs, through his bedroom and into his spacious bathroom. Within seconds the Jacuzzi bubbled. The light scent of vanilla filled the air.

Standing behind her, he released her satin rope outfit and then slowly slid his hands down her body as he removed it. He pressed his lips to her neck. She trembled and sighed as he feathered kisses along her throat into the dip of her shoulder blade.

Shawn moved away, releasing the catch on his toga, the cloth sliding down his already heated body. He removed his sandals and took a step into the recessed pool. The water was warm, inviting. A rainbow of iridescent colors shimmered, caused by the fiber optics in the pebbles lining the tub. Together their shadows elongated and then shrank against the walls as the candles' yellow-orange flames flickered. The skylight overhead rolled back to reveal the night. Dual moons snuggled close to one another like lovers as stars dotted the heavens.

Shawn extended his hand. "Come, let me bathe you." She hesitated only briefly before reaching for him. Hand in hand, they went deeper, bubbles caressing, the water soothing.

Gliding upon the lounge seat, Shawn placed Kitty in front of him so her back lay against his chest.

Her movements were tentative, but as she eased into the depths, she hummed, "Mmmm…"

"Relax—"

The suggestion no sooner left Shawn's lips than both of his brothers burst into the room. Neither was smiling.

Kitty startled, sitting upright.

"We had an agreement." Even in the dimly lit room, Shawn could see the veins in Tor's neck bulge. His eldest brother was angry unlike Shawn had seen in some time.

"Get out," Terrance barked. Kitty rose to oblige, while Shawn pulled her back against him. She released a tight squeal as she fell and water splashed over the side of the pool.

"No." Shawn's voice was calm but firm as his arms folded around Kitty. "She's not ready. Now leave us." There was no way he was sharing her with his brothers, tonight or any other night.

"The contract—"

"Damn the contract," Shawn growled at Tor. He had had just about enough of this. "The woman is mine. I'll do with her what I want. Now get the hell out of here."

Both brothers stood speechless. It looked like Terrance might object. His mouth opened then snapped shut.

Shawn had never defied his brothers, had never placed his own desires before the good of their business. But he was now. Whatever it took he was going to make Kitty his own. His hand rose, water dripping, as he pointed to the door. "Leave us."

Without a word Tor and Terrance left.

Shawn knew there would be hell to pay upon the morrow, but he didn't care. Tonight belonged to him and Kitty.

* * * * *

Okay, now that was amazing. She'd never seen three large men so mad before. Their bodies shook with anger. It had been frightening at first, but when Shawn took over, when he said she was his woman, she had been filled with such sweet sensations she'd forgotten about the incriminating evidence she'd left in her room. Some of the documents flashed in her mind. Accounts closed. A fortune lying yards away. Someone went to great lengths to frame her. It was hard to think. Her mind wandered.

Should she take the money run? No, she'd be running forever. What kind of life was that? One thing she had learned in the last couple of days was life was worth living. And she owed it all to Shawn.

Something had to be done with the stuff, but not now. She couldn't think with Shawn whispering in her ear, stroking her body.

His deep, caressing voice plucked at the taut strings of Ciarra's libido as he dried her with a warm fluffy towel. It felt as if her breasts were growing larger, but it was only desire filling them, tightening her nipples with an ache she felt clear to her toes. She still couldn't believe he called her "his woman"…if only that were true.

Strong hands moved between her thighs briskly, moving up and down, her legs parting of their own accord. He was expertly playing her like a musician transforming wood and strings into a concerto of sweet, sweet melody as he seduced her. Yeah, she knew what he was doing and it was working. He had only to command and she bent to his will.

He stepped away. His gaze was hot on hers as he threw the towel to the floor. "Lie down before the fire."

The breath she held escaped in ragged pants as she exited the bathroom. What was she doing? She tried to remind herself that Shawn was a stranger. Still, she knelt before the flames then slid gracefully onto her side. The *albutra* rug beneath her was downy soft. All thoughts of what she'd discovered earlier—the documents, the money—disappeared from her mind as if it were all a bad dream. Instead her heart fluttered in her chest.

Before her stood the epitome of a perfect man. His erect cock arched, its crown resting just below his bellybutton. He didn't speak, didn't move. In quiet solitude she drank her fill, stroking every masculine inch of him with her gaze. Then he slid down beside her.

Resting his head on the palm of his hand, his other hand danced lightly across her hip.

"So you're ticklish, angel?" His fingertips dipped into the curve of her waist then tapered along each ridge of her rib cage. The most exquisite sensation feathered up her side.

"Yes," her voice was breathless.

"Where is your most ticklish spot?" His hand went astray smoothing the skin beneath her breasts.

"My underarms." Her response escaped upon a gasp.

"Mmmm...really?" His hand drifted back to her waist, sliding along her side, grazing the fullness of her breast, then her arm, then her elbow, until he grasped her wrist. He dragged her limb up and over her head and held her wrist firmly.

Their eyes locked. His lips mere inches from hers. Ciarra wanted to taste him, wanted to feel his tongue tangle with hers, to feel it move in and out of her mouth.

He draped his leg over her pelvic area, pinning her to the floor. His weight trapped her, rendering her partially helpless. And, God, did she love the feeling of being held beneath his control and dominated by muscle and steel. Shawn's cock pressed against her stomach, teasing her in a whole different way.

Now this was erotic. Sweet, sweet torture that chased every thought of her predicament away. Yeah, it was still there in the back of her head, but while he sensually teased and stroked, her body's desires overrode her mind again.

He drew closer, his warm breath licking at her desire. Gently he outlined her mouth with his tongue. She arched, wanting to kiss him, wanting him to kiss her, but he retracted his head. Instead he pressed his lips to her ear.

"You are so beautiful." His soft praise stroked the flame burning in her belly. "So, beautiful… Even here." He swirled light fingertips over the sensitive spot of her armpit. She jerked beneath him, goose bumps prickling across her skin.

"Please," she moaned.

"Please, what? Please torture you?" He nipped her earlobe, touching the area again.

"*Ahhh*," her voice quivered. "I-I don't think I can bear it."

When his tongue slipped into her ear, Ciarra thought she would climax. Her pussy clenched tight, spasms pulsating against the walls of her womb. She was wet and ready. Putty beneath his hands.

He blew lightly on her ear, sending chills up her back. "For me, will you try?"

Short, quick nods were her answer. What was it about him that melted her control?

"Tell me you want me to torture you." His dark sexy voice was a hum in her ear.

If she'd had any resistance before, she didn't now. She would do anything to feel his touch. "Yes, yes, please."

"Call me Master," he purred cupping her breasts and kneading. "Say, 'Yes, Master, I want you to torture me'."

The man was going to kill her. She needed to feel his lips pressed to hers, his cock buried deep inside her. She had never connected with anyone like this before. The warmth of his body pressed to hers felt right, as if she belonged here in his arms.

"Yes, Master, please...I want you to torture me." *Ohmygod*, did she just say that? And what was even more disturbing was she meant it. Yes, she wanted him to do wicked things to her. Then she hesitated. What was happening? She couldn't be falling for this guy, not when her life was such a mess, not when she didn't even know whether she still had a life.

As if he knew she was faltering he crossed her mouth with his. Gently he moved his lips, coaxing her surrender, working the tightness from her body, from her soul. Slowly he moved his tongue in and out, emulating the motion with his hips, working his cock gently over her hip and abdomen.

When he broke the kiss, Ciarra whimpered in protest. "Please, I need—"

"Quiet." His sharp tone startled her. "You will not speak unless I give you permission." The intensity of his gaze startled her. Then he smiled, leaned into her and took control of her mouth, again, this time hard, punishing.

And man, did she like it.

But all too soon it was over and he resumed the position of his mouth near her ear. His hips began to move again. Pre-come from his hardened cock moistened her stomach, assisting his smooth strokes across her sensitive flesh.

"Angel, I know what is right for you." He sucked her earlobe into his warm mouth, his tongue teasing and stroking. "Will you allow me to take control, to see to your needs? Will you surrender completely to me?"

Ciarra felt a tug at her soul as he drew her into his sensuous web. His voice, his touch blinded her senses and mesmerized her body.

She groaned deeply as he cupped her sex, forcing a "yes" from her mouth. Her voice was taut, almost inaudible.

When a finger delved into her heat, Ciarra thought she would explode. She attempted to move her hips but the leg over her pelvis grew heavy, immobilizing her. His grasp tightened on her wrist, driving her arm up higher, stretching the length of her body.

Fuck me, she silently begged. *Fuck me until I can't think about anything but you.*

He crammed another finger deep inside her. A cry broke from her trembling lips. His fingers stilled.

"You will abide by my rules and not question me?" He was baiting her, she knew he was, but she was helpless.

"Yes, anything. Just fuck me, fuck me now," she begged.

He cocked a brow. "Master?"

"Yes, Master."

Light laughter caressed her ear. "You are too impatient. You must learn control. Learn to pleasure your Master. Your pleasure will be a reward for my pride in your behavior."

"What?" What was he saying? What did he expect from her?

Yet before she could rationalize his words, her thoughts, his fingertips swirled around her clit.

"*Ahhh.*" Another cry ripped from her throat.

"Do you willingly agree with my demands?"

A wonderful ache was tightening every muscle in her pussy. A fresh flow of moisture dampened her thighs. "Yes, yes." It was too late to worry whether she had just made a pact with the devil. She was lost in his voice, his touch.

"You have pleased me and have earned your first reward." He pinched her clit, hard.

Ciarra's body convulsed, sharp jerky movements as her climax burst throughout her body like an earthquake splitting the core of the planet. She screamed. Her high-pitched wail was captured by Shawn's mouth. His finger continued to stroke her nub, wringing out every spasm, while his tongue caressed her mouth, skimmed her teeth and danced with her tongue.

Another orgasm struck. Lightning-hot liquid shot up her sex, raced across her abdomen and spread currents across her body. Ciarra's breath caught. She had never experience soul-shattering climaxes like Shawn had given her and this time had drawn out of her with a single finger.

He released her lips. Lust darkened his green eyes, hunger raged, hot and intense, sending a shiver up Ciarra' spine.

Shawn drew an unsteady breath. His heart pummeled against his chest. He wanted Ciarra, needed to feel her heat, her body taking him inside, joining together. And he wanted her forever.

As she whimpered, lost in the afterglow of ecstasy, Shawn straddled her hips and nudged the head of his cock against her swollen folds. So wet and hot. Her scent caressed the air. He inhaled, held it, as he reeled in his control. With his palms he skimmed her abdomen, up past her rib cage until his large hands cupped her full breasts.

Heavy, sated eyes opened, bluer than any sky he had witnessed, lovelier than any erotic flower blooming on this planet. Hell, any planet. Then she graced him with an innocent smile that nearly undid him. He pressed his cock an inch into her sex, watched as she arched, lifting her hips in welcome.

Slowly, Shawn smoothed his hands over her soft flesh, drawing her other arm over her head. Her hands were so small pinned beneath his. The light kiss he stole was unavoidable.

"Shawn," she whispered. Her tongue swept along her lips, tasting him. What he'd give to feel them wrapped around his hard erection, taking him into her mouth, sucking and licking. He grew harder, inched further inside her. Any deeper and he would take her, fuck her right here, right now. But he wanted her to beg for his cock, beg for him to fuck her.

It took the strength of God and all his disciples to withdraw from the warmth cradling the head of his cock. She whimpered and he assuaged her by pressing his member tight against her slit. He pumped his hips and slid against her clit until her long lashes floated upon her cheekbones.

When she started to open her eyes he said, "No, keep your eyes closed." Without hesitation she yielded. Without words she surrendered.

Now to test her.

He stood, scooping her into his arms. As his bare feet padded across the floor, he wondered how he had fallen so quickly for this woman. Gently he laid her upon the bed, her eyes still closed tightly.

"Angel, I want you grasp the bed railings above your head and keep your eyes closed. No matter what I do to you I don't want you to let go. Do you understand me?"

"Yes," she whispered gazing up through half-shuttered eyes.

"Yes?" He dropped his tone.

She licked her full lips. Breasts rising with each accentuated breath. "Yes, Master."

"Good. Now I'm going to explain what I'm going to do to you." He delighted in the shiver that passed through her body. Consciously or unconsciously her hips rose. Her desire for him to join with her was obvious.

"I'm going to tickle you." Her tongue darted across her bottom lip. Her face tensed. "Believe me you will enjoy every agonizing minute."

He barely touched her underarm and she flinched, giggling as her fingers released the head rail.

"Don't bring your arms down." His voice lowered, growled his warning. Immediately she grasped the iron. "Don't forget or you will force me to punish you."

When Shawn stroked her underarm this time her knuckles paled, holding tight to the bed. Her teeth clinked together as she gathered her resolve not to move.

"Prepare yourself for my touch. *Tickle,*" he whispered in her ear, allowing his breath to tease her skin.

She tensed at the simple suggestion of being touched. He eased his cock against her slit, his bodyweight pinning her to the bed. With featherlight fingertips he softly grazed the flesh of one armpit.

She strained beneath him. Her body lurched, but he forced her back down. "Nice," he groaned, as her skin prickled and her nipples pebbled harder. "You're so very soft and sensitive. So reactive... *Tickle.*" His voice was light and airy.

He repeated his touch and reveled as she clenched her eyelids, fought to accept his delightful torture without a sound.

"*Tickle,*" he breathed, as he brushed the tips of his fingers across her flesh. Then gave his attention to her other underarm, alternating and drawing his nails down the side of her body to wrench the moans she struggled to hold back. When soft sounds seeped from her delicious lips, he had to taste her.

She was putty beneath his mouth. Without coaxing she opened and took him deep. The woman tasted of desire and lust. Hot, moist need called to him, begged him for more. He kissed a path to her ear.

"*Tickle.*" She flinched at the word without him even touching her.

A desperate gasp left her as he lightly stroked, then he pulled away.

"Master, please." A hint of urgency filled her breathless tone.

"Please what, angel?" He barely touched her and a shiver shook her from head to toe.

"I need —" Her voice cracked.

"More torture? Remember it is not about your pleasure, but mine. More torture?" he repeated firmly.

She swallowed hard. "Yes, Master, more torture."

With wisps of her own hair he teased her underarm. She arched against him, fighting the torrent of sensations that flooded her body. Her head thrashed side to side, her soft, red hair feathering across the pillow.

"Stop, Master," she cried, moisture seeping from her closed eyes. "I can't take any more."

But he knew she could — would. She had only entered the dimension of pleasure, the space of time where the word *tickle* became heavy with erotic power. Where not only sensation but sound lit the fuse to her arousal.

"And remember," he kissed her neck, "you must not come without my consent."

"What?" Her breathing was labored. Her breasts heavy with need, rose and fell sharply. Just the mere touch of his hand, her own hair, sent her writhing beneath him.

Shawn moved so that he lay beside her. He cupped her sex. She threw her head back, grinding it into the pillow. Slipping a finger inside her warm, wet channel, he leaned forward and began to lick a path from her navel, across her taut stomach, over the delicate mound of one breast. He nipped lightly at her nipple, eliciting a sharp cry from her trembling lips.

Shawn felt the walls of her pussy flex against his finger. She was close, so close.

When he whispered, "*Tickle*," against her moist skin she groaned aloud. She raised her hips, searching, seeking. He trapped her again with a leg across her pelvis.

Shawn was pleased, she never released the bed rail and continued to keep her eyes closed. Kitty was an adept student in the art of bondage and domination. She would make an exquisite lover and wife.

Yes, that's exactly what Shawn wanted. He wanted Kitty Carmichael as his wife. A quiet confidence filled him.

"Kitty, I have a surprise." His voice had an amazing effect on her. She trembled, squirmed, and then quietly whimpered. "Only one..." he kissed her nipple, "more..." he nipped the bud, "hour of *tickling*." His tongue stroked the sensitive skin of her underarm.

She shrieked. Her passionate cry nearly threw him over the edge of ecstasy. Bowed beneath him, her climax ripped through her. Shawn had never felt so much power. Yes, he had dominated many women, but this one was different. Her responsiveness made him feel as if he was king, the Master of her body and soon to be Master of her soul.

As the last of her orgasm drew to the end, she gazed into intense eyes. Oh shit. She came without his permission. When his lips parted she tensed, ready to hear what her punishment would be. Instead he asked, "Kitty, will you wear my collar?"

Chapter Thirteen

❧

Ciarra opened her eyes and released the bed frame. *Uh, did Shawn just ask me to wear his collar?* She had heard the phrase, "Will you wear my ring?" but never collar. Arms aching as they slid beside her, one hand came to rest on his chest. Beneath her palm she felt his heart thud, hard. The man was serious.

The pads of his fingers slid up her arm, barely skimming her flesh, yet it was so arousing, she felt her nerve endings tingle and burst into flames along the path he stroked.

"The giving of power to another is magical." His voice was sultry, enticing. "The collar is an emblem of submission, ownership and control." She couldn't miss the gravity in what he said as his eyes darkened. "Permitting someone to collar you can be a deeply significant act."

Sadness crept into her heart. Even if there was chance for the two of them, her father was a murderer. Her life was a mess, and after Shawn discovered the truth he'd push her aside like a pair of worn-out shoes.

"Kitty."

"Please don't call me that." The indiscretion slipped out before she could halt it. She wanted to hear her name on this man's lips, not some other woman's as they made love.

The crease in his forehead deepened, confusion surfaced. "What?"

She shrugged and said, "Nothing. Never mind," as she looked away.

"Look at me." She didn't miss the authority in his voice. "Do you understand what I'm asking?" A sober expression met her.

She swallowed, hard. "You want to make me your pet, your plaything."

Shawn flinched as if she'd slapped him. "No," he said firmly, before his deep voice softened. "I wanted to give you a glimpse of freedom, exhilaration. Bondage and submission is rewarding because there is an excitement, an intensity that cannot be achieved with vanilla sex. The dark side of your dream world is where you tuck your fantasies for no one to see." He brushed his knuckles along her jawline. "I want you to share your dreams with me, and mine with you. I want you to be my—"

Shawn stopped in mid-sentence. A look of uncertainty crept across his face.

His tenderness was killing Ciarra. She couldn't take much more.

"Let me make this easier for both of us." Ciarra gathered her resolve in one breath, when all she wanted to say was, *yes, I'll wear your ring—your collar—whatever you want.* Yet there could be nothing between them. "I'm on vacation and will be leaving, sooner if a transport comes available." Emotion knocked on the back of her eyelids. She squeezed them shut and counted to five. When she opened them she saw the disappointment in Shawn's and it broke her heart. "While I'm here I'll wear your collar, be your slave, but you'll have to let me go in the end."

A nerve twitched in his throat. He clenched his jaw. Suddenly his worried expression disappeared, replaced with a smirk that made Ciarra a little uneasy. He pushed from the bed, stood, and then padded across the room to a dresser. The drawer scraped wood against wood as he opened it and withdrew a blue velvet box. When he returned to her side, he raised the lid and withdrew a beautiful white leather collar etched with sapphires, a matching leash attached. He gazed admiringly at the set before he sat the box down on the bed stand. With agile fingers he began to disconnect the collar from the leash, which he laid on the bed stand before crawling upon the bed.

Ciarra's heart lurched forward, bouncing off her rib cage as the smooth leather slid around her neck. A click of finality sounded as it locked into place. Gently Shawn moved his fingers between her skin and the collar. It was loose, but clearly not large enough to slip over her head.

Immediately a sense of belonging, of being divested of all freedom, flooded her body. It was frightening, but at the same time exciting. She wanted to belong to this man. Wanted to share in his dreams—his fantasies. Ciarra couldn't think, her heart was racing so fast. Slowly she glanced up at Shawn and saw him smile, a semblance of pride brightening his eyes. Before she knew what was happening he jerked her into his arms and squeezed. Then he kissed her lightly on the top of her head. It was tender and sweet, but oddly strange as if she had agreed to something beyond being his slave and plaything for the remaining time she was on Ecstasy Island.

Shawn gripped her hips, tugging, so that her length lay flat upon the bed. He followed, spooning himself against her side, his head resting on his palm as he gazed down upon her. With gentle strokes he played with the collar and caressed her skin around it.

"Tell me about yourself. Who is Kitty Carmichael?"

Ciarra tensed then relaxed. She realized it didn't matter what she said, even the truth would work here. "I don't know who she is." Hell, she didn't even know who Ciarra Storm was anymore.

"Then tell me about your family?"

"I don't have any family. Tell me about yours." She forced a smile, attempting to change the subject.

He laughed. "You really want to know about Tor and Terrance?"

She skewed her mouth and shook her head. "Are your mother and father still alive?"

Shawn's hand paused on the collar, her neck. He leaned closer and kissed her forehead. "No. Mom and Dad have been gone for some time. But I do have a sister."

"Really?"

He chuckled again and he sounded so young. "Really. Actually Taryn and Terrance are twins."

Ciarra's eyes widened. "Holy shit." She slapped her hand over her mouth. "Sorry," she said through parted fingers, before removing her palm. "I just can't imagine a female Terrance."

This time Shawn burst into a full body roar. The cheerful sound warmed Ciarra as she placed a hand on his rippling chest. His mirth was contagious and she couldn't help joining him. For a while they simply shared in laughter and the developing closeness.

"You pretty much nailed Taryn, but she's much, much prettier than Terrance." Shawn cupped Ciarra's breast then rolled her nipple between his fingers. Her other nipple grew taut, longing for his touch.

Desire began its sweet ascent, higher and higher, so that her next sentence came out breathy. "Does she live on Zygoman?"

"No." He leaned forward and took her taut nub between his lips. Gently he suckled, his mouth making a popping sound as he released her. Then he snuggled his face between her breasts. The warmth of his breath teased her sensitive skin. "Taryn is a defense lawyer. She really doesn't call anywhere home. She travels from one planet to the next, wherever she's needed."

"She's a lawy—"

Shawn placed his palm over her mouth. "No more talking. I need to be inside you."

Eyes dark with desire burned into her. His fingers danced along her leg as he parted her thighs then moved between them. With a single thrust he entered her, filling her with such exquisite fullness, air left her lungs in a rush. His slow, sensual undulations heated her blood and made her inner muscles clench tight as he brought their bodies together in a steady rhythm.

"You're so hot and wet," he murmured, moving in and out of her body. "So, fucking wet." He released a groan along with his weight as he pressed his chest to hers. She sank deeper into the mattress and his earthy scent surrounded her like a veil. She inhaled, savoring the moment. Head-to-head, she could hear his breathing quicken as fire licked up her core.

Ciarra scored her fingernails across his back. He arched, pushing deeper inside her, harder, faster. Her palms smoothed down his heated flesh and then grasped his ass. His firm muscles clenched and unclenched as his body steadily rocked. Then he struck the special spot inside her that bowed her back, squeezed a ragged cry from parted lips and shattered her world into a million pieces. White-hot liquid heat poured through her like steam hissing from an open valve.

"Mine," Shawn cried aloud as his orgasm exploded. He pounded his hips against hers one final time, before his body went tense and he filled her with his hot seed. Several tremors assaulted him, flowing through her as if they were one instead of two separate beings. Together they transcended time. His chest rose and fell on a heavy sigh. He rolled to his side, taking her with him.

Without a word he began to stroke her collar again, then before she knew it he fell softly to sleep.

Ciarra listened to the light rattle of Shawn's breathing, watched the rise and fall of his masculine chest. She placed her hand over his heart, felt the beat and warmth against her palm.

What am I going to do? The image of her clothing hanging in her bungalow closet, the damaging documentation and the knife still tucked in that damn purse came to mind. Emotion stuck in her throat, a knot that wouldn't go down or up. Somebody had broken into her apartment — rifled through her personal belongings and exchanged Kitty Carmichael's things with hers. Had they also tampered with Brody? Her sedan was supposed to be safe, fail-proof. And what about Kitty Carmichael?

Someone was setting her up to take the fall for Stan's murder and embezzlement. But who? And why?

A deep masculine sigh brought her attention back to the man beside her. She snuggled closer, inhaling his fresh scent of earth and warm musk. Even in sleep he reacted, sliding an arm around her and hugging her nearer. She bit down on her bottom lip, fighting the emotions swimming to the surface.

What she feared had become a reality. She had fallen for Shawn. It might not be love, but it was enough that she knew when their time came to end this farce it would hurt.

Silent tears fell as she too drifted off into slumber.

* * * * *

Just before dawn crested over the horizon Shawn stirred. The smell of sunflowers and the soft female body touching brought him fully awake. He wasn't alone. Curled against his chest, Kitty had one palm cradling his cheek, the other flung over his waist. The flames in the hearth waned, but were still alive enough for firelight to flicker across her soft features. While she slept, the dip of her nose intrigued him, as did her full lips that were parted as if awaiting his kiss, and the flutter of her auburn eyelashes. He inhaled, breathing in her scent, then pressed his lips to her temple because he had to. Contentment like he had never known penetrated the recesses of his mind.

Damn. How did he get so lucky?

A numb, tingling sensation in his arm edged into his reverie. He battled with easing the pain and possibly waking her, or sticking it out until she awoke. In the end he had to move. When he rose far enough to pull his arm forward, her hand cradling his cheek softly slid around his neck.

Then both arms closed around him like a vise. A strangled cry pushed past her lips. Her body trembled. She began to mumble. The inaudible words made no sense, but her soft whimpers where those of distress.

A bad dream?

Folding himself around her, he held her close. "Shhh, angel, it's just a bad dream." She didn't wake, but became quiet, seemingly taking comfort in his voice. Something was bothering her, so much so that it had seeped into her dreams. Shawn only hoped she would confide in him soon. Trust between two people was everything, something he expected in their relationship.

"Time," he whispered and a holographic laser beam flashed four o'clock against the wall. Too early to rise, but he needed to relieve himself. Still he didn't want to wake her, so he waited.

"Time," he whispered sometime later. The need to use the bathroom was growing into an ache. The virtual image of 4:50 lit up the wall in green neon. He couldn't wait any longer. Carefully, he eased out of her arms, off the bed, and then rose. Reaching for the covers, he tucked them snugly around her, before padding across the marble floor to the bathroom. The door squeaked as he drew it shut.

When he finished relieving himself, he moved away from the urinal and activated the faucet with a swipe his hands. He rubbed them briskly beneath the stream of water. He splashed his face, the coolness against his skin invigorating. The towel followed and when Shawn looked into the mirror he was smiling. He liked having Kitty in his bed. Waking up with her in his arms felt right. Having her wear his collar felt right.

A wave of uneasiness shook him. What would Tor and Terrance say? He pushed the anxiety aside as quickly at it surfaced. It didn't matter. No matter what either said or thought, Kitty was his. She didn't know it yet, but there was no way he would let her go.

As he entered the bedroom, he noticed Kitty stood before the picture window. Her naked silhouette was a striking image against the colors of yellows, oranges and blues that formed as the rays from the solar disk—an artificial sun and lighting source for Zygoman—began to radiate over the ebony horizon, introducing its approach. He moved toward Kitty, startling her when his hand touched her shoulder. She twisted around. He caught her in his arms.

"This is my favorite time of the day," he said. A chaste kiss followed. "Open window one hundred percent." Immediately a gush of morning air greeted them as the glass rose. The sweet scent of the island, tropical flowers, rich fertile soil and the stirrings of life smelled clean and innocent.

He turned her in his embrace and folded his arms around her waist as he pulled her back to his chest. His cock hardened with the feel of her silky skin.

"It's like a fresh start over and over again," Shawn whispered. "No matter what happened the day before, you always have the dawn to begin anew." Kitty released a heavy sigh as if she wanted to believe what he was saying was so.

Slowly night ebbed and the day completed its journey, lighting the sky. Without a word, she turned in his embrace, lifted her chin and pressed her mouth to his. Her kiss was tender, surreal. She snuggled closer.

For a moment Shawn held her in their blissful state. His fingers played with her silky hair, sliding through the long red tresses. Soft hands caressed his back, her warm breath fanning over his skin.

"What would you like to do today?" Shawn asked.

She pushed away from his chest. Her brows furrowed. "What?"

He pressed his lips to her forehead. "What would you like to do today? Or would you rather stay here?" He jerked his head toward the wall where the bed awaited them.

The hard lines in her face softened. She laughed a delightful sound that was music to his ears. For the first time since Kitty had arrived on Zygoman she appeared happy, almost peaceful. Or maybe it was the backdrop of a new day. No matter the reason, he wanted to make each day of her life just like this one. If only she would let him.

"Why don't I show you around the island?"

Her eyes widened. "Really? I mean, what about this Master/slave thing we have going on? No, wait." A troubled expression hardened her soft features. "I-I need to do something first."

He held her at arms' length and wished he could vanquish whatever made every fiber in her body tense. Instead he chose to ignore it. She would reveal all in time. In the meantime he would keep her occupied, busy with the art of bondage and lots and lots of sex.

"It's time to explore your sexual nature, Kitty." She cocked a brow and for a moment it appeared whatever caused her stress was forgotten. "Break down the resistance that has burdened you far too long." She shifted her feet. "Zygoman is a place where you can experience those fantasies, chasing them into the playground of your mind." He stroked a path down her chest, cupping a breast before drawing her nipple between his fingers. "What we do here is a mutual exchange of pleasure, of trust, of love." He pinched and pulled, drawing a cry from her lips. Her eyes darkened with the beginning signs of arousal. "There is pleasure for both of us when one is allowed the freedom to play and other permits his or her body to be the toy." He bent so that they were eye to eye. "Can I play with you?"

The laughter that spilled from her lips and the softness in her eyes was a heady win. But when she said, "Yes," his body reacted with a rush so intense that it took his breath away. He could almost imagine her stepping beyond the mental chains she had arrived with and into the dawning of a new revelation.

Chapter Fourteen

ॐ

To say Ciarra was not excited about the coming adventure would have been a lie. Yet, she had some hard decisions to make. What lay in her bungalow, the damaging evidence, could put her away for eternity. A man was dead. Her conscience struggled, knowing he deserved justice, but what would happen to her? The choices were few. Destroy the evidence and let a killer run free or turn herself in and hope that the law believed in her innocence. And if they didn't...

What about Shawn?

She watched him move around the room as she lounged on the bed. He brought out strong emotions in her that no one ever had. Passion. In the past, sex was recreational, something she used to fill an empty void in her life. She'd been searching for that all-elusive love, the kind she read about, had seen in a pair of lover's eyes, but never been quite close enough to grasp.

She was curious about this dark side Shawn spoke about. He made it sound so mysterious—so appealing. She wanted to discover her limits and she wanted to experience them with him.

Her current dilemma had not been forgotten, neither had the need to find a way to get back to Earth. Yet while she was here she would damn well enjoy what this man had to offer. Who knew what the future held—or if she would even have a future after the dust settled on all this mess.

Shawn moved away from her, heading toward one of many doors leading out of his bedroom, and disappeared behind it. In mere minutes, he returned dressed in boots, tight black leather pants and a matching vest. Ciarra's pulse raced.

The man had the bad-boy look down pat. His wild blond hair, malachite eyes and bulging muscles only added to the sinful ambience.

Okay, she had a lot to do today, but surely a couple more hours would not make a difference. She moved off the bed and stood before him.

In one hand Shawn carried a white leather ensemble—a short skirt, a halter top and delicate silver chains. In his other hand a pair of silver sandals dangled from his fingers.

Without a word he began to dress her. First the halter top slid over her neck, the smooth, cool leather caressing her breasts, pebbling her nipples tight as he hooked the back. Talk about raising the blood level. Ciarra had never been dressed by a man. Undressed, yes—but dressed, no. And it was a delicious feeling as his strong hands moved over her body.

The skirt hung low, really low on her hips. He laced the delicate chains around her waist, three of different lengths so they layered across her abdomen. Then he knelt, brought her foot to rest on his thigh and slipped one sandal on her foot. His eyes darted to the apex of her thighs, bared and spread wide. He licked his lips, sending a shiver up her spine. He slipped her foot off his thigh and lifted her other one, slipping on the final sandal.

All the time his eyes grew darker, hotter. His breathing had risen. The silence was heavy, adding to the moment. Then he stood and reached for her.

She went willingly into his arms.

"Damn, you're beautiful." He nuzzled her neck, his hand stroking the skin beneath the collar she wore.

A woman could never get tired of hearing a man refer to her as beautiful, but Shawn actually made Ciarra *feel* beautiful. Of all the gorgeous women he could have on this planet he had chosen her and it wasn't out of duty. No. He had broken a contract and defied his brothers. And there was that other identifier, the tender way he held her, made love to her. Unless he was a helluva actor, the man was more than attracted to her.

Feelings of loss, of disappointment that this would end and Shawn's feelings could be hurt overwhelmed her. She felt her circle of control closing in on her. This wasn't going to be an easy breakup for him or for her.

"Tonight is a masquerade ball." His voice deepened as he nibbled on her earlobe. "Tatiana will show you the costumes that are available. It will be your choice—surprise me."

His hands floated down to the halter-top strap at her back and the material snapped, coming undone. She startled and then softly moaned as he pressed his lips to the hollow of her neck. "Are we going out or have you changed your mind?" she murmured.

"Out," he said slipping a finger down the back of her skirt into the cleft of her ass. His soft, but firm lips slid down her chest between her breasts. He inhaled her scent.

"Out," she repeated on a sigh that forced her head to loll backwards.

He pulled away and stood staring at her for a moment, before he began to redo the clasp of her top. "Out." Then he threaded his fingers through his blond hair. "But I can't promise what will happen. You're too delicious to avoid. I can't seem to keep my hands off you."

She laughed, not remembering when she had felt so wonderful, but at the same time so lost and scared.

Should she confide in Shawn? Lord knew she needed someone to talk to. His palm brushed up and down her bare arm. The warmth in his eyes as he leaned forward and kissed her softly on the lips was all she needed to see to know she didn't want those eyes looking at her with suspicion and doubt.

He grasped her hand and pulled her forward. "There's something I want to show you." Almost like a child, he bounded down the stairs with her in tow. The soles of her sandals slapped the marble floor as they moved through the large hall, while his booted footsteps echoed. Reaching the front door, he pushed it wide and they exited.

The solar disk was high in the sky. Heat rays penetrated her skin, causing her flesh to tingle, making her feel alive. She breathed in the fresh air, smelled the sweet flowers sprinkled all around and listened briefly to the sounds of free-flowing water. Ecstasy Island was truly a paradise. A place she could live forever.

Ciarra cut her gaze to Shawn. His nose tilted to the sky as if he too was taking in the fragrance of the day. A peaceful, almost reverent expression softened his features giving him a boyish quality. Yet he was all man. There was no doubt in her mind as she reached and stroked the leather-clad bulge between his thighs.

What had come over her she didn't know, but it was exciting to feel his cock harden beneath her touch. The growl that surfaced from his throat before he caught her in his arms and kissed her passionately was worth her forwardness.

When their lips parted, he again took her hand and started off toward a dense forest. How far they traveled Ciarra had no idea, but when Shawn halted, the sight took her breath away. Slowly her gaze followed the waterfall that sprang out from a verdant-covered mountain. The gentle splash as it spilled into a small pond created a prism of colors that gave it a mystical halo effect. A flutter of wings made her turn her head. A rainbow of parrots squawked and chattered, sitting in the branches of the trees. She even saw a monkey swinging through the limbs on a vine.

"It's called Temptation Springs." The reverent sound in his voice made her realize he had brought her to a special place — his special place. The knowledge squeezed her heart. This man was a mystery. He had so many layers to his character that Ciarra wondered if a lifetime would be enough to discover all his intricacies.

"Why Temptation Springs?" she asked.

A roguish grin raised the corner of his mouth. "Because it makes you want to tear your clothes off and fuck."

She laughed then became quiet as she reached around and unfastened her halter top. Slowly she let it drop on the grassy bank at her feet. With only a tug on her skirt, the *Glootium*, a substance discovered in the mid twenty-first century that replaced buttons and zippers, released and the material slithered down her legs. As she stepped out of the skirt, his hand reached for his vest.

She shook her head, stopping him. "Let me." She kicked off her sandals, wearing nothing but the three delicate silver chains layered across her abdomen and the white leather collar dotted with sapphires.

His broad chest rose, stilled, as he trapped air in his lungs. When she touched his arm, felt the firm muscle beneath tight skin, his breath released in one gush. She looked up at him through feathery lashes, ran a single finger along the edges of his vest before taking her time to pull the material apart. When she did she placed both palms on his chest, savoring the heat of his skin as she brushed the vest back and down his arms.

He reached for her and again she shook her head. A vein ticked in his neck. His jaws grew taut.

With a single finger she drew a path down his chest, across his abdomen, to his waistband. A lift and a tug and he spilled out into her hands, hard, thick and ready. Her tongue made a swipe between her dry lips. She wanted him with a passion. Her nipples ached, sending the radiating sting through her heavy breasts. Desire dampened her thighs, and already her clit throbbed with anticipation.

Still she dragged out the moment.

Remembering how he had teased her body with his expectant touch urged her to run her hand a breath away from his engorged erection. His green eyes flared then a visible tremor assaulted him as she released her warm breath upon him.

Again he reached for her. Again she shook her head.

Leaning close so their bodies almost touched, she placed her palms on his stomach moving them to slip beyond the leather to cup his firm ass. Tight muscle bunched beneath her hands as she tugged his pants down his legs. Black leather boots kept them from coming off completely.

"Sit," she said, offering him a hand for assistance. The sun heated the silver chains at her waist while beads of perspiration formed beneath the collar around her neck. She knelt as he obeyed her. One boot came off easily. She had a little difficulty with the other boot, until he used the ball of his foot to force it off. Then she slid his pants off and let them slip through her fingers to the ground.

His arms extended toward her. "Come here."

This time she tested the waters, wondering whether they still played the Master/slave game. "No," she whispered.

He cocked a brow, but the twinkle in his eye gave him away. He was aroused by her efforts at seduction. She had never really tried to seduce a man, but with Shawn there appeared to be a lot of firsts.

Curiously, he watched her. His arms came up and he laced his fingers behind his head. The quirky lift on one side of his mouth seemed to say, "What are you going to do next?"

With little effort she bent his knees, then dragged them apart, spreading him wide. Over his impressive chest he looked at her, eyes shaded with desire. Her pulse jumped in her throat. Damn he was good-looking—good enough to eat.

On all fours, wearing nothing but his collar and the jewelry he had gifted her with, she crawled between his thighs. She circled his ankles with her palms then smoothed them over his calves and along the sensitive spot behind his knees. She continued over the inside of his thighs, stopping just before she reached his member, which jerked in anticipation. Her eyes met his playful ones. He grinned then waved again at her with his erection.

An uncontrollable giggle bubbled up from her throat. Ciarra couldn't remember a time she had laughed during foreplay or sex. There was something magical, something that seemed to bond them closer together.

No. That was just her overactive mind again wanting to latch onto anything that felt safe. Still, she wasn't about to let her negativity ruin what she had started.

She folded her fingers gently around his cock and stroked. He hissed, slowly. His eyelashes brushed his cheeks before his gaze returned to hers. Opening her palm and using her other hand she rolled his member back and forth…back and forth.

"Mmmm…nice." Shawn moved his legs further apart, his hips rising slightly to slide between her palms.

There was so much power in making his body react to her touch. It raced through her veins, heating her blood. The pressure in her breasts rushed to her nipples, white-hot lightning pulling and straining for release. Ciarra's skin shrank all over her body, increasing the tight and tingling sensation as she slipped her mouth over his cock.

Every muscle is his body tensed beneath her as he groaned and arched his chest off the ground. She fondled his sac, pushing on the sensitive spot directly beneath it.

"You're killing me, woman." The throaty sound he made came from deep inside him and flowed over her like silk.

Her tongue followed the length of him, swirled around the crown and then dipped into the small slit, tasting the salty masculine flavor that was all his.

As she fucked him with her mouth, his hips began a gentle rhythm meeting each stroke. His fingers tangled in her hair, slight pressure forcing her to take him further, deeper. Their cadence increased, picking up speed as their breathing became shallow, ragged.

"I'm going to lose it, angel, if you don't crawl up here and fuck me." His grip on her hair tightened, pulling her away so he slipped from her mouth. As she crawled atop him she licked her lips. *"Damn,"* he said as she straddled him and he speared her with his cock.

Thick and hard, he filled her completely. She remained still, enjoying the feeling of taking him into her body, sharing with him the only thing she had to offer. Just looking at him, the intensity of his desire, made her pulse stutter. If this was heaven then she never wanted to leave.

The feel of his warm hands on her hips, the scent of his earthy musk and glow in his eyes made her rock gently against him. Something about the moment was so precious, so tender she wanted this to last forever and not be lost in the heated fury of sex. She needed to feel more, believe there was more, something tangible she could hold on to.

When he cupped her breast she arched into him. He kneaded softly then began drawing circles around her globes, the circles growing smaller as he reached her nipples. They stung, like electrical currents forced through her chest and exploding outward.

Her clit throbbed against his member as he pumped in and out. The muscles inside her clenched around him almost as if they were grasping him, afraid he would disappear. Desire became a fire inside her burning brighter and brighter.

Their gentle rhythm continued, enhancing every movement—every sensation. Her skin was so sensitive she could feel his pulse in his fingertips as they moved across her body like a flame, hot and needy.

The pressure between her thighs climbed higher, stronger. She tried deep breathing to prolong the inevitable, but her climax washed over her like a wave, taking her breath away. Shawn groaned low and deep, following her to the summit. Together their bodies vibrated in a series of tender and sweet aftershocks.

Softly she pressed her chest to his. His arms flowed around her like a blanket, holding her close. Listening to the beat of his heart, she released a sigh that said it all.

Ciarra felt contentment for the first time in her life.

Gently Shawn rolled Kitty beneath him. He stared into her blue depths, wondered what her dreamy expression meant. He bent forward and pressed his lips to hers. She was soft, pliable, as he moved his mouth over hers.

What followed were long—slow—kisses. Each more tender than the previous. Sweeter than any dessert he could imagine.

There was a pause in time, an almost bewitching period that held him spellbound. He was falling too hard—too soon.

Abruptly Shawn did a push-up with his arms, raising himself above her. He moved aside and got to his knees, and then stood and offered Kitty his hand. "I want to show you something."

She slipped her palm in his and he helped her to rise. Hand in hand, through white glistening sand, they walked to the edge of the water. There was a crispness to the blue that made the pool inviting as he stepped in. It was cool and refreshing against his heated skin.

Kitty's eyes widened at the first touch of the water upon her flesh. She hesitated briefly, a slight resistance against his grasp. Rosy nipples puckered and a delightful rash of goose bumps spread across her flesh. She took another step.

"Do you swim?" he asked pulling her further into the water.

She nodded, finally becoming accustomed to the temperature.

They stood chest deep before the spray of water falling from the rocks. A lone dove spotted the blue sky and it released a cry. The sound was forlorn as if the bird was searching for something — perhaps its mate.

"I'm glad you swim, because we're going under." He plunged beneath the water taking her with him.

When they surfaced on the other side of the waterfall, she sputtered and struggled to catch her breath on a gasp. A formidable curtain of water separated them from the pool. The crystal window distorted the beauty that lay beyond. Behind them it was pitch-black.

And then he turned her toward the blackness. She blinked as water trickled down her face. *Damn.* He hadn't allowed her to take a breath before diving.

"You okay?" he asked, pausing for her response before searching for the rock shelf he knew lay before them.

"Yes." Her response was a little strangled. Silhouetted by the daylight behind her, she twisted the excess water from her hair and tossed the mass behind her. Again he took her hand.

"Step." As his foot landed on the stone platform, flames came to life in the sconces lining the walls. Another step and then another and he rose out of the water to lead the way into the blackness ahead.

Kitty startled as dark suddenly became light. She twisted around, her wide gaze scanning the room as her eyes adjusted, her pupils dilating.

"Sensing devices — heat activated," he explained guiding her further into the grotto.

On the moss-covered floor lay a makeshift bed of furs. White angora and zebra-striped furs complemented the two robes — one black, one white — thrown across it. Rose petals were sprinkled about, the light fragrance perfuming the air. A stone-top table and two satin pillows were off to the left. Upon the table sat a fresh basket of fruit — grapes, plums, strawberries and a variety of other sweets — arranged next to a bottle of wine with two goblets.

Kitty's surprised expression sank into a frown.

"What?" He tried to draw her to him, but she stepped away.

"Do you bring all your women here?" Sarcasm and a little hurt cut through her words.

"Like all the features of Ecstasy Island, Temptation Springs is refreshed frequently throughout the day. Nothing but the finest for our guests is provided." He reached for her again, catching her hand and dragging her to him. "But this is my sanctuary." Each of his brothers had their own little getaway. Temptation Springs was his. "I come here to get away from the chaos… I come here alone."

Her smile was full of relief as she went on tiptoes and kissed the tip of his nose. He pulled her to his length and captured her mouth. She was warm and inviting. Still he broke the kiss. They had a ways to go as he grabbed her hand and strolled deeper into the cave.

The rock floor beneath them was uneven, but not so much as to make it uncomfortable or difficult to walk on barefooted. The walls had patches of velvety dark green lichen growing out of crevices. Several long strands hung from the ceiling. A light tinkle of water flowing from the pool further into the cave could barely be heard over the rushing waterfall outside.

"It's beautiful," Kitty whispered. They still held hands and as she turned she moved into his embrace. Firelight danced in her blue eyes. Her breath was warm against his shoulder.

As they continued to walk, the sconces lit their way, but dimmed to leave a little mystery to what lay ahead. The stone walls maintained their ruggedness, but they were shining, polished to where their reflections were clearly visible.

The last of the sconces lit, causing Kitty to stumble. "Shawn?" She spoke his name with an air of unease. He watched an array of emotions creep across her face—surprise, concern, perhaps even a little fear.

Kitty pulled her hand out of his and scanned the walls where whips, chains, and a variety of other playthings hung. A dungeon had a way of bringing out an individual's stronger feelings. It was as if it stripped away the top layer of skin and left one's soul revealed.

It was time to set Kitty's soul free, but the look on her face said she expected something totally different.

"I-I thought you said you come here alone," she stuttered.

"I do, but I'd hoped to find someone, some day, to share my life with, to make this our sacred playroom of love."

"And you brought me here?" She pressed her palm to her mouth as if she thought it would hold back the emotions that showed in her eyes.

"Yes." He answered before reaching for her.

Chapter Fifteen

✑

Ciarra's pulse jumped in her throat as Shawn slipped his fingers between her skin and the collar around her neck and pulled her to him. The dark look in his eyes made her tremble, a shiver of uncertainty slithered up her spine. She stubbed her toe on the rocky surface but the sudden sting was quickly forgotten as he drew her against him.

This just couldn't be happening. Not now with her life in shambles.

She was falling for this man. Her heartbeat pummeled her chest. What would he say when he discovered the mess that awaited her on Earth? The image of Stan Mayhem lying dead on the bed, covered in blood, made her tense. The room full of evidence that needed to be destroyed or revealed flashed before her eyes.

"You're frightened." It wasn't as much a question as an observation as his fingers around the collar brought her a breath away from his lips.

She wanted to say *no*, but the darkness in his green eyes gave her pause. More than anything she wanted to forget for the moment her dilemma and accept whatever he had to offer.

"Kitty, you came to Ecstasy Island for a glimpse of freedom, of exhilaration through what we offer here. Let me help you to deepen your emotions and set your passions soaring. You'll never experience anything so blissful than spiritual exploration and fulfillment through erotic surrender."

She wanted to believe him—needed to.

He held the truth in his eyes—a level of intensity coupled with warmth that should have felt conflicting, but didn't. While she stared into the depths of his gaze it was difficult to believe he would hurt her. Discomfort yes, but arousal and heat that most definitely would lead to a spectacular ending.

"Will you let me play with you?" he whispered in her ear, sending shivers up her back.

The word "yes" was out before she knew what was happening.

In the next minute the cave came alive. Vines fell from above, swaying and swinging. The floor began to move as they emerged from breaks, crevices in the stone. She couldn't hold back the high-pitched squeal that pushed from her lips as the long, thin stems climbed across her feet, then twisted around her ankles. At the same time her wrists were enclosed by greenery.

"Shawn," she cried.

"Heat sensored." He gave her a reassuring smile. "Relax."

Heart pounding like drums against her chest, she had to will herself to stand still as the vines wound around her limbs like snakes crawling across her skin. When the ones around her wrists and arms reached her chest they split. One set of tendrils encircled her breasts and tightened. Her globes began to swell and turn pinkish-red.

"You are so beautiful." His eyes darkened while he watched the usually small veins in her breasts become fuller with restrained blood. When he stroked them she gasped. They were so tender, so sensitive to his touch.

The other set of tendrils wrapped around her throat, placing pressure on her collar. For a moment she panicked, felt her eyes widen as she struggled to breathe, jerking against her bindings.

"Do you trust me?" Shawn's voice dropped into a deep caress that halted her fight.

She swallowed, forced herself to think. Did she? For some reason she trusted him more than she'd ever trusted another person.

"Yes," she finally said. "I do."

"Then relax, angel," he encouraged.

Ciarra tried, she really did. But she was so preoccupied with the breast and throat bondage she hadn't noticed what was going on below her waist until a vine slipped between her legs. The coolness gliding across her pussy was a surprise, but an interesting one that released a flood of desire which caused the vine to split. One stroked her labia, the other moved around her anus. Then the two vines invaded her body.

"*Shawn*." She hated the fear in her voice as she began to struggle. Tears burned behind her eyes. She didn't want to let Shawn down, but she didn't think she could do this.

His gentle hand cupped her cheek. "Resistance heightens emotional pitch and intensifies physical sensation. It's okay to be frightened. The key is to find your way to pleasure in the end." He captured her mouth in a firm, demanding kiss that stole her breath and for a moment her anxiety. Then he stepped away. "Look at yourself in the reflection of the walls."

Amazingly she could see all around her. The roughened stone around, above and below her had taken on a mirror effect. Naked, bound tightly in vines, she looked wicked, sinfully wicked, and a little of her fear subsided.

"You're beautiful." Shawn moved behind and brushed her long red hair aside before feathering his fingertips down her spine and into the cleft of her ass. "It pleases me to have you bound and at my command." His other hand struck out and landed solidly on her ass cheek with a loud slap.

Ciarra jerked, a cry bursting from her lips. His swat stung, but it was more surprise than pain that caused her to shout. In reflection on the smooth surface, his image bent at the waist and kissed the angry pink impressions reflecting against the wall.

"I love making my mark upon your beautiful body." Another sharp slap and she had matching palm prints, one on each cheek.

Then with both hands he began a brisk rub across the marks. The friction was vitalizing. It woke every nerve ending in the area, making it sensitive, alive to his caress. The beat of his pulse through the pads of his fingers was amazing. The heat was incredible, even the lingering throb was wonderful.

Warm hands burned up her back, across her shoulders and down her arms as if the vines didn't exist and there was only his touch. Then he pressed his body to hers, wedging his firm cock between her thighs. His hips pushed back and forth along her wet slit, teasing her clit and causing the silver chains across her abdomen to sway. She felt the vines inside her pussy and anus began to swell and to fill her orifices.

"Do you trust me?" His voice dropped another octave. It was deeper, richer and slid over her skin like silk. His large hands glided over her hips, his splayed fingers and palms spanning her abdomen across the waist chains.

She closed her eyes as more of her juices made the glide of their bodies smoother, hotter and the vines inside her to pulse.

He stilled. "Do you trust me?" he repeated firmly this time. His hot breath caressed the skin along her neck.

Did she really trust him?

Her heavy lids flickered open. "Yes," Ciarra murmured, not knowing why. It was a feeling, a sensation that Shawn would never hurt her. She wanted his touch. In fact she needed it. Her nipples were aching, her breasts heavy with desire.

When he stepped away a cool breeze filtered up her back. She shivered—not from the chill, but from what was yet to come.

Her gaze caressed the lines of his broad back, his tapered waist and firm ass, as he moved in front of her. Sinewy muscles rippled beneath golden skin. He walked with an air of confidence and control that sent another tremor up her spine. Power. It rolled off his flesh, thick and forceful.

When he turned to face her, Shawn had a flogger in hand. His face was a blank mask. His strides were heavy as he approached her. As the eight silver thongs glistened in the firelight, Ciarra couldn't help the sliver of fear beneath her skin.

She startled, jerking against her constraints as the straps brushed across her shoulder, down her back and over her ass. The downy hairs on her body seemed to stand straight up as she trembled.

A slight movement and Shawn was standing so close behind her that she could feel his body heat against her skin and smell his earthy musk. Another shift and his cock wedged between her thighs as the flogger's thongs dangled over her shoulder and teased a breast. It was so sensitive that even the light brush brought a mixture of pain and pleasure. As his hips moved, so did the ends of the whip. Lightly, oh-so lightly, it moved over and over her nipple until the nub tightened into an aching peak and felt like it would burst.

"Shawn," she whimpered, needing to feel his hands on her breast, her body.

"Master." There was a hard edge to his voice, dominant, commanding.

"Master," she repeated breathlessly. "Please."

"Remember you are here to please me, not me to please you." He stepped away. In the wall's reflection she watched him stroke her body with his gaze. A hoarse sound rose from his throat. "It would please me to whip you, mark you." His touched the small of her back. "So beautiful."

Ciarra didn't know what to expect, but the featherlight swat on the cheek of her ass was not it. Before long Shawn had touched every inch of her body with soft gentle caresses as he moved around her, dragging the whip across her skin. When he stood behind her again, he stopped.

Crack. The sound of the flogger snapping was nothing like the sting as it connected with her ass and forced a cry from her lips. Her back arched and she struggled against the vines holding her firmly in place. The cold, hard tendrils didn't give an inch. Another *crack* sounded. Another sharp burn touched her skin, this time on the other ass cheek.

"Breathe," he said, at the same time the vines moved deeper inside her wet pussy and ass. She gasped as they began to move in and out, in and out, fast and hard, blurring the lines between pain and pleasure. Just as her body tensed, the vines halted their action.

The whip sounded, struck the tender skin of her thigh, wrapping around her leg close to her sex. The sweet, sweet pain nearly threw her over the edge. Over and over, the lashes landed on different areas of her body than before.

Ciarra's body trembled. She was so close...so hot...so ready.

"You will not come until I grant permission." His harsh command caught her unaware. She closed her eyes and struggled to concentrate on breathing, and to focus less on the delicious fire streaking across her body and burning between her legs. She was fighting a losing battle.

But before she found release the vines inside her slipped away. The tight green ones restraining her body slowly unwound, disappearing across the floor and ceiling, and slithering into the dark crevices of the stone. When her shackles were released, Ciarra's knees buckled. She started to fall toward the floor as Shawn caught her in his arms, picked her up and cradled her to his chest. His heavy footsteps padded against the stone floor as he carried her through the cave.

The softest of furs met her backside. Her eyes shuttered closed and she felt Shawn's strong hands part her thighs none too gently. Then he was between them, piercing her pussy with a single thrust.

Ciarra cried out at the exquisite sensation of being filled. She squirmed beneath his weight, seeking the right spot that would give her release.

"Hold," he growled, moving in and out, pounding her body with his. Breathing labored, his movements quick and desperate.

Flesh slapping flesh was a heady sound as he fucked her hard and fast. The scent of his arousal was thick, heavy in the air. Her body coiled tighter and tighter. She clenched her jaws and prayed for control.

"Now," he yelled as his body slammed into her with a force that shook her, shattering her release into a massive wave that flowed through her veins like a raging river. It poured over her hot and steady. Throbbing, pulsating every corner of her being until she screamed from the intense sensations. When the last of the tremors subsided, he rolled over and drew her close.

In the aftermath she lay sated, her head on Shawn's chest as it rose and fell. The soft sound of his breathing hummed in her ear. He tucked several fingers between her neck and the collar she wore, giving it a tighter, more secure feeling as his other hand stroked her hair. She felt cherished, and if they had known each other better — loved.

But that was just a dream. The days were dwindling. She would be leaving soon to face the unknown. Tonight she would have to tell Shawn about Stan Mayhem. Tonight she would bare her soul.

In the calm of the moment something made Kitty tense. It drew her skin taut against Shawn's body. Even still she was fighting something — something that would not let her rest or even enjoy what they had shared. She had been an ardent student, as he had known she would be. Her body was made to love.

"What is it?" he asked.

"Nothing." Her voice sounded lost, forlorn. Her response felt like a ton of bricks on his chest.

"You still do not trust me." What must he do to break through to her?

Kitty pushed up on an elbow and caressed his cheek with her fingertips. "I do, but let's not ruin what we have here, now. Make love to me, Shawn." There was desperation to her words as she took him into her arms. Then she pressed her lips to his.

Her kiss was violent, a mesh of mouths, tongues and teeth, as if she fought to forget, fought to lose herself in his arms. Shawn didn't want her like this. There was something wrong about it, something that cheapened what they had. Something that made him feel used.

Gently, but firmly he pushed her away. "We don't have time, Kitty. The masquerade begins shortly." He peeled her arms from around him and made to rise. "You still need to choose your costume." He pushed himself to his feet. "We need to get back." The disappointment in her eyes spoke loudly. But until she could confide in him, he wouldn't make love to her again.

Emotions warred inside him as he extended his hand and helped her to her feet. He wanted Kitty with a vengeance, but he needed her to come to him free of her demons. Free to build a foundation on which their feelings could grow, not be weakened by her past — whatever that may be.

Silently, they walked through the grotto. The rush of the waterfall grew louder as they approached. Reaching the water's edge, Shawn plunged into the coolness without hesitation. He broke the surface on the other side of the waterfall. The sun was bright, causing him to squint against the rays as his powerful arms moved and he swam to shore and strode from the water. Warm sand heated his feet, water pebbling off his skin as he reached for his pants.

Shawn needed time alone to consider how he should approach Kitty. He waited on the beach, unsure whether she could find her way back to the citadel. In the next moment he saw his angel breaking the waves and gasping for breath. He wanted her so badly his body tensed, his cock grew hard. Each stroke of her slender arms brought her nearer, and made his body riper.

Her skin was still pink from their play. He knew her pussy would be wet and inviting. It was difficult but he eased his erection into his pants, sealing the flaps and closing himself from her. As he put his boots on she began to dress. Her forehead was creased. She frowned. What was she thinking?

After Kitty dressed they walked through the forest without speaking or touching. At the door of her bungalow, Shawn stopped.

"I will send Tatiana to assist you with dressing for the masquerade," he said, already moving away from her, knowing he would be unable to feel her skin beneath his hands without taking her.

Her lips parted as if she meant to say something and then they snapped closed. The look in her eyes gave him pause. It was clear she wanted to say something, but instead she turned and disappeared through the open door.

Damn. Shawn threaded his fingers through his blond hair. Tonight she would reveal her secret, or he would force it from her.

Chapter Sixteen

ဢ

Tonight was the night. Anxiety crawled across Ciarra's skin like a million bugs. Tonight she would confess what had happened on Earth before she arrived on Ecstasy Island. She would tell Shawn what had occurred and ask him to assist her in resolving it. If nothing else, it would definitely get her a quick exit off the planet.

"Stunning," Tatiana remarked. Ciarra moved before the mirror in her bungalow and gasped. Tatiana was right. She looked amazing.

A lavender half-mask glittered beneath the light, framing her eyes. At her hairline a feathery headdress began and swept down her back. Like the feather structure of a bird's wing, the mask began with a layer of lesser covert feathers, then middle and greater coverts, each firm but soft. Every row grew in length, blending the lighter shades of purple into deeper hues for the different types of feathers. Finally two-foot, vibrant, purple plumes completed the mask as they jutted high from the headdress in one-inch intervals.

Downy feathers, soft and fuzzy, were placed on each breast, layer after layer, covering each nipple and the gentle swell of each mound. More were used to design a thong to cover her mons and glide across her ass. She turned and looked down at her buttocks where Tatiana had made a swirly design on each of her cheeks.

Ciarra laughed and Tatiana joined her. "The sticky substance used to apply the feathers to your skin will dissolve with extreme body heat," Tatiana explained. "This will allow you to be plucked and feel no pain."

Ciarra felt her brows pull together. "Plucked?"

"Master Shawn has to get you out of the costume somehow. I doubt you will be wearing it very long. You look absolutely fantastic." Tatiana raised the lid on the box lying on the bed and brought out a pair of three-inch stilettos. "This should finish off the ensemble." She held them out and Ciarra reached for the glittering heels. "I have to go and get dressed now. You have about thirty minutes before you are to arrive at the ballroom in the main citadel." Tatiana began to gather all the excess feathers and the bottle of adhesive. Then her gaze darted to Ciarra. "Will you be able to find your way?" She crammed all the stuff into a white bag and heaved it over one shoulder.

Ciarra brushed her off with a wave of her hand. "Yeah, don't worry about me. What costume will you wear tonight?"

As Tatiana moved toward the door she said, "Don't know yet." She smiled, a mischievous lift to her mouth. "But I have thirty minutes to make up my mind." The door closed behind the woman, leaving Ciarra alone.

Anxiety struck immediately. How would Shawn take the news? What would he do?

Ciarra walked to her dressing table and picked up a bottle of sunflower perfume. She placed a squirt between her breasts, then one on each wrist, then rubbed them briskly together. In the reflection of the mirror she saw her briefcase and her suitcases packed and ready to go after she spoke with Shawn tonight. Tatiana had told her there was a shuttle arriving first thing tomorrow morning. Conveniently, Shawn had forgotten to tell her that shuttles left every other day to other planets that would provide a ride home.

A melancholy feeling seeped into Ciarra's bones. This was her last night with Shawn and she would make the best of it, enjoy what he offered before shattering everything they had built between them over the last week.

Too antsy to remain in the room, she slid through the door that opened upon her approach. Fresh air was what she needed to clear her thoughts. As she strolled along the cobblestone path into the garden, a shadow stepped beyond the bushes.

She startled. Her palm pressed against her chest.

"I'm sorry if I frightened you." Even behind the pirate getup, Ciarra knew it was Matthew Collins. "Do you have a moment to talk?"

Apprehension brushed across her skin as quickly as the breeze that kicked up and fluttered the large plumes of her headdress.

"Now? The masquerade is about to begin." She glanced over her shoulder toward the huge citadel in the distance. Had Collins been watching and waiting for her to leave her bungalow? A healthy dose of fear made her take a step backwards as he approached.

"It's just that I can never get close to you with that Thorenson brother always hanging on you." His hand whipped out and caught her wrist.

Feet planted firmly on the ground, she attempted to resist as he pulled her to him. The smell of liquor flooded her senses as his warm breath hit her hard. He brought their faces inches apart.

She wrenched her head back and raised her chin. "Collins, let go of me."

"Kitty," he whispered as he started to nibble on her neck. "You're so beautiful," he slurred stumbling back and taking her with him.

"Stop it," she insisted, attempting to pull away but he held firm, his fingers digging into her flesh. She'd have bruises in the morning. "Right *now*, stop it." Before she could close her mouth he assaulted hers in a sloppy, wet kiss. He crammed his tongue between her lips and she gagged at the taste of whiskey.

It was more a reaction than anything when she brought her knee up and caught him squarely between his legs.

Collins doubled over. His hands cupped his groin as he groaned, falling to his knees.

Ciarra bolted toward the looming shadow of the citadel where she knew Shawn awaited.

Running wasn't easy in three-inch stilettos. Twice her heels lodged between the cobblestones. The presence of several people ahead of her made her feel more secure. She slowed her pace to a brisk walk as she tried to catch up with them. Her pulse was racing, her heart beating out a mad staccato, as she constantly looked over her shoulder. The one time she hadn't glanced over her shoulder, strong fingers folded around her arm, pulling her off balance.

She whirled and swung with her free hand. Before making contact with her attacker, her wrist was caught— stopped in midair.

The man at the end of that firm grip was Shawn. A look of surprise hardened his handsome face.

Ciarra gulped in a breath of relief. Her body swayed toward his. He caught her in his strong embrace.

"Kitty, what's wrong?" Concern was obvious in his frown and tense facial features shadowed by the light from the dual moons above. A blue-gray hue gave him a dangerous mien. He didn't wear a costume, only the black leather pants and vest he had on earlier.

She tried to quell the tremors that shook her. "I had a run in with—" She pursed her lips and then said, "Nothing. Everything is fine." But who was she kidding? He knew she wasn't okay.

"With whom?" he asked, his voice dropped dangerously low.

Before she could answer, a high-pitched scream rented the air.

Shawn's hands dropped from around her. He swung around and without hesitation fled toward the woman's continued screaming.

The individuals in front of her spun and dashed past her toward the woman's cries. Others joined them. Ciarra attempted to follow, but her shoes made it nearly impossible. She reached down and tore off first one stiletto then the next, and raced to catch up with Shawn.

A trembling Cherry was wrapped in Shawn's arms. The crowd had formed a circle around something. Several women released tight gasps. One man darted off to the side and heaved. The sickly sounds of being relieved of his dinner turned another man's stomach sour and he joined the first in retching. Two women's faces were waxen, pasty from whatever lay before them.

As Ciarra approached Shawn and Cherry, the woman screamed, "No, get her away from me. She did it. She killed Master Collins."

Ciarra's feet stopped before her body and she swayed, attempting to gather her footing. Cherry was crying now, her face buried against Shawn's chest. The crowd was staring at Ciarra, but none of them felt as condemning in her eyes as the look of surprise on Shawn's face.

"Shawn?" Ciarra's voice cracked like the ground she felt shifting beneath her. The crowd parted and a few feet away lay Matthew Collins covered in blood. His body lay in an awkward position, one leg beneath him, his torso twisted as if he had attempted to see his attacker, but his feet refused to cooperate and move. The hilt of the knife protruding from his back was the same dagger that killed Stan Mayhem.

Ciarra staggered. She tried to swallow the lump caught in her throat. Instead her knees buckled. She fell, her knees hitting the ground hard.

"Let me go," she heard Shawn say, but Cherry was glued to him. Was he going to come to Ciarra's aid? The hopeful thought picked her head up. She locked gazes with him, praying to see a shred of support. But before she could contemplate the heaviness in his eyes, she was jerked to her feet. Two galactic-officers had her by the wrists. Two more had laser guns pinned on her.

"*No*," she cried fighting their holds. This wasn't how it was supposed to end between Shawn and her. "*No*."

The officer with black hair began to speak, but Ciarra only heard threads of his words. "Ciarra Storm...anything you say can and will be..." She felt her wrists being drawn behind her, felt them bound tightly together. "...if you have need of an attorney..."

Ciarra blinked back tears, unable to bear the expression in Shawn's eyes, or the gleam behind Cherry's moist ones as she snuggled closer to him.

"I didn't kill Collins." Ciarra looked at one officer and then the other, before facing Shawn again. "Shawn, I didn't kill him."

"Ciarra Storm?" Her name was a whisper on Shawn's lips. His face had gone expressionless. "You're not Kitty Carmichael?"

Before she spoke, the officer to her right said, "Miss Storm is being arrested for the murder of Stan Mayhem. However, it appears that she has struck again." Her gaze followed his toward Collins' listless body.

"*No*! Shawn," she pleaded, struggling to turn and face him. "I didn't kill those men. I can explain, please."

But Ciarra was yanked away by the four galactic-officers. She struggled to look at Shawn over her shoulder. Prayed to see one ounce of forgiveness or that he believed her, but there was none. He just stood there. His eyes were pinned on her, but not seeing, as if he looked straight through her. A chill embraced her as he turned his back, shattering any hope that she had held onto.

Shawn didn't believe what he was hearing—seeing. Numb was what he felt clear down to his bones. Kitty—no, someone by the name of Ciarra Storm—had lied to him, deceived him. His body tensed, growing hot as anger built quickly. Dismay followed on quick footsteps. With a rush his heart seemed to drop from his chest to feet. This couldn't be happening. The woman he had fallen in love with couldn't be a murderer. She just couldn't be. Confusion swamped his thoughts, making it more like a swirling whirlpool.

It was true Kitty was a virtual stranger, but still he couldn't believe that what they shared had been a farce. That the way her body reacted to him — his caresses, his kisses — was just the act of a desperate woman trying to hide from authorities. Their souls had touched.

He didn't resist Cherry spinning him around so that his back faced Kitty's departure. The pleading in Ciarra's eyes was too much for him. Yet her panic-stricken expression remained burned into his mind, her cries lingered in his head. Shawn attempted to move to free himself to run after Kitty and bring her back, but his feet felt heavy and Cherry arms were still wrapped tight around his waist. She sniffled from time to time, burying her head into his chest.

No, he refused to believe what had just occurred. The woman he knew, had shared the last wonderful days with, was incapable of murder.

"Cherry." He peeled her arms away and held her at arms' length. "Did you actually see Kitty…uh, Miss Storm, kill Master Collins?"

The woman wiped tears from her cheeks. "Well, no, but they were fighting earlier. I saw them kissing, then my Master doubled over and that woman ran away." She tried to fold her arms around him again but he held her wrists in the air.

"Then you didn't see her stab him? Double over? Was she standing in front of him?"

"Yes, but…" Cherry's brows dipped in frustration. Her lips twisted into a tight knot. "No. But remember she killed that other man, the-the one on Earth five days ago." She spoke quickly as she pulled her arms from his grasp. She took several unsteady steps backwards.

He narrowed his gaze. "How do you know that?"

"Uh...I...well, the officer just told us she did. Weren't you listening?" Her tongue swiped across her lips. "She killed Collins *and* she killed Stan Mayhem."

Something didn't feel right. Cherry's tears had dried too quickly. Her fear shifted to a panic, clearly wanting to ensure the guilty finger pointed to Kitty—or whoever the woman really was. Shawn got the oddest feeling that Cherry was withholding information.

"A man stabbed in the back wouldn't double over. And you said that she stood before Collins."

"I meant behind him," she corrected.

"If you know something, tell me." He moved toward the woman who continued to mimic his steps, except in the opposite direction. "A woman's life is in jeopardy."

"*What*?" Cherry came to a dead stop. Her fists dug into her hips. "What about the men she killed?"

Shawn took her brief pause to catch her by the wrist. "You don't know that." He was trembling as his fingers pressed firmly into the woman's tender skin.

Cherry jerked against his hold. "No. No, I don't. I mean, she's guilty." Then her posture shifted. Her fiery gaze snapped up to meet his. There was no fear, no terror, only anger.

"How do you know this?" he growled, needing to discover the truth—to save the woman he had fallen in love with.

"Fuck you. You're only mad because your woman is a murderer," she snapped. "Now let me go."

"Let her go, Shawn." It was Tor who spoke. Beside him stood Terrance. Where they came from Shawn had no idea. Nor did he recall the large crowd that watched the interplay between them.

Shawn grudgingly released Cherry. She knew more than what she was sharing.

"I ought to sue you, or at the very least have you arrested for assault," Cherry bit out, rubbing her arm that held the angry impressions of his fingers.

Shawn was shaking so bad now that he didn't trust himself to respond. He had to see Kitty-Ciarra. He had to tell her he knew she was innocent. He knew it, felt it deep inside him.

Terrance moved to stand beside Shawn. With his most intimidating scowl, he growled, "Try it." The woman almost tripped over her feet as she stumbled to get away from Terrance's advance as he stepped forward. Then she turned and fled toward the bungalows.

"She didn't do it." Shawn's voice sounded small, unsure even to him.

"How can you say that? You don't even know that woman." Tor's attempt to reason with Shawn was met with a frown. "Don't look at me that way, Shawn."

"She's innocent." Shawn drew himself up to his full height. Kitty—no, Ciarra—was innocent.

"Damn it, bro, you're not thinking straight," Terrance insisted.

"Fuck you both," growled Shawn as he raked a hand through his hair.

Tor said, "Now wait. We didn't say we weren't going to help. We just want you to be sure." He shook his head discouragingly. "Man, Shawn, you didn't even know her real name until five minutes ago."

Shawn hated the reasoning behind his brother's words. He didn't know Ciarra Storm and it had been clear from the beginning she was running from something. Hell, it was obvious she'd been running from someone just before they met tonight. "Tor...Terrance, just help me. I don't know why, but I know she isn't guilty."

"Then we better call Taryn." Tor looked to Terrance and then to Shawn. Shawn knew he was waiting for one of them to offer to call their sister. When neither did, Tor said, "Okay, I will." Then Tor turned and walked away.

Shawn released a sigh of relief joined by Terrance's exhale. It wasn't that either was scared of Taryn. She was just hell on wheels, more so when she knew that any of them were in trouble.

Terrance stood for a moment staring at Shawn. He didn't speak—just stared. Then his hand rose and settled on Shawn's shoulder. Terrance nodded before he pivoted and headed after Tor.

His brother's support meant more than he could say.

Family was everything and Ciarra had no one but him.

Chapter Seventeen

ஐ

The room was a six-by-eight cell. Cold metal bars imprisoned Ciarra, but were hardly necessary. It was more psychological as everything else was these days.

Her trembling hand touched the electric device that now ringed her neck, instead of Shawn's collar. It alone was enough to keep her within the defined limits. On the way back to Earth their transport had stopped to pick up a prisoner from Deltron. He had tried to escape, once. After the man's convulsions calmed and he was carried back into the transport, red angry burns rose beneath his neck-bracelet.

Once on Earth, no escape was possible. No attempts were made—by anyone.

Disheartened, she gazed around the room taking in the toilet that looked like it hadn't been cleaned in over a year and stunk of urine.

Guess the government couldn't afford the self-cleaning ones that were now available. No more scrubbing, no more ring around the commode, the same amoebas she had experienced on Zygoman were also used to take the dirty task out of a person's hands.

Ciarra continued to scan her small jail cell on Earth noting the small sink was in no better shape than the john. A cot that swayed in the middle with one blanket and a sheet folded upon it was the only other thing in the room.

Time was elusive. How long she stood in the corner, her back pressed tight against the bars, she didn't know. She couldn't move. She was lucky that her legs held her up at all.

Moisture gathered in her eyes but she fought the tears. She was alone with no one to rely upon but herself. *I will make it through this – I will.* Still she couldn't forget the expression on Shawn's face. The horror in his eyes when he stared at her was demoralizing. He hadn't even known the details, yet still he presumed her guilty.

Hell, the evidence was enough to convict her. What had she expected?

When a hand clutched her shoulder, Ciarra jumped, banging her head against the bars. Pain splintered her skull and it began to throb.

"I said your attorney is here," barked the short female officer who looked like she was a cross between a Pit Bull and Siamese cat. Dirty brown hair was pulled so tightly into a ponytail it looked painful. She snarled and for a moment Ciarra thought the woman would bite.

Ciarra had been so engrossed in her problems, she hadn't heard the officer enter the cell, much less grasp what she had said. Did she say attorney? Ciarra didn't have an attorney. She hadn't even used the tele-communicator.

"What?" she finally got out.

"Damn, woman. Are you an idiot? I said your attorney is here," the officer snapped as she waved a metal rod over the lock. There was a click and then the door swung open.

Still Ciarra couldn't move. Her feet refused to listen to the commands the officer gave.

"Get the fuck out there or I'll drag you out by your shitty red hair." The officer took several steps toward Ciarra before she shuffled her feet as she decided to obey. She took several unsteady footsteps toward the open door.

Okay, so the officer didn't like redheads. Well, Ciarra didn't much care for assholes.

The officer brought her stun wand out and waved it an inch away from Ciarra's nose. "Try anything and *zap*!" She made a hiss and then a popping sound with her mouth. "You'll be wishing I'd killed you." There was a gleam in the woman's eyes that told Ciarra the officer would relish the opportunity to use the weapon. The officer wanted Ciarra to make a run for freedom.

Freedom. Yeah, right. Like she'd ever know what that was again. Didn't matter that she didn't kill those men. She'd been framed, perfectly.

The smirking woman waved her wand in the direction of another door. "Over there. Miss Hotsy-Totsy demanded a conference room."

Miss Hotsy-Totsy? What was going on?

When Ciarra entered the room, a statuesque blonde stood before her in a designer suit that Ciarra swore cost more than she'd made in a month's salary at the advertising agency. The three-piece, midnight-blue ensemble was highlighted by a red silk shirt. Her short skirt showed off a pair of shapely legs. Her two-inch heels put her over six feet. The woman was a classic beauty, but the stern expression on her face could freeze water. Five-foot-eleven of pure, unmovable and cold, very cold female steel.

She was immaculate from her high-shine heels to her long, groomed fingernails that she waved dismissingly at the officer. "That will be all. And *don't* slam the door on your way out." There was authority in the woman's tone that was unmistakable. Confidence and, yes, even arrogance. In fact, when she spoke, Ciarra swore the lights flickered and the air grew heavy as if the woman controlled even the elements in the room.

The smartass officer must have felt the same way, because she didn't hesitate to move through the open door. She closed the door as directed, but not before she released a huff of displeasure.

Ciarra would have been glad for the officer's departure except that it left her alone with the haughty woman who was now looking at her as if she was a bug under a microscope ready to be dissected one limb at a time.

The demeaning inspection started at Ciarra's toes and worked upward over her face, taking in her baggy shirt and pants. Black and white stripes looked strange next to this impeccably dressed woman. The silence was eerie. The icy glare in the woman's eyes made a shiver race up Ciarra's back. Then the blonde moved, approaching in long lithe steps that nearly undid Ciarra.

Fuck. Who was this woman? And where did she get off treating Ciarra like she was a piece of meat to be examined?

The intensity of the woman was unnerving. Still Ciarra couldn't help but think that this was a test. She was gauging Ciarra's mettle. *Damn her.*

Ciarra drew herself to her full height, never diverting her eyes. If the woman wanted a pissing contest, hell, Ciarra had nothing to loose.

"Are you innocent?" There was something about the way the woman asked the question that made Ciarra feel as if her answer determined more than just the lady's representation.

"Yes," Ciarra responded quickly, raising her chin a notch higher. The blonde cocked a questioning brow. Ciarra's bravado faded and she slipped into the chair before her like her bones had melted. Hell, she was holding on by a thread. This woman might be her only hope. "Yes, but...no one is going to believe me."

"Why?" That one word slipping from the blonde's perfectly sculpted lips was filled with more than power, it elicited the truth.

Strange, but there was something familiar about the woman that began to nag at Ciarra. An uneasy burst of laughter broke from her mouth.

"Haven't you seen the evidence? Shit." Another despairing laugh escaped Ciarra. "I'd convict me." She rubbed the ache at the back of her head before she placed both elbows on the table in front of her and buried her face in her palms.

She fought the tears beating behind her eyelids. She wouldn't cry—she wouldn't.

The click of heels against tile made Ciarra glance up. She met hazel eyes that cut into her like a knife. Another feeling of familiarity struck Ciarra, hard.

Did she know this woman?

Then the intimidating blonde took a seat across from Ciarra. Her back remained rigid, her face expressionless. "I've seen the evidence." She paused, her voice hardening more. "Are you guilty?"

"No, but..." Should Ciarra confide in her lapse of memory? What about what happened on Ecstasy Island the first night she was there? She had been so out of control, so lustful for Shawn. Just the thought of him made her body ache, her soul cry out.

"But?" the woman asked.

"There are things that I can't explain." Ciarra just did not know how much to expose. Did she trust this woman? Their eyes met. Ciarra felt caught in the woman's magnetic pull.

"Like?" Damn, the gal was like a dog with a piece of meat—she would not let up.

Ciarra clasped her hands together, felt tension tighten her jaws. "Like waking up with a dead man's leg pinning you to the bed, holding a dagger with blood on it. His blood." Her eyes pooled with moisture. "Or—or the shower verifying that you'd been there before, when you don't remember seeing the place—ever. And then your turbo-sedan programmed for your escape. Or how about all your clothes and evidence showing up on a Godforsaken planet you never planned on arriving on?" Ciarra gulped on the emotion choking her. "Fuck, woman, I'm beginning to think I did do it." Big watery tears rolled down Ciarra's cheeks, one after another, like someone had released a flood behind a swelling dam.

Again, Ciarra buried her face in her palms and wept. It was the first time since she had been arrested. The flow wouldn't stop and right now she didn't want them to. The release was for more than her predicament, it was for the life she'd never live, the freedom she'd lost. But mostly she cried for the man she'd never see again.

"Do you think crying is going to help you?" The woman's insensitive words dried Ciarra's eyes immediately.

Sudden anger broadsided Ciarra. She jerked to a standing position, her chair tilting and then crashing to the floor. She shook uncontrollably. "Who the hell are you?"

The chair scooting across the tile and Ciarra's raised voice brought the officer into the room. Simultaneously, Ciarra and the attorney turned to the official and yelled, "Get out of here." Wide-eyed, the officer backed out of the room, closing the door behind her quietly.

Then Ciarra's glare snapped back to the woman before her. "Listen, lady, I don't know who you are or who assigned you to me, but I'm innocent. Furthermore, I don't give a rat's ass if you believe me. If I have to do this myself—I will. Now get the hell out of here." Ciarra didn't know where the rage came from, but it felt good—damn good. "I'll find someone to represent me who does believe me."

Miraculously, the woman's face softened, not much, but enough to take the chill from her features. "You already have found someone who believes in you."

"Yeah, right." Ciarra shook her head.

The attorney jutted out her hand. "I'm Taryn Thorenson. My brother, Shawn, has sent me to represent you."

The hairs on Ciarra's arms felt like they'd been charged with a hundred volts of electricity as goose bumps raced across her skin. She shivered as if a cool breeze stroked her. Then her knees buckled and she almost fell, grasping onto the table to steady herself.

The attorney rose and retrieved the chair Ciarra had thrown across the room in her outburst. "Sit before you fall."

"I don't know if I can," Ciarra whispered as she struggled to stand.

"Bend your knees and let the weight of your ass take over." The woman inched the chair beneath Ciarra. She felt the pressure on her legs and again her bones dissolved, unable to hold her as she fell onto the chair.

"Shawn?" Ciarra's voice cracked.

Taryn took her seat across from Ciarra. "Apparently he feels that you are above reproach." She studied Ciarra with a critical eye. "His leg pinned you to the bed."

For a moment Ciarra starred at the woman confused. "What?" Shawn believed in her enough to send his sister, Terrance's twin. Ciarra gazed at the woman's features. Her eyes. Those lips. Yes, she could see the resemblance now.

"You said you woke up with the dead man, Stan Mayhem, his leg pinning you to the bed."

"Yes...I-I dropped the knife." The horrible scene began to play through Ciarra's gauzy mind. "Pushed, shoved, until I could get out from beneath him." Her stomach churned. "Blood—it was all over."

"Tell me about the blood."

Ciarra licked her dry lips. "It was all over me, my clothes tossed on the floor, the room, the bed." Acid crawled up her throat. God, she was going to be sick. She buried her face in her palms.

"Miss Storm—Ciarra. I need you to focus. What did the blood look like?"

Ciarra gazed across the table. Was the woman mad?

Red.

Dark Crimson.

Black.

It was blood. How the hell did she think it look like?

"Red, wet, sticky," Ciarra responded with an agitated lift to her voice.

"No. Think patterns. How much? Where was the largest amount of blood? Did the room look like there had been a struggle? The crime scene was cleaned up in the pictures. Your doing I would suppose." Taryn cocked an accusing brow.

"Pattern? Like a splatter?" Ciarra asked confused.

"No, there wouldn't be splatters with a knife. The blood would gush and pool. If he crawled away there would be a path. There weren't any defensive wounds. It didn't look like he put up a fight." The vision the woman created in Ciarra's mind made a shiver race up her spine.

"The bed. Most of the blood was on the bed. It was as if it was painted on my body."

"Your clothes?" the attorney asked.

"Like they were used to wipe up some of the mess."

Taryn's eyes gleamed. "How many drinks did you have that night?"

"One—that I remember. Why?"

"Are you a heavy drinker?" Taryn whipped open the small computer on the table. Her fingernails clicked over the keys as she started to take notes.

"No, I seldom drink." With Ciarra's family history she was always careful.

The woman sprang from her chair and began to pace. "How did you feel when you woke up? Was your head cloudy? Was there a bitter or foul taste in your mouth?"

Ciarra swallowed hard, remembering the awful taste in her mouth. "Dizzy, nauseated and yes, there was a foul taste in my mouth—bitter—metallic. But—" She paused, remembering the lack of control, the hazy sensation she had felt on Ecstasy Island when she nearly attacked Shawn out of lust.

Taryn drew to a sharp halt. "But?" She turned and glared at Ciarra.

"When I arrived at Ecstasy Island…uh, your brothers— Well, there was this three-cornered table—" Heat raced across her face like a rush of steam. "I felt so horny, out of control. Not myself…"

"*Philter*." Taryn shook her head and long lashes swept across her high cheekbones.

"Shawn kept repeating that word. What does it mean?" Ciarra asked.

"*Philter* is an aphrodisiac, a drug. Let me guess, Terrance gave it to you." Ciarra could see the woman fighting the grin that wanted to push through her tight lips. Even still there was a brightness, pride in her eyes when she said her twin's name. "He is the devil reincarnated."

"An aphrodisiac?" Anger built swiftly. Ciarra had thought she had lost it—gone crazy. Thought she had truly killed Stan Mayhem. "I'll kill the son of a bitch."

The blonde's face tightened, then she burst into a deep laugh. "Terrance does have that effect on many people, especially women." Her laughter died as abruptly as it had appeared. She cleared her throat, her expression hardening. "Tell me about Kitty Carmichael."

Ciarra went through the events one by one. The woman's conversation, disposing of her ticket, dropping her gloves, and her suitcase filled with all of Ciarra's own clothes.

"Sounds like you've been set up. Who would want to harm you?"

Man, it felt good to hear someone else confirm she was framed. "No one. I can't think of anyone who hates me enough to do something like this."

"Then you're a patsy for someone—some other reason. Let's see…" Taryn patted her index finger against her lips. "We know that Collins and Mayhem were business partners. Was Mayhem actually stealing from Collins? If not, why or who would want to see both of them murdered? We know that Kitty works for the same advertising agency you do. That's the connection between the four of you. I've tried to locate Kitty Carmichael, but she has disappeared. Her boss said that she never showed up for work. My guess is she's dead and that one will be pinned on you too." More questions rapidly fired from her mouth as she took up pacing again. Her heels clicked solidly against the tile.

The creases in Taryn's forehead deepened as the woman's thoughts became quiet, her steps slowing. "I bet Brian can help."

"Who's Brian?"

Taryn shut the cover to her computer, picked it up and headed toward the door, ignoring Ciarra's question.

"We'll talk later," Taryn said over her shoulder as the door slammed behind her, leaving Ciarra alone and wondering what would happen next.

Chapter Eighteen

ഇ

The last person Shawn expected to see at the Los Angeles Courthouse as he stepped inside was Morris Dawson, the wealthy businessman who Shawn and his brother had eighty-six'd off Ecstasy Island. When their eyes met it was an exchange of fire hot enough to create an explosion. Not a word was spoken, nor greeting exchanged. In a slow calculated movement, Dawson's lips curled into a snarl. His eyes appeared to laugh as if taunting Shawn. The evil chuckle that surfaced from the man as he took a seat across the way made Shawn's fingers clench into fists. He took a step toward the man, but a firm hand on his biceps halted him.

"Shawn?" Taryn's voice lowered as she looked from Dawson to him. "Who is he?"

"Morris Dawson."

"Ahhh, yes." She nodded her acknowledgement. "The asshole who gave you trouble with that model, Chastity Ambrose. Why is he here?" Taryn methodically scrutinized the man.

"How the hell do I know?" barked Shawn. "He's a sadistic bastard—" The last word caught in his throat as Ciarra was ushered by two female officers into the room. He moved to go to her, but Taryn's hand tightened on his arm, stilling him.

"You can't approach her, Shawn," warned Taryn. "Now sit down." Shawn shook off Taryn's hold. "Shawn, sit down!"

When his gaze met Ciarra's, she bowed her head, breaking the connection.

Fuck. He wanted to hold her. Tell her everything was going to be all right. He wanted to peel her navy blue suit off, feel the silk of her white shirt slip through his fingers before he revealed her breasts. His fingers dug into the wooden barrier separating them. His cock grew firm, his balls drew tight. The memory of her kiss, the smell of her skin was the only thing that had kept him going over the last week. He needed to touch her, hold her.

"Shawn, you're making her nervous. Now sit the fuck down." Taryn's voice was a whisper. Still, the iron in her tone drove him down upon the bench.

Ciarra moved directly in front of him and took a seat, her back facing him. Her unique scent of sunflowers caressed his senses. Leaning forward, he reached out to touch her, his hand stopping midair when his gaze met his sister's glare. A glare that said, "Touch her and you're dead." In fact, the two female officers moved closer, their hands resting on their laser wands.

The air crackled, electricity shooting between them as if it were alive. Her hair was pulled back in a long braid and he had the urge to release it. To feel his fingers slip through her cool tresses, to feel them slide across his body. He gulped down a breath he hadn't even known he'd been holding. God, he needed to hold her, part her thighs and delve between her legs to reinforce in his mind as well as hers that she was his.

But there would be time for that later.

Right now he needed to focus. If anyone could prove Ciarra's innocence, Taryn could. His sister knew people, knew the system and if he knew Taryn she had already primed the pump even before the proceedings got underway.

Taryn and Ciarra stood and faced the judge and his staff—all holographic images. Several years ago, after the murder of four judges, the judicial branch decided that it was prudent to safeguard themselves and the jury. Now the courtroom contained only the prosecutor and defendant's team, plus the audience.

The three-dimensional figures before him flickered. The virtual images became sharper, clearer until the judge in his black flowing robes, his court reporter and bailiff sat beside him.

Shawn listened to the charges read. Shit! Ciarra was being charged with three murders. Apparently the woman she had impersonated had washed up on the shores of Muscle Beach last night.

Kitty Carmichael was dead.

From behind he watched Ciarra's shoulders fall on a defeated sigh.

"How do you plea to the charge of murder in the first degree of Stan Mayhem?" the judge asked. His hologram might not be steady and firm, but his tone was.

"Not guilty," Ciarra responded. Her voice quivered, showing signs of anxiety.

The big man beneath the seal of justice raised a bushy brow, his image flickered once more. "How do you plea to the charge of murder in the first degree of Matthew Collins?" the judge asked.

"Not guilty," Ciarra responded again. Her voice dropped to a whisper.

"How do you plea to the charge of murder in the first degree of Kitty Carmichael?" the judge asked.

Ciarra remain silent. Her palm clasped her mouth.

"Miss Storm—" the judge frowned with impatience, "answer the question."

Taryn leaned into Ciarra, murmuring. Her words were lost to Shawn as Ciarra mumbled something back before facing the judge.

The strain on her face as she swallowed hard made Shawn's fists clench.

Finally, Ciarra murmured, "Not guilty."

With that aside, both lawyers began to present their arguments about bail.

The district attorney stood. He walked toward the judge and then spun on a heel. "Ciarra Storm is a threat to the community. We ask that no bail be posted."

Shawn wanted to strangle the short man, balding, with glasses perched on the tip of his stubby nose. Bad posture and his cheap suit did nothing for his image.

Taryn drew herself to her full height of five-eleven. A light chuckle of disbelief left her lips. She shook her head at the man. Then she opened her mouth, dropped her eyebrows, the expression plainly showing she thought the prosecutor an imbecile. "Miss Storm has no priors." She gazed back at Ciarra sorrowfully and again shook her head. "It is clear to all except the prosecutor that Miss Storm is a victim in this travesty." He watched his sister with pride as she worked the judge who began to nod along with her.

When the prosecutor huffed, "Flight risk," Taryn turned her fiery glare on him. The man went literally weak in the knees, holding onto the table beside him, then he regained his composure to continue. "She has run once before. She will do it again."

Innocent one moment and then fit to kill the next was Taryn's specialty. She had the hard-ass and angel character down pat. But let no one underestimate her. She was not a woman to fuck with. "She ran because she was framed."

"You have no proof," the DA countered.

"Proof! Even an imbecile can see everything is too neat, too perfect." Taryn flashed the man a look that clearly stated she thought the prosecutor to be *that* imbecile. "Your Honor…"

The ensuing battle went on a good ten minutes longer before the judge's gavel hit the desk hard with a thud. "Enough! Since there are no priors, bail is set at fifty million dollars." He grinned at Taryn. If the situation wasn't so dire, Shawn would have laughed at the coy smile his sister returned. "However, Miss Storm will continue to wear the neck-bracelet." He looked toward the prosecutor. "That should satisfy the fear of flight." The judge again turned his attention to Taryn. The burly man's gaze stroked up the length of bare leg Taryn presented from where she sat.

Ciarra audibly gasped, her head snapping around to face Taryn. She mouthed, "Fifty million dollars." Wide-eyed, she stared at Taryn. His sister leaned into Ciarra whispering. Shawn knew what Taryn was relaying to Ciarra. He had already promised to pay whatever the bail was.

Ciarra shook her head. She turned and their eyes met, sending a heat of desire straight to Shawn's cock. "No," she mouthed.

Her refusal made Shawn love her even more. She was innocent and he would go to his grave proving it. How? He didn't know, but he would and then they would be together. He tried to present her a genuine smile, but somehow he knew it fell short. He just nodded, continuing to refuse her rejections. Nothing short of an earthquake would keep him from holding her in his arms tonight.

From the corner of his eyes he saw Dawson, and by the man's reddened face, the twist of anger distorting it, he was fuming. Dawson flung around to face a three-piece suit, obviously an attorney, and began to mumble. The guy shrugged, receiving another tongue-lashing from Dawson. Then he pushed past the guy, but not before his eyes met Shawn's. Dawson's menacing glare flashed anger, and then the man shoved past a man and woman before disappearing out the door.

Damn the man. What did he have to do with Ciarra? The thought made Shawn cringe. But before he could think further on the subject, Taryn drew his attention with the wave of her hand. Ciarra stood quietly beside his sister, her eyes cast downward.

"I'm going with Ciarra to see that everything is taken care of. Where are you staying?" Taryn asked.

"With Ciarra," he responded without haste. Ciarra's head jerked up, her eyes widened in the sweet, shocked way he remembered. "She isn't getting out of my sight." He grinned and received a weary smile from Ciarra until the two officers sidled up to her. The tension in her shoulders stiffened further, the vein that bulged in her neck and the clench in her jaw made anxiety slide up his spine. How much more could she withstand?

"Fine. You can wait for us in the lobby," Taryn shot over one shoulder as she followed Ciarra, the two officers one on each side clutching her by the arms. Anger built as Shawn watched them haul Ciarra through the door that opened on their approach. The thud that followed sealing Ciarra away made his gut quiver with disgust.

Shawn smelled a rat. It had the unnerving scent of revenge. He would have to ask Taryn to look into Dawson's involvement, because he knew there was a link. There had to be.

* * * * *

Morris Dawson paced the length of his office, taking time to kick the wastebasket so hard it crashed against the wall. Chunks of drywall splintered and fell to the floor. His breathing was heavy, his pulse elevated. Anger heated his face hotter than an iron over coals.

"I paid the prosecutor a helluva lot of money to ensure bail was denied," he growled, slamming a fist on his oak desk causing pens, pencils, a clock and an array of papers to rise and fall. "What went wrong, Smith?" he demanded from the man who accompanied him to the Storm woman's indictment.

Cautiously, the man stood, moving behind the brown leather chair that was a little too close to Dawson's desk and way too close to the man himself. "Last minute change of judges. There was nothing I could do. I don't know how that Thorenson bitch pulled it off." Perspiration beaded the tall, thin man's brows. "But I know she had a hand in it."

"Fucking Thorensons. Sister, you say?" Dawson's fiery glare made Smith take several more steps to increase the distance between them. "I want the remote to Miss Storm's neck-bracelet." The thought made him smile. "I want to fuck her, and then slowly kill her while that Thorenson bastard watches."

"Can't be done."

"What!" Dawson yelled as he swiped at the items on his desk, throwing them into the air before they tumbled to the floor. He took several menacing steps toward Smith.

Smith moved so the chair was wedged between them. "I-I mean...well, it can't be done." The man began to tremble. Dawson could taste his fear—it was exciting as his cock hardened. Anger was a great aphrodisiac. "Judge Clausen has been given the only remote."

Fuck, I need a woman, maybe two, to work off this anger. "Then kill the son of a bitch."

Nothing was going as planned. Well, almost nothing. Ciarra Storm would rue the day she shunned his attention. He reached up and rubbed his cheek, still feeling the sting of rejection.

"Judge Clausen?" The surprise in Smith's voice came out a squeak.

"Get it from him. I want to finish this tonight." Dawson thought of Ciarra and what he planned to do to the little bitch. A smile creased his lips. He'd make her scream—before she died. He began to pace again. Smith stood quietly off to the side.

"Everything had been going so well and then Collins' death." Dawson shook his head.

"Well, sir, it wasn't exactly Collins' death, but the timing of it," Smith reminded Dawson.

Dawson growled low and deep in his throat. "Your damn galactic-officer should have followed Storm from Earth to Zygoman after he offed Mayhem."

"Yes, but there was that bit of trouble with the real Kitty Carmichael. Who knew that she'd get cold feet about setting Storm up? Remember you asked Taylor to take care of that loose end before he left—" Dawson spun on a heel and faced Smith, causing the attorney to stop short his comment.

"Fucking woman," Dawson growled.

"Kitty, sir?" Smith flinched as Dawson raised his hand as if he would strike him. Instead, he curled his fingers into a fist and slowly lowered his arm.

"Cherry. If Taylor hadn't exchanged the knife she used on Collins—" Dawson felt his blood pressure soaring. Heat and pressure built in his chest, fanning across his neck and face. He pulled at his neckline and tried to calm his erratic breathing. "Let's just say that we were lucky that your man confiscated the knife from Storm's room earlier. As it stands, Storm was blamed for the murder instead of Thorenson. Not exactly what I wanted."

Damn woman. Cherry had really thrown a monkey-wrench into Dawson's plans. Taylor had drugged Collins with a tumbler of whiskey. The mere mention of "Kitty Carmichael" and her long legs made Collins hot and horny. Taylor didn't even need to suggest Collins' visit to the woman. All the galactic-officer had to do was ensure that Collins was headed in the right direction. With Miss Storm's abrupt presence outside and Collins un-orchestrated attack, Taylor had to act quickly to exchange knives. Before he could make it look like Shawn Thorenson did the deed, Cherry had pointed the finger at Storm, to save her own ass. At least that's what the halfwit had informed Dawson after the galactic-police arrested Storm.

Yes, Mayhem's and Collins' deaths were the driving factors in this little plan of his. The two dolts had been stealing from his company in the West Indies. Artifacts and a great deal of money were missing. Hours and hours of surveillance and one or two people paid off had revealed what Dawson needed to know. The path led back to these two men.

Dawson pummeled his fist upon the desk, blood seeping from his torn knuckles. "No one, absolutely no one steals from me. Money or women." Dawson swore beneath his breath remembering how Shawn Thorenson had foiled his plans to taste Chastity Ambrose. That sweet morsel should have been his, not Seth Allen's.

"Yes, sir, but you do have to admit that it was a fluke of good luck that Collins and Mayhem had planned a vacation on Ecstasy Island, even a bigger streak of luck that you noticed Ciarra Storm and her likeness to Chastity Ambrose on your last business trip to New York several months ago." Smith's attempt to appease his boss was failing miserably.

"Everything seemed so perfect, as if it had been aligned with the planets. I could get rid of Mayhem and Collins, and take care of Shawn Thorenson and Ciarra Storm in the process. With her father's history I knew she would run."

"What if she hadn't?" Smith asked.

Dawson smirked. "Either way she was dead. It was just a matter of time." The headhunter he sent her way, the new job at one of his other companies ensured he knew where she was. Reprogramming her turbo-sedan hadn't been easy. Storm reacted just like he had expected, and then Collins—

Dawson's fist swung viciously through the air. "Damn that bitch. If Cherry had waited a mere hour, Collins would have been dead and Thorenson blamed for the murder."

"Now what, sir?" Smith's question brought Dawson's glare straight at him.

"Where is Taylor?" Dawson asked.

"He has yet to arrive from Zygoman." Smith shifted nervously from foot to foot.

"I need Storm taken care of immediately. The ultimate would be a lovers' quarrel and both Thorenson and Storm dead. I'm tired of dealing with these two. I want results."

"Dawson. After indictments, the judges go into hiding. There isn't a way to locate the judge," informed Smith. He swiped his tongue across dry lips. "It was wrong to present yourself in court. I saw the look in Thorenson's eyes."

"The man knows nothing," Dawson barked.

"Not him, his sister. Taryn Thorenson is one of the top intergalactic attorneys. She's a bitch, but she is smart, cunning and fair. I don't trust her."

"Fuck! Then it looks like I will need to take care of this myself." Dawson ignored his lawyer's objections as he stormed from the room and into the adjacent room he used for private visits from his lady friends. A plan was already forming in his mind that made a smile creep across his face. He had seen how Thorenson looked at Miss Storm. The bastard was crazy about her.

Well then, both would die.

Ciarra Storm and Shawn Thorenson would not live to see the morning light and perhaps neither would Thorenson's sister.

Dawson's balls drew tight remembering the female attorney's long legs. His hand clutched his groin. The bitch, as well as the slut who looked almost identical to Chastity Ambrose, would be a nice addition chained to his dungeon wall.

Yeah, it would be a very fulfilling night.

Dawson unfastened his pants and took himself in hand. He stroked his firm flesh while thoughts of torturing and then fucking the two women heated his blood and brought his climax swiftly to a head.

Chapter Nineteen

৪১

The lobby was swarming with people, young and old, each with their own story as to why they were in court today. Ciarra couldn't help cringing each time someone stared at the neck-bracelet around her throat. It was like a beacon or perhaps a homing device drawing attention. The worst was when a six-year-old boy jutted his little finger out and yelled, "Look, Mommy, a crem-men-amal." If it hadn't been so demeaning she would have laughed at the way he said criminal.

Ciarra's aplomb dipped slightly as an arm slipped around her shoulders and she looked up into Taryn's hazel eyes. "He's a child." The chill had left the woman's façade. For the first time Taryn gifted Ciarra with what appeared to be a genuine smile. Could Shawn's sister be warming up to her? At the very least Ciarra needed her to believe in her innocence. She couldn't ask for any more. Who would want their brother associated with a woman up on charges for murder—not one but three?

"From the mouth of babes isn't the truth supposed to flow?" Ciarra asked as acid churned in her stomach. She needed to get out of this building with tall ceilings that echoed every voice, every step and every movement. The ominous structure felt like it was pulling the oxygen from the room. As a sliver of anxiety slid across Ciarra's skin, she had the unnerving feeling to run, but she gathered her courage and the hand firmly holding her arm helped her to walk through the crowd of gawkers and straight for the door leading outside.

The warm salty air was welcome as she gulped down a breath. Just after she had been released she was allowed to make a call. She had programmed Brody, her sleek black turbo-sedan, to be waiting outside the courthouse for a quick getaway. Which she discovered was much needed as Taryn and she fought the onslaught of newscasters.

"Miss Storm, do you really think you will get away with three murders?" a flashy blonde with too many teeth asked.

"Miss Storm has no comment. However, I do," Taryn promptly added. "Miss Storm is a victim." She stared down the lens of the camera. "I will find you." The steel and conviction in the woman's voice and expression sent a shiver up Ciarra's spine. "And when I do—you will pay." Then a smile lit Taryn's face. "Please excuse us." And just like that the crowd parted.

Ciarra's feet rooted to the ground. She couldn't move the moment she glimpsed Shawn. He looked so handsome, so male in his jeans and T-shirt, leaning up against her car. As always he left her breathless, struggling to inhale. Her pulse sped and the beat of her heart pounded against her chest.

"Partner, get away from my grill," growled Brody in warning. The light purr of his engine roared deeply once, twice. "Do *not* force me to run over you."

"Quiet, you worthless piece of tin," Shawn murmured as he pushed away from the ebony car.

"Tin," Brody huffed, obviously insulted. "I'll have you know that I am constructed with the finest—"

The vehicle's dispute faded as Shawn took long, determined strides to close the distance between Ciarra and him.

He opened his arms. "Come here, baby."

Ciarra flew into his embrace. Like a chocolate bar too long in the sun she melted, loving the feel of his arms, his body pressed tight against hers. She couldn't help the tears that instantly fell.

"Don't cry, angel." He held her like a child, rubbing her back and rocking her to and fro. But the firm bulge pressing into her stomach was anything but childlike. She tipped her head up and he caught her mouth in a light assault. At first it was just a brush of lips, a gentle nip, then he took control, melding her body to his, thrusting his tongue deep inside to taste her.

Ciarra's fingers desperately clutched his T-shirt as her nipples drew taut, her breasts heavy. God, she had missed him—needed him. The palm on her ass was driving her crazy, but before anything more could evolve, Taryn's, "Get into the car," broke the spell they were under. "Now. The police are holding back the newscasters, but for how much longer I don't know."

Ciarra tore herself from Shawn's embrace and quickly punched in her identification code. Brody's doors rose high. Ciarra slipped inside, followed by Shawn and then Taryn.

When the monitor brightened and a sexy, shirtless cowboy appeared, tipping his Stetson, Taryn's eyes widened and she tilted her head to look across Shawn to stare questioningly at Ciarra.

The machine purred his excitement of Ciarra returning home and began to undress, his hands slowly peeling away tight blue jeans.

Shawn said, "This thing has got to go."

Both women burst into laughter.

As Shawn reached to disable the monitor, the image on the screen thrust a palm forward. "Back away, partner, only Ciarra can stroke the goods."

"But— I was just— Fuck, Ciarra, turn this contraption off," growled Shawn.

Another burst of laughter filled the car.

"I kind of like him," Taryn said, receiving a scowl from her brother.

"Brody, dim the monitor," Ciarra demanded.

"As you wish, kitten." Brody's sexy, deep voice was enough to force another growl from Shawn.

"How much further?" Shawn pulled Ciarra into his embrace, frowning at the monitor. Damn if the man wasn't jealous over an inanimate object. The realization was like a warm breeze flowing over Ciarra.

"Not much," Ciarra responded as she snuggled closer. Tonight she would forget her plight and enjoy what time she had with Shawn. That was unless Taryn planned to stay with her too.

Brody dipped into the parking garage and came to a stop in front of the *skytron* leading up to her apartment. As they exited the vehicle, Shawn slammed the door and Brody blurted, "Hey, buddy, was that necessary?"

Shawn raised a fist, stopping midair before striking the vehicle's hood when Ciarra said, "Uh-uh, no dents." Even though she knew that the flex-metal could take the impact.

Once inside her small apartment, Ciarra felt her tension miraculously drift away, maybe because she was home, but more likely because Shawn was with her once again. His arm still circled her as if he was afraid to let her go. Fine with her. In fact she wanted more of him. She glanced at Taryn as she paced the floor, making one tele-communicator call after another.

"Does she ever sit down? Relax?" Ciarra asked, turning in Shawn's arms.

"Not Taryn. She's like a dog with a bone. She isn't going to let go until she has uncovered every possible lead or avenue." Shawn began to unravel Ciarra's braid. The tug as he played with her hair felt wonderful. When the red tresses hung loose, he threaded his fingers through them, cupping the back of her head and pulling her closer until their mouths met. His lips were warm but firm as he moved gently, nudging her own apart with his tongue. When he entered, she savored his masculine taste. Loved the way his hands caressed her body, sealing them together as the kiss grew ardent.

"I ordered Chinese." Taryn's interjection made them break their connection and Ciarra stepped away, embarrassed that she had forgotten that Shawn's sister was in the room with them.

Taryn moved around them, appearing oblivious to their need to be alone. "I've started the ball rolling." She finally took a seat in one of Ciarra's overstuffed chairs before the cinemax screen. Then she jumped back up to her feet. "There's a link somewhere here." She began to move again. "Something isn't right."

"Like?" Ciarra asked as Shawn pulled her back into his arms.

"Forget about her. Taryn talks to herself when she's trying to figure out a problem. She doesn't expect us to answer." Shawn chuckled. "Hell, I doubt it even matters if we're listening."

"I heard that." Taryn came to a stop. She opened her satchel and retrieved her computer. "Ciarra, do you know Morris Dawson?" Within moments she pulled up a picture of Morris. The smirk on the handsome man's face made Ciarra's stomach roll.

Ciarra frowned. "Oh yeah, I know him." Shawn tensed beneath her palms.

"How?" Both Taryn and Shawn asked in unison.

Ciarra felt their hot glares pinned on her. She squirmed in her chair. "It was really nothing." Well, if she could call being propositioned and fired nothing.

"Tell me everything you know about the man. Don't leave anything out," Taryn warned.

Shawn's face grew redder and redder as Ciarra shared her story. "Son of a bitch." A menacing growl rumbled deep in his throat.

Taryn slapped her palms together. "There's our link." She smiled, continuing her pacing. "Both you and Carmichael worked for Kohler. Collins and Mayhem were clients at

Kohler. If I can find the smallest connection with Dawson we might be able to blow this case apart."

Even after the Chinese food had been delivered and set upon Ciarra's small kitchen table, the woman was still pacing.

Taryn sat long enough to eat a few mouthfuls and then bolted from the table. "Gotta go," she said, disappearing through the open door that slammed shut behind her.

There was an awkward silence between Shawn and Ciarra. Then she said, "I didn't kill either of those men or Kitty."

Shawn reached for her hand across the table. "I know, honey."

Ciarra pulled away and he frowned. He had to listen, know how sorry she was. "I'm sorry."

He made to rise. "For what?" He stopped mid-rise and then sat again.

"Lying to you. I had no choice. I didn't know what to do."

For the first time tonight Ciarra could see his disappointment. "You should have told me the truth from the beginning."

She searched his face, knowing the obvious. "Would you have believed me?"

A sheepish grin curled his lips. "Perhaps not at first. But now, yes."

"Shawn, I had planned to tell you at the Masquerade. Then Collins…" Her voice drifted off.

He rose and moved around the table to stand beside her. "It's okay, angel, I understand."

"Do you? Do you really understand? Do you know what it is like to doubt yourself—doubt your sanity? That little aphrodisiac Terrance slipped me didn't help," she grumbled.

Shawn had the decency to blush. He knelt beside her. "Damn him." He rubbed his palms up and down her arms.

Emotion crept into her voice. "I thought I was crazy."

"You're not crazy, baby." He stood, pulling her to her feet. "Taryn will take care of everything and we'll get back to our lives," he assured, taking her into his embrace.

But what did the future hold for them? Even if she was cleared of the charges, what would become of them? He lived on a pleasure planet swarming with women. She lived on Earth in this little apartment. Her only friend was Brody, a computerized car.

"I love you," Shawn murmured as he slipped his fingers between the seal seams of Ciarra's silk blouse. "I've wanted to get you out of these clothes since I saw you this morning." The shirt parted, revealing her lacy white bra. His finger traced the contour of the material, slipping across Ciarra's nipple. The bud tightened instantaneously. A flick of his fingers and the bra snapped loose.

Ciarra's heart stuttered. *Did he say, I love you?* She couldn't help the warm sensation that enveloped her. She wanted to believe him. But how? They really didn't know each other.

He must have sensed his declaration startled her, because he cupped her cheeks in his palms. For a moment he stared deeply into her moist eyes.

Could it be true?

"I love you, Ciarra," he repeated in a definite tone that left no doubt. His long, strong fingers closed around her biceps. He pulled her close, so that their chests met. Slowly, his eyes dropped to her lips, before he captured them. With a firm and demanding caress he sealed his promise.

When the kiss ended, a smile touched her lips and eyes. So this was what it felt like to be loved. Giddiness bubbled up inside her. She could live with this feeling.

With a toe she nudged one shoe off, and then repeated the action until she was barefooted.

Grinning like a fool, she tugged at Shawn's T-shirt, pulling it up and over his head, baring his broad golden chest.

Her palm slid over his warm flesh, muscles and curves creating a tightening low in her belly. A gush of liquid heat between her thighs followed.

She gazed up at him. He stared back with such wonder in his eyes. Her expression grew sober. "I want you." It might not be an avowal of love, but the truth sang in her breathless tone. She did want him and more importantly — she needed him.

She slipped her hand down his pants, parting the seams and at the same time backed him up to a living room chair. As the back of the chair struck his legs, he sat.

Shawn slid his buttocks forward on the chair, slumping back against the backrest. His cock thrust upward from its nest of blond hair and his balls hung full and heavy in her palm. She licked her lips, forcing a groan from his throat.

Shawn never dreamt a week without Ciarra would be such hell. A lifetime without her was simply unacceptable. His breath caught in his throat as her fingers circled him and began a gentle stroke. As her hand slid up and down he promised himself this woman was never getting out of his sight again.

Bright blue eyes met his as her head lowered into his lap. Then her warm wet mouth closed around him, sending his thoughts into a tailspin. He closed his eyes, savoring the feel of her tongue along his length, relished the slow, seductive rhythm of her lips gliding over him.

His cock jumped in her mouth, muscles twitching, veins throbbing. The sensation was beyond blissful going straight to heaven. He was so close to climaxing. Then the creak of the front door opening made him jerk his eyes open. Half expecting Taryn, he stilled Ciarra's head, his cock buried deep in her mouth.

Instead Morris Dawson stood in the open doorway and he was holding a gun. A large silencer was on the end of the barrel. In his other hand he held a small gym bag.

"Well, well, it looks like I'm just in time." His ominous voice frightened Ciarra and she fell backwards, landing on her ass. Breasts bared, she scrambled on all fours to rise as Shawn pushed from the chair, staring down the cold metal barrel pointed dead center of his chest.

"Isn't she a treat, Thorenson?" Dawson asked, moving further into the room, his eyes pinned on Ciarra as he closed the door behind him. "I hand-picked and delivered the fiery redhead."

"What?" Confusion filtered across Ciarra's face. Her gaze darted from Dawson to him. "What's he talking about, Shawn?" Her hands attempted to cover her breasts, her skirt was gathered up to her thighs. If she pulled her skirt down she would expose her breasts. She left her hands where they were and remained on the floor.

"Did Shawn tell you that you are the spitting image of his last lust affair?" Dawson's chuckle made Shawn cringe. "What an idiot you are." Dawson rolled his eyes. "You made it simple, so very easy. But then again I fell for Chastity too." A wistfulness in the man's voice almost made Shawn think the man was human.

"You wanted to destroy her." Shawn took a step, stopping when Dawson pointed the gun at Ciarra.

"I wanted to love her," Dawson insisted. There was a softness in the man's eyes. But Dawson was a cruel man, bent on having his way.

"You don't know how to love," Shawn responded as Dawson moved closer, deeper into the room.

"Perhaps you're right." Dawson's hungry gaze raked over Ciarra's body then he turned his eyes on Shawn. "But you have taught me to hate. You ruined everything."

"I ruined nothing. Chastity wasn't mine and she wasn't yours," Shawn said, as Ciarra rose and inched her way to his side.

Cautiously, Shawn moved Ciarra behind him, securing her before he tucked his now semihard cock into his pants, sealing the seams with a press of his hand. He couldn't miss the warmth of her breasts against his back, or her fingernails digging into his arm.

"Playing the hero again, eh, Thorenson?" Again Dawson released that menacing laugh, causing a chill to race up Shawn's spine.

Ciarra moved from behind Shawn to his side. Confusion waged across her face as she stared up at him. "Shawn?" Then she glared at Dawson. "Why?" Her voice was tight and small. He looked down at her bulging eyes as she gaped at the gun in Dawson's hand. Her pulse thrummed through her fingertips gripping his biceps.

"Why? Did you think that you could get away with shunning me? You little bitch. I should have killed you after you slapped me."

"But what does Shawn have to do with all of this?"

The hate in Dawson's eyes deepened as he glared at Shawn. "I'm Thorenson's worst nightmare." Dawson wagged the hand holding the gun toward the bedroom door. "Let's continue this discussion in the bedroom. I thought we'd have a little fun before you both die."

"Die?" Ciarra's gasp was warm across Shawn's shoulder. He reached for her trembling hand and held tight, squeezing it to assure her everything would be all right. How? He didn't know.

"Dawson, let Ciarra go. She had nothing to do with what happened a year ago." Shawn pushed Ciarra behind him again, ensuring she and his nemesis were separated as Dawson moved slowly around them, driving them toward the destination he wanted.

"True, but I have my own score with her." He chuckled. "Of course, she wasn't supposed to be the patsy for Collins—

you were." Dawson waved the gun again toward the bedroom door. "Now get going."

As Shawn moved, he knew he needed a plan and quick. If he rushed Dawson, the man would shoot. Was he good enough to fell Shawn with one shot? If so, then Ciarra would be left unprotected.

There was a sharp tug against Shawn's hand as Ciarra stopped dead in her tracks. "What?" he whispered, but Ciarra was focused on Dawson and if he didn't know better the woman was pissed. Her face was red with anger, her brows dipped low as she frowned.

"*You* framed me!" Her accusation came out in a gust of disbelief as she glared at Dawson. "You killed Mayhem and Collins? You son of a bitch. Do you have any idea what I've been through?"

That was his girl. Even in the face of danger she had spirit, but now was not the time.

"Don't forget Kitty. Now she was a lovely morsel I will miss." Dawson shook his head. "To answer your question — not personally — no, I didn't kill them, but I ordered it." He said it with such authority, such power and pride. "But I will see to your demise, before Thorenson here."

Shawn tried to calm Ciarra down with a touch of his hand. She jerked away, anger spreading across her face like a flame. "You mean all of this is revenge because I slapped you? Because another woman I never knew chose a different man over you — not even Shawn? You're fucking crazy."

"Beautiful and smart. What a shame we will only have tonight. But no, darling, you and Thorenson were only a small part in my plan. Sorry. Collins and Mayhem were stealing from me." His lustful eyes slid over Ciarra's bared breasts. "Now get your fucking asses in this room." Impatience slithered into Dawson's tone. He kept his distance as Shawn and Ciarra entered the bedroom. Perched beneath the doorframe he said, "Strip. Both of you." He set down the bag and from his pocket he extracted a condom. "After Thorenson fills your sweet pussy with his seed, I plan to have some fun."

Just the thought made Shawn's fingers curl into fists. "Over my dead body."

"Exactly." The bulge in Dawson's pants grew firmer. His licked his lips. "Two lovers reuniting." He bent and opened the bag, extracting a length of coarse rope. "Things get a little out of control." He tossed the rope on the four-poster bed. Next he brought out a flogger that looked like it had spurs down the thongs, their silvery tips glistening in the light.

Ciarra's grip tightened on Shawn's hand.

"Lover A accidentally kills Lover B and is so remorseful that he commits suicide." He snapped the whip. "Any guess as to who's A and B?"

"What do you want, Dawson?" Shawn's heartbeat thundered. Damn, what was he going go do?

"Your death," Dawson replied simply.

"Then *do* it, but release Ciarra." Covertly, Shawn scanned the room for a weapon, but it was a woman's room. A fluffy, lacy comforter lay neatly across a queen-size bed. Typical knickknacks, perfumes and make-up graced her dresser. Nothing was out of place, not even a pair of nylons he could strangle the bastard with.

"I'm tiring with your stalling tactics. Can't you see Miss Storm is a loose end? Killing her will tie everything up nicely." His lips curled into an evil grin. "See, Thorenson, not everything has to do with you." Dawson's gaze fell on the rope lying on the bed. "Tie her to the bed. I'll watch while you fuck her, then I'll take over and you can watch." He pulled a pair of handcuffs from his gym bag. "I actually brought a couple of toys to make this party a little more interesting." He drew out an electrical probe and waved it side to side.

"*Shawn.*" His name was a mere whisper on Ciarra's lips. He took her into his arms and pressed a kiss to her forehead.

He murmured, "I love you."

"Touching." Dawson's sarcasm lit a fire deep inside Shawn. If it was the last thing he did he would see Dawson dead. There wasn't an opportunity to tell Ciarra to fall to the ground when he planned to attack Dawson, because out of nowhere Taryn appeared behind the man. She moved fast as she buried her shoulder blade into his back, throwing him forward and off balance.

Then everything happened at once. Taryn lost her balance, going down with Dawson, falling atop him as they hit the floor with a thud. Dawson's "Bitch," was countered with Taryn's "Bastard," as they struggled, rolling, before the gun exploded with a loud pop that sent a deafening echo throughout the small bedroom.

Shawn's ears rang as he shoved Ciarra to the floor. Her unexpected landing pushed a scream from her lungs, drawing Dawson's attention as he jumped to his feet. Before he could aim and shoot, Shawn flung himself upward, soaring through the air and striking Dawson. They both went down, hard. Each sucked in a breath the fall had robbed them of, as they watched the gun skid across the marble floor.

Shawn lunged for the gun at the same time as Dawson did. His fingers touched the metal, but the impact of Dawson slamming against him sent the weapon skidding once again across the tile and beneath a table.

From the corner of Shawn's eye, Taryn lay motionless, a pool of blood forming beneath her. Pain and anger detonated like a short fuse sizzling against a stick of dynamite. In the mere second he took his eyes off Dawson, the man rose and headed for Ciarra. Shawn caught up with him, jerking Dawson about as he swung. His knuckles connected with Dawson's chin, bone crunched and gave. An impact that should've felled the man, but Shawn had underestimated his opponent's strength. He staggered back, quickly regaining his balance. Dawson reciprocated with a left hook that Shawn dodged.

The sounds of their heated breathing filled the room. They faced one another, circling like two angry bulls, then charged before locking horns. Again Shawn slammed into Dawson, this time his fingers closing around Dawson's neck as the man's fist gave him an uppercut to the ribs.

An *umph* pushed from Shawn's thin lips. There was no pain, only fury as he squeezed, his grip tightening.

Wide-eyed, Dawson frantically waved his hands then grasped Shawn's wrists, fighting to free himself. He was strong, but Shawn's fingers continued to tighten. All he could see was his beloved sister bleeding, if not already dead, before him.

A knee to the groin Shawn successfully avoided. Then there was a loud pop that shook the room. Dawson's hands fell to his side. His body went slack, limp in Shawn's grasp. He grunted. His eyes rolled back into his head and his body slid out of Shawn's hold and onto the floor in a heap.

Shawn raised his gaze to Ciarra and the gun she clutched in both hands. Her eyes were agape with fear. She trembled.

"Lower the gun, angel." Shawn moved carefully toward her, watching the barrel shake unsteadily. She blinked hard, swallowed, yet held the gun firmly toward the man lying upon the ground. "Ciarra, honey, give me the gun." When he tried to peel her fingers from the weapon she refused to let go—refused to look at him. He knew he needed to calm her further, but his gaze darted to Taryn.

He turned away from Ciarra and with a silent prayer he fell to his knees beside his sister. He felt for a pulse. There. It was light, but it was there. She'd been shot in the side. The blood flowed so quickly he was afraid she would bleed to death, even if no vital organs were hit. Either way paramedics needed to be called and pressure placed on her wound. The glossy look in Ciarra's eyes gave him no hope that she would be able to help him.

As he scrambled to his feet, heading toward where he thought he'd seen a tele-communicator, another gunshot startled him, tossing him forward and onto his belly for cover.

His first thoughts were of Ciarra as he rolled over. Dawson stood over him, a knife in his raised hands ready to plunge. The man's body swayed, the knife fell with a clunk, and then he crumpled backwards, hitting the floor with a loud thud. A small hole in the middle of his forehead oozed blood.

Damn, Ciarra was a good shot, or lucky as hell.

"Ciarra, I need your help—call the paramedics. I've got to stop the bleeding," Shawn said, making his way back to his sister's side.

Like a light switch, Ciarra's eyes brightened, she tossed the gun to the ground—thankfully it didn't discharge—as she ran toward the small dresser next to her bed. She fumbled with the tele-communicator, but managed to punch in the emergency number.

As Shawn applied pressure to Taryn's side he murmured softly to her. "Sis, hold on. You'll be fine." His sister's eyes fluttered, she mumbled something inaudible. "What, Taryn?" He leaned closer as her eyes inched open.

"I said, 'fuck it hurts'. Did you kill the son of a bitch? Ouch!" Taryn's face was skewed with pain.

Shawn gave a soft laugh. "No, Ciarra did."

"Good," she groaned in agony. "But I wish I'd had the chance to shoot the bastard. He shot me. The bastard shot me." She lifted her shoulders and started to rise. Shawn held her down with a gentle hand.

"Not a good idea. Just lie still until the paramedics arrive," he ordered, before he realized he'd done so. No one told Taryn what to do.

"Damn you, Shawn, help me up." She groaned again. "I don't want anyone to see me like this."

He shook his head in dismay. "You're hardheaded."

"Not any more than you were with Ciarra's innocence," she bit back, but there was a hint of a smile beneath her thinning lips.

Shawn looked about the room for Ciarra but she was gone. Carefully, he helped Taryn to her feet. She nearly cold-cocked him as he tried to scoop her into his arms. "Don't you dare." The slap on his arm was weak, not the strength his stubborn sister was known for. So, arm around her waist, he moved slowly to the front room where she collapsed in a chair.

"I need to find Ciarra. Will you be all right?" He headed for the front door.

"Hell yes. It will take more then a bullet to put me beneath the ground." Shawn released an uneasy chuckle at his sister's bad joke.

As he reached for the doorknob, the door sprang open and two local enforcement officers entered. Behind them several more officers and paramedics approached. Shawn looked around them to see one of the officers suddenly subdue Ciarra.

Shawn reacted. Before he could reach her two officers took him down. His breathing was labored. He was seeing red as they cuffed his hands and feet, rendering him helpless. In front of him he saw the officer place restraints on Ciarra's wrists. She wasn't crying, but he could see the glistening of tears forming in her eyes.

The next thing Shawn knew Taryn was on her feet. She growled and one paramedic actually released her and took a step backwards. Grasping her side she fought off the other paramedic with a balled fist. "Once again you officers fucked up. The man you want to arrest is lying dead in the bedroom. Now release both of my clients this instant unless you want assault charges brought against you." She gave them her firmest scowl and fainted.

Chapter Twenty

ॐ

Ciarra nearly jumped out of her seat when the holographic form of Shawn's sister appeared beside her in the courtroom. The image flickered and then sharpened. Taryn turned and looked directly at Ciarra, giving the feeling that the woman actually sat beside her. From her hospital bed Taryn had demanded to handle wrapping up the case. Ciarra was amazed at how omnipotent one woman could appear from a sickbed. She raised a haughty brow at the DA and then turned a dazzling smile toward the judge. In seconds Shawn's sister had both men eating out of her hand.

The short, balding prosecutor looked toward the three-dimensional figure of the judge in his black flowing robes. Beside him was his court reporter and bailiff. He cleared his throat. "Based on the evidence supplied to my office, the State of California wishes to drop all charges against Miss Ciarra Storm."

The judge's gavel slammed the wooden pedestal as he declared, "Case dismissed. Miss Storm, you are free to leave."

Ciarra breathed a sigh of relief as she rose. Taryn showed no emotion except for the slight lift of her shoulders, a proud movement few if any saw other than Ciarra. The woman was an enigma, but then again so was her infuriating twin brother, Terrance.

Ciarra was free. She turned to find Shawn directly behind. She squealed as he picked her off her feet and swung her around. Both threw back their heads and filled the courtroom with their laughter, a joyous sound that Ciarra thought never to hear again.

"Shawn. Ciarra." Taryn's firm voice brought them both back to reality. "I know that you're heading back to Zygoman tonight. I need for you to stop by this damnable place—" she swung her arms about, "so that I can apprise you of dates and events that both of you will need to be involved in."

Taryn frowned. "Shawn, get your hand off her butt and get your ass over here, pronto." The woman's hologram flickered, and then *snap*, it was gone.

* * * * *

Nothing like a sterile hospital to subdue a happy occasion, Shawn discovered as he and Ciarra entered Taryn's room. By her bedside stood Terrance, Tor and Passion Flower. Amazingly, each of them was wearing suitable attire for Earth. His brothers were each attired in a three-piece, gray suit and tie, while Passion Flower wore an elegant navy blue pantsuit. Shawn felt his eyes bulge.

"Don't they clean up nicely?" Taryn asked. She grasped Terrance's hand and his brother's burly stance softened. He leaned over their sister and pressed his lips to her forehead. Shawn saw her squeeze Terrance's hand before she shoved it aside.

"Now, there are a few things we need to settle." From beneath her pillow she pulled out a file. Terrance cocked an inquisitive brow. "Damn nurses keep messing with my things."

"You need to rest." Tor tried to grab the file, but Taryn was quicker, pulling it aside.

"I know what I need. I need to get out of here. Passion Flower, find the doctor. Get me the hell out of here." Passion Flower nodded with a brief smile on her lips as she left the room.

Taryn's gaze cut to Shawn and Ciarra. "Okay, both of you will have to return to Earth for the trials of Cherry and the officer from the LA transport station." She looked through her file. "George Taylor. It appears that the officer was in actuality a hit man for Dawson." She extracted a picture of George Taylor and handed it to Ciarra. "Is this the man you saw in a LA transport galactic-officer uniform the day you left for Ecstasy Island?"

Ciarra's fingers shook as she gazed down at the photo in her hands. "Yes," she said and handed the ominous picture back to Taryn.

Taryn tucked the glossy paper away. "Taylor is responsible for murdering both Stan Mayhem and Kitty Carmichael. Kitty. What parent would name their daughter, Kitty?" Taryn shook her head. "Anyway, Kitty —" she said the woman's name with a hint of sarcasm, "had been Dawson's latest squeeze. Evidently after leaving you in the restroom she began to have second thoughts — thoughts that got her killed."

"What about Matthew Collins?" Tor asked, making another grab for the file and again was left clutching thin air. Taryn frowned at him.

"It appears that Cherry had killed Matthew Collins. His blood had been found on an *Impressionist* glove with her fingerprints behind a bush by a Pandorvia vampire, Paolo de Rimini."

"He's the vampire who—" Ciarra stopped in mid-sentence.

"Who?" Shawn asked, watching her squirm. He knew the same Pandorvian had attempted to seduce Ciarra, but he wanted to hear her admit it.

"Uh, he tried to seduce me." A delightful blush tinted her checks.

"Well, it appears your vampire had been involved in an *affaire de coeur*. Another client who has retained me," she added before continuing. "Apparently, he was about to do the dirty when he heard the argument between Collins and Ciarra. He was getting busy as the last argument between Collins and Cherry took place. The man had not immediately come forward because he knew his sorry ass was in for a heap of trouble."

The confusion on Ciarra's face prompted Shawn to explain. "He was with a woman—a human woman, which he knew would bring repercussions."

"Exactly." Then Taryn smiled, an actual smile that brought out her beauty. "The final *coup de grace* was Caldwell Smith, Dawson's attorney—the slime ball. The man sang like a bird to cut a deal with the DA's office. All the sordid details of Mayhem and Collins' dealings to swindle Dawson were revealed. Dawson's plan to frame both Ciarra and Shawn. Quite an elaborate scheme I might add."

"But why?" Ciarra asked.

Taryn gazed at Ciarra, taking her measure. "Dawson was obsessed with Chastity Ambrose, and these three big morons for throwing him off Ecstasy Island. You were a look-alike who attracted Dawson. When you rejected him too, Smith said he cracked. Then when Collins and Mayhem mention Zygoman, Dawson's plans took form. In fact, Kohler's Advertising Agency was another of Dawson's shields. After he fired you in New York he arranged for you to be offered a job, so he could keep an eye on you—have you available when he decided to strike." She shifted, sending her face askew. It was clear Taryn was still in considerable pain but would not admit it.

"But what about the documentation I found in the bungalow? Papers showing Mayhem and I were embezzling funds from Collins," Ciarra asked.

"Just another cover-up for Dawson to retrieve his monies." Taryn inhaled carefully and placed a palm over the wound at her side. She extended the folder to Tor. "Now, big brother, you may have the file and go look for your wife. I expect that doctor to be in here in ten minutes or I'm checking myself out of this damn place. Do I make myself clear?" She turned and motioned Ciarra to her side with a wave of her hand. "Ciarra, I welcome you into this family, *but*—"

Shawn did not like the tone of that "but".

"But," she continued, "if you ever hurt my little brother I will hunt you down like a dog and believe me it will not be pretty." She reached out and squeezed Ciarra's hand. "Now come here, Shawn."

Shawn went to her side, leaned over and kissed her forehead. She curled her fingers into his shirt, holding him near. "Be happy," she whispered and Shawn thought he heard a tear in her voice. Then like was typical for his headstrong sister she pushed him away. "You two get out of here." She turned to Terrance and snarled, "Get the damn doctor in here *now*."

Chapter Twenty-One

The warm male scent of Shawn wrapped around Ciarra like a blanket. She wiggled closer, her back against his chest, the length of him spooning her. Over the bedcovers she gazed around the room that she and Shawn now shared. A sigh of contentment eased from her lips. From the moment she stepped from the transport onto Ecstasy Island's platform yesterday, it had felt right—like coming home.

The nightmare was over.

Lost in her thoughts, Ciarra startled as a strong arm wrapped around her waist, his warmth slid across her chest to cup her breast. "You're tensing." Shawn yawned, his sleepy voice sensual and low. "I thought we were going to put all this behind us." He rolled her nipple between his finger and thumb, drawing it into a tight nub. "You don't want me to punish you, do you?" he teased, his warm breath caressing her ear. She pushed her chest into his palm, relishing his touch. "I'll take that as a yes." He flipped her over on her back, causing a squeal to squeeze between her lips.

His weight felt good pinning her to the bed. He drew her wrists above her head as he pressed his body over hers. His cock jerked against her mons. Her womb clenched then released liquid desire that dampened her thighs.

She stared into his green eyes filled with such tenderness. His long blond hair had that slightly mussed, just-fucked look.

Her palms itched with the need to touch him as she jerked against his hold. "Shawn, make love to me." Her breasts ached. She fought to widen her thighs, invite him in, but he held her legs together beneath his own. "I need to feel you inside me," she whimpered, arching her chest into him.

His lips lightly skimmed across hers, up her jawline. Soft kisses followed across one eyelid, forcing it closed. So gentle, so sweet it made Ciarra's heart skip a beat.

Shawn had professed his love. Never experiencing the elusive thing called love caused doubt to muddle her mind. Still Ciarra knew she would be a fool to not hold on to what he offered. Buried inside she wanted to believe, needed to see where this relationship would take her. A chance to be happy was all she wanted.

Without a word, Shawn released her legs. His strong hands widened her thighs as he pressed his cock against her slit. Slow, drawn-out strokes kindled the fire inside her as back and forth, he caressed her clit. With each thrust he moved more easily, anointed with her juices.

"Fuck me." She was breathless with desire and the need to join with him completely. "She squirmed beneath him. "I need you deep inside me," she breathed and then moaned as he thrust, driving deep.

Ciarra felt him tremble as he settled in her cradle. The knowledge of how deep his emotions ran for her was humbling. His hunger tore at her heart, touching places she never knew existed. Tears of happiness swelled.

"Angel?" he whispered, stilling his hips. A crease furrowed his brow. He released her hands and used his own to hover above her. His eyes searched hers.

"No, I need you," she insisted rubbing her palms over his strong arms. A single tear beaded and rolled down her face to pool in her ear. "Happy tears." She managed a smile as another fell.

"Happy?" His face softened into a grin and he lowered himself slowly upon her. His weight, the smell of him so close was intoxicating.

"Happy because I've found a man worth his weight in gold," she teased wrapping her arms around him, holding him tight.

He cocked a brow. His grin grew. "I'm heavy?" He filled her completely as he ground his hips into her.

"A ton." She squirmed against him, loving the feel of their bodies united.

"Too much?" he asked moving in and out faster, deeper, harder.

"Never enough," she gasped as her pussy clenched, a tightening growing low in her belly. Her breasts were heavy, her nipples aching as lightning zinged from them to her womb.

"Promise?" His breathing was labored, his eyes growing dark with desire. He took her mouth in a fiery kiss, tongues dueling as she drank in his essence. "Promise?" he whispered again, but his voice held a note of uncertainty.

"Promise," she screamed as her climax burst, surging through her like electricity rupturing, branching hot and steady throughout her body. Nerves raw with emotion cried as he pumped in and out, wringing every sensation from her. The sound of his voice as he groaned his own release, the feel of his seed filling her, the rich scent of his desire was so arousing that her vaginal walls spasmed around him, drawing him deeper, releasing another exquisite orgasm that made her cry out his name.

"Shawn," she exhaled. They felt so perfect together, so right. So when he said, "Promise?" again she replied, "Forever and ever." Lying in his arms there was no other response, because she knew she had found forever in his embrace.

Also by Mackenzie McKade

About the Author

෨

A taste of the erotic, a measure of daring and a hint of laughter describes Mackenzie McKade's novels. She sizzles the pages with scorching sex, fantasy and deep emotion that will touch you and keep you immersed until the end. Whether her stories are contemporaries, futuristics or fantasies, this Arizona native thrives on giving you the ultimate erotic adventure.

When not traveling through her vivid imagination, she's spending time with three beautiful daughters, a devilishly handsome grandson, and the man of her dreams. She loves to write, enjoys reading, and can't wait 'til summer. Boating and jet skiing are top on her list of activities. Add to that laughter and if mischief is in order—Mackenzie's your gal!

Mackenzie welcomes comments from readers. You can find her website and email address on her author bio page at www.ellorascave.com.

Tell Us What You Think

We appreciate hearing reader opinions about our books. You can email us at Comments@EllorasCave.com.

Why an electronic book?

We live in the Information Age — an exciting time in the history of human civilization, in which technology rules supreme and continues to progress in leaps and bounds every minute of every day. For a multitude of reasons, more and more avid literary fans are opting to purchase e-books instead of paper books. The question from those not yet initiated into the world of electronic reading is simply: *Why?*

1. *Price.* An electronic title at Ellora's Cave Publishing and Cerridwen Press runs anywhere from 40% to 75% less than the cover price of the exact same title in paperback format. Why? Basic mathematics and cost. It is less expensive to publish an e-book (no paper and printing, no warehousing and shipping) than it is to publish a paperback, so the savings are passed along to the consumer.

2. *Space.* Running out of room in your house for your books? That is one worry you will never have with electronic books. For a low one-time cost, you can purchase a handheld device specifically designed for e-reading. Many e-readers have large, convenient screens for viewing. Better yet, hundreds of titles can be stored within your new library — on a single microchip. There are a variety of e-readers from different manufacturers. You can also read e-books on your PC or laptop computer. (Please note that Ellora's Cave does not endorse any specific brands.

You can check our websites at www.ellorascave.com or www.cerridwenpress.com for information we make available to new consumers.)

3. *Mobility*. Because your new e-library consists of only a microchip within a small, easily transportable e-reader, your entire cache of books can be taken with you wherever you go.

4. *Personal Viewing Preferences.* Are the words you are currently reading too small? Too large? Too… ANNOYING? Paperback books cannot be modified according to personal preferences, but e-books can.

5. *Instant Gratification.* Is it the middle of the night and all the bookstores near you are closed? Are you tired of waiting days, sometimes weeks, for bookstores to ship the novels you bought? Ellora's Cave Publishing sells instantaneous downloads twenty-four hours a day, seven days a week, every day of the year. Our webstore is never closed. Our e-book delivery system is 100% automated, meaning your order is filled as soon as you pay for it.

Those are a few of the top reasons why electronic books are replacing paperbacks for many avid readers.

As always, Ellora's Cave and Cerridwen Press welcome your questions and comments. We invite you to email us at Comments@ellorascave.com or write to us directly at Ellora's Cave Publishing Inc., 1056 Home Avenue, Akron, OH 44310-3502.

COMING TO A BOOKSTORE NEAR YOU!

ELLORA'S CAVE

Bestselling Authors Tour

MAKE EACH DAY MORE *EXCITING* WITH OUR

ELLORA'S
CAVEMEN
CALENDAR

WWW.ELLORASCAVE.COM

erridwen, the Celtic Goddess of wisdom, was the muse who brought inspiration to storytellers and those in the creative arts. Cerridwen Press encompasses the best and most innovative stories in all genres of today's fiction. Visit our site and discover the newest titles by talented authors who still get inspired - much like the ancient storytellers did, once upon a time.

Cerridwen Press

www.cerridwenpress.com

Discover for yourself why readers can't get enough
of the multiple award-winning publisher
Ellora's Cave.

Whether you prefer e-books or paperbacks,

be sure to visit EC on the web at
www.ellorascave.com

for an erotic reading experience that will leave you
breathless.